Living Badly

Walter Cummins

Living Badly

Selected Stories

Walter Cummins

You live badly, my friends.
It is shameful to live like that.

—Anton Chekhov

SERVING HOUSE BOOKS

Living Badly, Selected Stories
Copyright © 2026 by Walter Cummins
ISBN: 9781947175976
Library of Congress Control Number: 2026933129

This book is a work of fiction. Any references to historical events, real people, or real places are used fictitiously.

Cover art concept by Walter Cummins

Cover design by Jacob Arms

Published by Serving House Books
Lawrence Landing Company
Raleigh, North Carolina 27609
www.servinghousebooks.com

Serving House Books is a proud member of:

Independent Book Publishers Association
 and
Community of Literary Magazines and Presses

for
Alison Cummins,
whom I miss very much

Acknowledgments

The stories in this collection first appeared in the following magazines and were reprinted in previous collections by Walter Cummins

Little Old Man—*Bellevue Literary Review*

What Eamon Did—*Georgetown Review*

Riding West—*Georgetown Review*

Islands—*Sonora Review*

Oxfords—*Virginia Quarterly Review*

Homemaking—*Green Hills Literary Lantern*

Awful Advice—*Confrontation*

Among the Gaytys—*da Cuhna*

Missing Venice—*Abiko Quarterly*

Baggage—*Florida Review*

The End of the Circle—*Bellevue Literary Review*

Little Life—*Perigee*

Saving Cimini—*Potpourri*

Another Person—*InkPot*

Habitat—*South Carolina Review*

Under the Deck—*Princeton Arts Review*

Structure—*Abiko Quarterly*

Roxanne's Ride—*The Panhandler*

Stef—*North Atlantic Review*

Pleasure—*Del Sol Review*

Telling Stories—*South85*

Contents

Preface / 9

Little Old Man / 13

What Eamon Did / 23

Riding West / 33

Islands / 44

Oxfords / 53

Homemaking / 67

Awful Advice / 81

Among the Gaytys / 93

Missing Venice / 107

Baggage / 117

The End of the Circle / 125

Little Life / 141

Saving Cimini / 149

Another Person / 156

Habitat / 162

Under the Deck / 171

Structure / 184

Roxanne's Ride / 194

Stef / 209

Pleasure / 219

Telling Stories / 222

About the Author / 231

Preface

First, I want to thank Bill Lawrence for inviting me to do a selected stories collection, but even more I owe him great thanks for leading Serving House Books into a very promising future with admirable new titles and excellent new authors with an international range.

Without doubt this collection is a swan song for me as I'm the cusp of becoming an nonagenarian and violating the expectations of longevity. In recognition, the first story here is titled "Little Old Man," written years ago before I was not so little or so old. Then I was just guessing what it felt like being of a great age. Beyond "old," "little" is appropriate too because I've shrunk about four inches as my disks compressed. Most people lose an inch or two. I've been excessive. Now I do consider it appropriate to contemplate death, awaiting the condition that will do me in, swiftly, I hope. There's no point lingering in a feeble state with morphine shots to kill the pain.

The order of the stories that follow the intentional first is random, just added to the list as the title came to me, not organized to make a thematic point. Some works are included to demonstrate a particular example of technique, though I may be the only one to care about that.

I do still like the stories, some better than others. Readers, of course, should feel free to dislike them all. That would bother me more if I were not so close to a conversion into unfeeling ashes. In defense of the stories I picked, I should say that at least one magazine editor liked each well enough to publish it. And some of my stories were nominated for submission for the Pushcart Prize collection though none made it, which leads me to conclude that there are a good number of story writers out there much better than I. Still, if writers did not write stories once they were aware that they wouldn't come up to their betters, they would give up and devote their time to reading the likes of Joyce, Chekhov, Hadley, and O'Conner. But probably every writer who sits down and turns out the opening words of a new story wonders if this time it's going to be him or her flirting with greatness.

Early on, my less pretentious hope was just adequacy. I'm not the only novice who used to think, if I could only have one story accepted for publication my writing life would be fulfilled. It took me a while to get that first, and then the second and third. After that I finally caught on, over the decades having around 125 accepted. At one stage I set myself the goal of one story for each year of my life. Then, once that was achieved, the goal became hitting a total of 100, after which I stopped counting. Now my hope is that some of them are good or at least deserve republication. Anyone reading this collection is a better judge than I.

Even at this final stage, I remain marked by my initial experience many decades ago of trying to be a fiction writer. With no thoughts about earning a living, I abandoned my post-college job as an executive trainee after realizing such a future terrified me. Then there I was in my first semester in the Iowa Writers Workshop with Philip Roth as my instructor, he just a few years older and having already won the National Book Award for Goodbye Columbus. My initial story submissions were turgid and all Roth did was write "Oh, no," "Too much," "Really?" in the margins. In one case he scrawled, "I can't finish this." Not once did he offer advice for revision. It may be that he found the drafts beyond redemption. Then near the end of the semester, I turned in a story he really liked, enough to have me submit it to an editor friend of his who did not like it as much. Still, even though for years afterward I imagined Roth-like comments on my attempts, I could tell myself, I wasn't so bad once.

I suppose my peak day as a story writer came in the 1980s when, before computers, we submitted manuscripts by mail. That afternoon three acceptances came in the return envelopes. All in all, over the years I received many rejections, but it got to the point that I reacted to a new acceptance with pleasure rather than excitement.

So what does it all mean now that my life span is terminating? I escaped being a corporate executive and enjoyed the satisfaction of turning out story after story, each one with imagined people in an imagined world that I feel good about creating.

I should warn potential readers that many of the stories in this collection have bleak endings, something a reviewer of one of my collections pointed out while affirming that they were worth reading. While much that I read in each day's news justifies that bleakness and some periods of my own life were, I plunge into my terminal nineties concluding that, all in all, it wasn't so bad.

Little Old Man

When Warren made the decision to die, he worried most about his wife, Julia—what would happen to her alone in a house a car ride from the nearest stores. She hadn't driven in years, would never drive again, her spine warped like an S, constant knives of pain stabbing her back and legs and face, her mind addled from frequent doses of Percocet. He wouldn't be around to monitor her pills, couldn't do it now anyway, barely inching along with his walker, wincing at the hurt in his own legs when he took a step. How could he stop her from opening the medication drawer any time during the day and sleepless nights? Sometimes she would call to him with her slurred voice, "Warren, did I take my pills?" He pictured her tongue wobbling in her mouth like a guppy on a table. "Yes," he would shout, "just an hour ago." But he would hear the drawer slide, the water run.

What would happen to her? He, ten years older, had been taking care of her for decades of her sufferings: first the swollen legs, then the rheumatoid arthritis, the scoliosis, the agony of tic douloureux. Teeth pulled, alcohol injected into nerves, procedure after procedure, specialist after specialist, to deaden the pain. Nothing worked. And now he was the one gravely ill, everything falling apart within months: a trickle of circulation below the knees, congestive heart failure, barely any kidney function. The EMTs call me every night before I call them, he told people. It seemed like every few weeks they had to rush him to Emergency for a lung pumping. "What else can I expect?" he would say, surprised that it was finally happening. "Hell, I'm an old man."

A little old man. A small boy had called him that even when he was still mobile, driving himself around the neighborhood. He had gone to bring a book to his friend Stan, a man he had known for fifty years. The boy answered the door chimes, no more than six or seven. When

Warren asked for Stan, the boy called back, "Hey, Grandpa, there's a little old man here to see you." Warren laughed out loud right on the spot, gripping Stan's arm when he appeared and still laughing. "Did you hear that? Damn it! The kid's right." Back home, Warren stood in front of a mirror and really looked at himself. There he was, grey and shrunken, his flesh ashen, loose on his face, his muscles just flab. "Goddamn!" he said aloud, amazed at what he had become. That night he called and ordered the boy a toy race car, asked that the card be signed "From the Little Old Man."

"Look at me," he said to Julia. "What do you see?" "You," she told him, "just you." She didn't recognize how he had changed, didn't care. He realized he was relieved that she was spared knowing. Dying was his problem, not hers. She lived for her pain killers, constantly checking the family room clock, sitting in her orthopedic chair just feet from the TV, the sound loud, but barely paying attention. She would talk over the sound, mentioning his name now and then, but really a monologue about things that had happened with her mother and father and sister a lifetime ago, agitated as she relived the same handful of days over and over.

Of course, Warren didn't blame the boy, but soon after he was identified as a little old man, he began becoming one, not deliberately, actually trying to will himself backwards, forcing himself to get out of the house, visit friends, attend meetings of his clubs. But the more he did, the more exhausted he felt, drifting off in his easy chair soon after supper, waking with a start at midnight, momentarily unsure where he was, then seeing Julia squinting at the TV screen, wondering how he could have slept with the speakers blaring.

His legs had been the first sign of disintegration, the poor circulation. For quite a while, they had been cramping when he walked the length of a block, and he had to stop to rest, knead the calves. Now he could barely get from the house to the car without a painful hobbling. His heart function declined from fifty percent of normal to thirty, and he had to take strong medications. But his kidneys were the most severe problem. For a decade, they had been weakening, and his doctor warned him that if his creatinine count went any higher, he would need dialysis. Then he did.

The procedure piqued his curiosity. Warren read pamphlets and tried to imagine the process. Fortunately, a dialysis center was available just five minutes from his house, and he could still drive. The treatment took three hours. One of a dozen patients, he sat tilted back in a molded chair hooked to a machine that droned a dull whirring. On a TV suspended from a wall bracket, contestants screamed at one another, the audience cheering and hooting. Warren spread a magazine on his lap but rarely read, eventually getting into conversations with the other patients lined up on two sides of the room, realizing he was by far the oldest of the group. Some, in fact, were very young, and he felt sorry for the years they faced. They talked about families and children, he relieved that his son was a continent away, his life and work there, too busy to be tied down by his parents' poor health. It wouldn't be fair, he realized, while he bragged about Richard's career, his promotions. Old people should fend for themselves, he declared. They've enjoyed their best years and had no right to rob others of theirs.

But the dialysis became more excruciating with each treatment, the machine drawing the fluid out of him so severely his sinews cramped into knots of agony. He clenched teeth, breathless, in spasm. The technician sympathized: "That's the way it happens at your stage." "Then," Warren told him, "it's no stage to be at." The technician just looked away.

Three times a week, home after dialysis, he could barely move from all the aches in his body, sitting in a chair and panting, unable to lift the newspaper or focus on the screen ten feet away. The next day he would sleep till noon, eat a slice of bread, and doze on and off till the evening, then lie awake, dreading the thought of enduring another treatment.

"This is no life," he finally admitted to Julia after several months of misery, wanting to spare her but finally having to say it aloud.

"At least you're alive," she told him.

"What if I wasn't?"

"What would happen to me?"

"I don't know." He touched her hand, the swollen knuckles, the brittle skin.

The conversation ended, but he continued it in his mind. What was he doing for her now? Driving slowly to a store for food and prescriptions, opening cans for meals she rarely ate and he had to force himself to swallow. One day, very soon, he wouldn't even be able to do that.

The accident convinced him. He was backing out of his driveway, a maneuver he had been making for years, when he lost control and shot across the street, smashing his taillight and knocking over a neighbor's mailbox. He apologized, wrote a check, and made it to his treatment. But when he drove home, he was trembling, afraid to creep faster than five miles an hour, a black SUV behind him blasting its horn. A month before he would have cursed the driver. Now tears steamed down his face. "I can't do this any more," he kept saying, "Can't." Right there, behind the wheel, a block from home on the most familiar street he had ever known, he decided to die.

Warren called his doctor to be sure what would happen if he stopped dialysis. "You'll get uremia and poison yourself," the doctor told him. "How long could I live that way?" Warren asked. "Three or four days. Why?" "Just curious," Warren said.

The first day he missed his dialysis appointment, he held himself tense in his chair, as if he would never get up again. Julia was prowling the house, hunched and twisted, dragging one foot as she moved from room to room, opening cabinets, slamming drawers. "Where's my pills?" he could hear her say each time she entered a room, going in and out the same doors several times, searching the same cabinets. The third time she returned to the family room, she gave Warren a look of surprise. "Are you supposed to be here?"

"I live here."

"Shouldn't you be somewhere?"

"Not any more."

"Whatever you say. Where's my pills?"

"Wherever you left them."

"If I knew that, I wouldn't be asking you." She moved into the kitchen.

Although he felt too weak too laugh, hurt too much, Warren knew that a stranger watching them might think it was comical—two old people having a ridiculous conversation, barely functioning, no thoughts beyond their hurts and their ailments. When he tried to look out into the family room, his vision was blurred, everything behind a grey film. But he knew what was there on the paneled walls, framed pictures of him and Julia when they were younger, faces touching, smiles broad, their son as a boy. Memories of a lifetime that he didn't care about recalling now. He wasn't even a little old man any more. Little old corpse, he kept thinking, the words swirling in his brain, a dimness spinning before his eyes, until he saw nothing.

When Warren looked out again, the light was dazzling, pouring in through the open Venetian blinds of a strange room, bright metal objects all around him, a pouch of liquid dangling from a steel stand, a tube in his arm. Hospital, he knew. And when he turned his head, there was Richard leaning over him with a rigid smile. "Hi, Dad."

"How'd you get here?"

"Airplane. The way I always do."

Warren made an effort to return the smile, not sure if his face were still functioning. Richard seemed so big, so strong and youthful, though he was a man close to sixty. It pleased Warren to see him and, once again, he realized how proud he was of his son, how much he had awaited his weekly phone calls, the sound of his voice. Richard was holding his hand, gripping it in a gesture of shaking, but pressing down with the other, the warmth of contact.

"You shouldn't have had to come," he said. "I didn't want you to see this."

"If not your son, then who?"

"Nobody. Nobody should see this. People should wander off into the woods like animals."

"People have other people who care about them."

"That's sad. In the long run, love is sad."

Richard was shaking his head, pressing his hand harder. "Only for a fraction of time. The rest it's good."

"How did you know I was here?"

"Mom called. It took me a while to figure out what she was saying. She must have swallowed a fistful of Percocet. But I finally understood that you weren't moving, barely breathing. So I called the EMTs and booked the next flight."

"What's going to happen to her?" Warren asked.

"What's going to happen to you?" Richard said, his tone flat, as if stating a technical dilemma. Warren smiled, once again surprised that he had produced an engineer.

"Not what," he said. "When. No more dialysis. I know you won't try to get me to change my mind."

"I wish I could."

"What good would that do?"

"None." Richard pinched the corners of his eyes and looked away.

Warren felt his head sink into the pillow, too heavy to lift, his throat dry as sand. He gestured to Richard for ice water, a wet towel pressed to his lips as he sucked on the cloth. "The funeral's all paid for. Five years ago. You'll find the papers in the top drawer of my desk. All the arrangements. My lawyer has the will. A couple of phone calls. That's the only thing you'll have to do. It's your mother we have to talk about."

"I'm not bringing her with us. Don't make me promise that, Dad. All she talks about is her pain. I guess she has a right to do that as much as she hurts. But I have a right not to be around it any more too. So does Bonnie."

Wait till you're a little old man and she's a little old lady, Warren thought, but didn't say it, knowing it wouldn't be fair. Let him find out when it happens. His eyelids felt so heavy. As much as he tried to force them apart, he drifted into greyness.

Each time he lost consciousness, Warren expected never wake again. This is it. He heard those words in his head, elongated, like a record on an old windup phonograph with a rundown spring. That was the image that occurred to him when he woke up again, seeing a memory of the first one he had every owned, hearing snatches of tunes. But it was all scattered, one picture fading into the next, people and places from decades apart flowing in and out of his consciousness. He couldn't make them hold still, couldn't will himself to focus on any one. This wasn't what he expected, not what he had read about dying.

No bright light luring him to another realm, no sensation of crossing a threshold. There was no other realm. For him, nothing but this room— the steel bars of the bed, the bulbs in the ceiling, the weight of the blanket that covered him. If he tried, he could think of Julia wandering through the house, opening cabinets, rummaging through drawers. But it all seemed so far away, a tiny image at the end of a tunnel.

When the nurses came into the room, checking his catheter, renewing the pain killer, sponging his body, rolling him this way and that to change sheets, he was alert, flirting with the young ones, teasing the old. He would gesture toward the morphine drip with a lifting of his chin. "Great stuff. I should have known about his years ago." His voice was thin. Some of the nurses smiled. One patted his hand. "Years ago they would have locked you up."

"If you came by every day," he said, "it would have been worth it."

When his doctor looked in, Warren asked what day it was. "Thursday," the doctor told him. "I mean day without dialysis." The doctor looked at his watch. "Fifth."

"I thought I was supposed to be dead by now."

"How bad is the pain?"

Warren winced and swallowed. "What pain?"

"There's still time to change your mind."

"A lot of good that would do."

"You're a tough old bird."

"Just a little old man."

Richard seemed to be in the room more and more. At least, whenever Warren awoke and looked up, his son was there, standing over him or sitting on a chair beside the bed.

"You don't have to come here so much," Warren told him.

"I want to be with you."

"Dying is boring. It must be more boring to watch."

"I'll miss you, Dad."

"Since you were born, it's been a treat just to think about you, to know you exist." Warren turned toward the window. "Is the sun out?"

"Dazzling. Do you want me to close the blinds?"

"Everything I look at now is in a haze."

Richard lifted Warren's hand, studied it. "Your fingertips are purple now, cold."

"I'm behind schedule. So much for medical predictions." Warren tried to look at his own fingers but saw only a blur. "What does your mother say?"

"She keeps asking when you're coming home. She's angry that you're away."

"What about her pills?"

"I locked them up. Give them to her on the prescribed schedule."

"That's what she's really mad about. Any ideas about what's to become of her?"

"I checked out a nursing home." Richard described the facility—the size of a private room where she could have her own furniture, the dining room, the nursing care, the monthly costs, but Warren couldn't hold on to the details. It sounded fine.

"She won't go," he said. "You'd have to tie her up and drag her out of the house." He imagined Julia shrieking, her warped body thrashing, summing up great strength in a furious resistance. Desperate to survive, obsessed with her Percocet. A strange life force.

Warren felt himself trembling, then realized there was a hand on his shoulder, light, barely pressing down. "Dad, Dad," he heard and turned his head to look up at Richard's face bending over him, just inches away.

Hi, he wanted to say, but it came out as a groan, a sound so quiet he wasn't sure his son heard.

"Dad. Mom's here."

"What?" Warren tried to lift his head and see the room. "Where?" He didn't want to see her, not in this place.

"In a room down the hall."

In an instant his mind cleared, as if a great rock had been lifted from his brain. "Why? What happened?" Now he could hear his own voice.

"She overdosed. She must have hidden some pills. I was getting into bed when I heard a loud crash from her room. When I found her on the floor, I thought she was dead. The rescue squad came in no time. They pumped her out in Emergency and brought her up here. That was last night."

"What is it now?"

"Past noon. You've been sleeping for hours."

"Did she do it on purpose?"

"I don't think so. I've been rationing her. She's been greedy for those damn pills. Probably found her stash and gulped them down. The hospital won't keep her overnight now. Insurance. I have to get her out by evening."

Warren strained to think, to made sense of it all. Both of them in the same hospital, on the same floor. It was crazy. Maybe it wasn't happening, just a delusion from all the poison in his body. The kidneys weren't filtering. Gone loony from his own waste and a morphine drip. He spoke his son's name—"Richard"—to see if he was truly there. When Richard answered, he knew what to say. "Take your mother straight to that nursing home. Hire an ambulance. Have them lash her to a stretcher so she can't get away. Somebody has to take care of her."

"I already made arrangements."

Warren tried to smile. "We think alike."

"She wants to see you," Richard said. "Cursing the nurses because they won't bring her down the hall. That's one reason they're so eager to get rid of her."

About to protest, to say, no, not like this, Warren realized it didn't matter any more. He shrugged. "Why not?"

He must have slept again, because when Warren opened his eyes at a shrill squeaking sound, it was dark outside the window, a ceiling light reflecting in the glass. He heard his name, Julia's voice, then Richard's. A nurse had wheeled her gurney right beside his bed, his wife stretched out alongside him, wrapped in a white sheet, fixed to the flat surface with dark straps.

When he looked out to her, he didn't see her, not as she was now, but his memory from decades before, shining brown hair, brilliant dark eyes, the joy in her face as she smiled at their child. He reached out an arm, barely able to extend it in his weakness. A hand touched his. It might have been hers. "Isn't she the prettiest thing?" he said to the nurse.

He heard them rolling her away and Julia calling back, insisting, "You'd better come visit me," and his son squeezing his hand, touching his face as he stepped away.

Even before they were out the door, Warren closed his eyes and knew it was over.

What Eamon Did

For a moment Carter thought he was standing at the end of the earth, alone on a dirt path on a bluff above the water gazing out at three island shapes in the mist below, and beyond them nothing but a dark sea fading back into the horizon. When he turned his head, he saw houses and stone walls scattered far behind him, the small square automobiles close beside the buildings looking as ancient as the boulders strewn across the landscape. He felt he was the only thing alive as he stepped slowly, boots grinding into the earth. Even the sheep far across a distant field were immobile, still white lumps. Then he saw two figures approaching in the distance, emerging from the dazzling haze of sunset. Carter knew they were human, erect, but moving with odd gaits. As they neared he could see that one of them stabbed the ground with a walking stick. It was a woman, a tiny, old, curved-backed woman barely taller than her stick. And beside her, her hand clutching his elbow, a young man in a grey suit and tie who stumbled forward with each step, arms rigid, right foot coming down hard but only the toe of the left touching the earth. He looked straight ahead with a glaring stare. Carter spoke a greeting as they passed. The man ignored him as if he were invisible, and he couldn't tell whether the woman nodded or was just bobbing her head. He stopped and watched them until they disappeared around a bend in the path.

For the first time in weeks he felt an urge to seek human conversation. Usually he walked alone, hours each day across remote fields, buying food in a local shop, spending the mid afternoon sprawled out on rocks or on the moist green soil reading a book, some ragged paperback that he had found abandoned in a bus station or in one of the bed and breakfasts where he stayed when the rain was too heavy to sleep outside. Reading was a diversion, but he never choose a book, preferring to take whatever came his way, random words on a page. The days were long in summer, and he sought most the sense of endless time that required nothing of him.

On the best days he could even forget this feeling of freedom was only an illusion, rationed to a few weeks in July and August with money always a problem, each expense entered in a notebook and immediately subtracted from his daily allotment. When that ran out, no matter how hungry or thirsty he was, he allowed himself nothing more. Some nights, chill in afield, wrapped from chin to toes in the single blanket he carried, he would chew the sweet damp clover grass and swallow it like a grazing animal.

The rest of the year Carter lived in a two-room flat in a crowded city neighborhood an ocean away, most of his furniture collected from curb sides or passed on by the janitors in his school, stiff wooden chairs, paint-chipped shelves, grey filing cabinets with twisted drawers where he stored his changes of clothes. Even at home he kept a running tab of expenses, obsessed with saving enough for his summer airfare and the cost of days in this empty green countryside.

He taught hostile twelve-year-olds, who by the time they had reached the seventh grade despaired of any future beyond furtive pleasures and the grind for subsistence. Every fall each new group repeated the same strategies for rebellion—dropped books, belches, obscene figures on the blackboard, firecrackers. But when they saw that Carter didn't care enough to be angry, they took no pleasure from their defiance and passed the periods in sullen boredom while Carter droned on and never bothered to learn who they were, calling them by the name of whichever past student they reminded him of.

Once he had worked at a desk in his own office, well paid for making decisions and devising plans. He received promotions and bonuses. But he hated listening to the others at lunches and meetings, all so serious about whatever project was at hand, craving recognition and advancement, ridiculous in their quests for picayune victories. For a quarter of his salary he found a school where he could teach without an education degree and kill the time between each summer escape.

His wife left when he stopped being an executive: "How can you do this to me?" But he knew she would leave anyway, sooner or later, that she would realize it was no life for her with a man who wanted to live like a stone in a field.

Even though he took the book from his pack and tried to read, he could not stop remembering the stare of the man on the path. The spine of this paperback had been folded a hundred times, twisted so much that chunks of pages had fallen out. The gaps made this book nothing but disconnected fragments that ended in a mid sentence limbo. But now the words seemed to slide off the paper, and Carter saw nothing but those dark fixed eyes.

Of course, he understand the actuality, that the pair were mother and son, that the man was not a boy but a person of his age, the flesh of his face starting to sink, lines forming around the mouth. And he knew the man had not been arrogant in his snub. This country did not hide its defectives. In the cities he passed through on the way to more open land he saw people with hunchbacks and goiters and open malignancies eating into faces. But this man troubled him more than any of the others in his fierce isolation.

As the sun began to set behind the shapes of the three islands, Carter shivered even though this was a warm evening. Unwilling to stay alone in a field, he walked the three miles into the village, rented a room for the night, and went out to the main street where people were strolling past the shop windows, studying the menus outside a small restaurant. A small hotel displayed a hand lettered poster by the main entrance—"Single's Night." From a window that opened to the sidewalk Carter could see inside to a bare room where four middle-aged couples fox-trotted on a pale wood floor to a recording of a song he remembered from childhood.

Carter turned onto the one side street, a road that curved downhill and led out of the village into farmland. Mid block he saw a squat stone building apart from the others with the sign "Tavern" over a wood plank door. Though he was not a tall man, he had to stoop to step inside.

It was a low windowless room with dark beams and a grey partition in the middle that stopped abruptly before the bar at the back.

The light was so dim, the air so heavy with cigarette smoke, that he had to blink and stand a few moments until he could see. All the tables were filled, on one side of the partition old men in black caps gazing down into glasses of thick dark liquid, saying very little to each other, the others nodding when anyone did. All the noise was coming from the other side.

Carter stepped over boots and outstretched legs to approach the bar. Someone had printed the word "Music" on a slate hanging next to the mirror. A boy no older than his students drew Carter a drink from the tap, tilting the glass, scraping off the head with a flat stick. Carter reached for the glass, but the boy snatched it back to top it off, giving Carter a snide look. Carter dropped coins on a yellow mat, turned, sipped, and leaned back against the bar.

From there he could see the source of the noise, people jammed at a dozen tables, courting couples in the corner, a group of well-dressed grey- haired ladies, obviously tourists, families of several generations, mothers with babies on their laps, young men in work clothes. They were shouting to one another, teasing the lovers, toasting the tourists.

Now Carter could see that every wall in the tavern was covered with postcards, each one pinned to the plaster with a thumbtack in the middle of the top edge. He stepped forward and bent over a table to look more closely at the cards directly in front of him. They came from all over—Greece, Spain, Belgium, Miami, Los Angeles. Without lifting them to read the messages, he was sure they were sent by the locals on their holidays, and as he glanced about the room, couldn't imagine people like these traveling so far from home. Then it struck him that at the end of this summer he could send his own card addressed just to the tavern in this village. He had no idea what message he would write on the back of a photo of a city he hated. Of course, no one would know who the writer was; no one would remember an anonymous stranger from a single evening.

He heard clapping, a sudden murmur, and followed glances to see two men enter through a side door just beyond the alcove with the toilets. They were the musicians, one carrying a small wooden pipe, the other a concertina. People greeted them by name, reached out and squeezed their arms as they passed—"Nick, Terry." The piper answered for them both, "Good to see you," in a rough, hoarse voice. He must have been Nick, a thickset man in a blue denim jacket with dark brows, deep eyes, and a sparse dark beard that grew high up his cheekbones. The man with the concertina, Terry, was pink and round-faced, skin so smooth he looked as if he never shaved. He wore a constant smile, but Nick seemed very serious, neck muscles taut, his pipe looking fragile amid the knuckles of large, hairy hands.

They sat on two empty chairs against the front wall. Someone handed Terry a glass of stout, but Nick only Schweppes and a lemon slice. Almost immediately they filled the room with raucous, lilting music. People began drumming feet against the stone floor, swaying heads, tapping tabletops. They were all smiling. Carter knew they would have leapt up and danced if there had been room in the tavern. He might have danced himself if he knew how.

Carter stopped slapping his hand on his thigh to watch a family enter the room, tiptoeing through the crowd against the partition, a pale, freckled little man with a puff of red hair, a small boy who looked just like him, and a dumpy young woman with a round, blank face carrying a baby sleeping on her shoulder. The man wore a dark brown suit that was too tight for him, short in the arms and legs, all three jacket buttons fastened over a tan sweater. The woman's cotton dress seemed faded, too cold for the night air. The boy had on a tie and jacket over dungarees. No one else paid attention to them, as if deliberately pretending they did not notice. Still tiptoeing, the man passed into the alcove and retrieved three folding chairs for his family. All through their entry, the unfolding and the sitting, the musicians played more loudly, wildly, Nick the piper stamping a foot and bouncing up and down in his seat.

The crowd cheered when they finished the tune. Even the old men in black were nodding. Nick studied his pipe, took out a handkerchief and wiped it very carefully, held it up to the dim bulb in the ceiling lamp and squinted one eye. Terry played a scale as if he could not keep his fingers still.

Then Nick looked straight at the little man and smiled; but Carter could see that it was more a twisting of his mouth, the straggly hair of his mustache sticking straight out, the grey fillings of his molars exposed. "Well, if it isn't Eamon," Nick said. "Out with the family on a night like this. And how are you, Eamon?" The voice rumbled, and Carter thought of all the stones in the fields.

Eamon, the little man, stared down at the floor and squirmed on the folding chair. His wife flushed and hugged the baby. The boy folded his hands and sat stiffly.

"It's always a great treat to see Eamon," Nick continued as if addressing an audience. "Isn't it great, Terry?" Terry nodded and sounded a long drawn chord, though Carter could tell he wanted Nick to stop.

Carter glanced at the boy behind the bar for a clue. This taunting seemed so unlikely, that a timid person like Eamon could have done something to annoy a man like Nick. Of course, they both could have grown up in this village, with Eamon the butt of ridicule since childhood, Nick's scorn an empty repetition of an old routine. Carter saw it in his classroom every year, one boy singled out as the butt, blamed for all misdeeds, evoking snickers each time the roll was called. But here no one else was participating, the tourists bewildered, the locals pretending to ignore it. Whatever had happened was between Nick and Eamon.

"Are you being good, Eamon?"

Terry pressed the concertina into a sound like a long sigh and then slid into a tune. Nick had to follow along, still half rising and pointing the pipe toward Eamon every time he played a high note. Eamon sat in silence, saying nothing, not ordering drinks, but giving his son a coin for a soda when the boy poked his side and whispered. Nick tooted a rhythm that followed the boy's shy steps to the bar, then leered at Eamon.

Carter was surprised that the mystery intrigued him. For all his summers in this country, he didn't know the people beyond a few brief conversations with people on buses and landladies, talk of weather and the outrageous prices. He had chosen this place for the landscape, the empty miles beyond the sight of any cottage, the stones, the layers of carbonized moss, the abandoned remnants of ancient habitation that suddenly appeared in the middle of nowhere. At night, alone in a field beneath distant stars, he felt a pure sensation of unremitting time, the insignificance of all that people allowed to obsess their lives. But now he was curious. What had Eamon done?

If what he did had been so awful, why was he here? He must have known Nick was performing this night. So why did he dress in his best suit and bring his family to hear him take abuse? Why was he so passive about it? Perhaps he felt so guilty that he was punishing himself with public shame. But to look at Eamon you'd think he was absolutely harmless, the most innocuous man in the world.

Carter had an eye for malevolence after so many years of teaching twelve-year-olds. On the first day of class he could spot the really nasty ones, boy or girl, no matter how seemingly sweet the expression, the ones who would do something cruel or corrupt before the year was over. But all he saw in Eamon was weakness, a man too craven to risk breaking a rule.

Even though he was exceeding his day's allotment, Carter signaled the boy bartender and ordered another drink. "Do you know that man in the suit?"

"Eamon? He's from the village."

"What does he do?"

"Works in a shop."

"Why does Nick hate him so much?"

The boy turned and plunged dirty glasses into a sink. "You'd have to ask Nick about that."

No one would tell him, Carter was sure. Perhaps only Nick and Eamon themselves, and why would they speak to a stranger? But he could try if he had an opportunity, though not now with the music so feverish, Nick piping with one hand and wiping his brow with the other, rubbing the handkerchief across the mat of chest hair showing from his open flannel shirt. Only Eamon and his family were not caught up in the rhythm, Eamon gazing fixedly as if he did not hear a sound. Now and then Nick would meet his eyes and wink.

Carter looked to the wife, Mrs. Eamon, for a clue. Perhaps Nick had seduced her or she had thrown herself on Nick in a moment of crazed passion. But she was so bland, so lethargic that he couldn't imagine Nick bothering or she having the spirit to act out her most secret desires. Unless Nick had seduced her for revenge. But that would have been a response to something that Eamon did, a gesture, not the root cause.

At the end of the tune, Nick began again. "Eamon, my boy. And how's life treating you, Eamon?"

Carter looked hard at Nick, trying to force his attention across the room, a recognition that would give him a sign. But when the man finally responded, in the instant he locked on, the eyes were hard and unyielding.

"Eamon, you're looking a bit peaked. Are you sleeping the way you should?"

Carter wondered what would happen if he bought Eamon a drink, a pint for the man and one for his wife. But they wouldn't have been able to talk, not with the music resounding through the tavern. People had to shout to comment to whomever sat next to them; he could see their mouths wide open, the lips forming sounds.

Then Eamon stood up and walked into the alcove with the toilets. For a few seconds Carter stayed at the bar, stunned by the sudden movement, before he followed.

They stood side by side at a urinal that took up one wall, a water tank above at the ceiling connected by gleaming copper pipes. Carter hadn't realized how badly he needed relief.

"How do you like the music?" he asked.

"It's what they do around here," Eamon said. It was the first time Carter had heard the man speak. The voice was soft and sullen, as if begrudging the words.

"Then you must live in the village." Eamon nodded.

"And know the musicians." He nodded again.

"What do you think of the piper?" "He's been playing all his life."

"He must be a friend of yours then."

"The man's no friend of mine"

Eamon zipped up quickly and turned to leave. Carter knew he would have to speak quickly and began talking about a subject he hadn't allowed to enter his thoughts all day.

"You wouldn't think my daughter's getting married tomorrow, would you?"

Eamon gave him a strange look. "Congratulations," he said in a tone that made it clear he did care.

"It's on the other side of the ocean, so I won't be there. Her sisters will and her brother, and her mother. She wanted me to come.

My daughter, not her mother. Her mother wouldn't give me a hand if I were drowning in front of her. My daughter called me before I flew over here. But I couldn't afford another round trip. It's hard to make exceptions when you have just enough money to live. It's only a formality anyway. Part of the show to have a father give her away. She's getting a husband. What does she need with a father anyway?"

"I guess so," Eamon said and reached out a hand to push the door.

Carter seized his arm. "Why does that man hate you?" But Eamon shook him off and plunged back into the room.

Carter splashed water on his face, rubbed at his eyes with his thumbs. The towel roll had reached his end, hanging half loose and filthy with hand smears. He had to wipe his face on a shirt sleeve.

When he went back to the bar, the musicians were standing as they played, sounding solo bursts and answering each other with a rapid tempo that got faster with each note of the tune. People were cheering, urging them on. The two of them kicked their chairs over and started threading through the crowded tables, playing and dancing, bringing the tavern to a pitch of excitement. Even the boy behind the bar was laughing now, beating a wash bucket with a wooden spoon.

Nick led Terry past the edge of the partition to the old men finally smiling and nodding their heads to the rhythm. Nick paused to drain a full glass of stout in one long swallow, and Terry gave him a look.

When they turned back to the other side of the partition, they had to pass right in front of Eamon's chair, and Carter expected something to happen. Nick seemed to ignore the man, but then stopped abruptly, backstepped, and swirled to face Eamon's wife. "What a night, eh darling? What a night to be married to a great man like Eamon."

In a second she was on her feet, thrusting the baby onto Eamon's lap. The baby was screaming, and she was shrieking, beating at Nick's shoulders, ripping the pipe from his hands and hitting the top of his head with it.

Two of the old men pinned her arms, stronger than she was no matter how she twisted and tried to kick at them. Terry took the pipe from her. But Nick was on the floor, shaking with laughter. "Oh, Eamon, my boy, what a hellfire you've got."

Eamon picked up the baby and dragged the boy by the wrist, heading toward the door of the tavern. The old men pushed his wife after him. When the door opened, Carter could see that it was dark outside, only a few stars visible in the black sky. The door closed quickly, and the room turned silent.

"The entertainment is over," Nick said as he picked himself up and studied his pipe for damage. "And the air is clearer in here. We can play some serious music."

Carter left, impelled by an urgent need to get away from the din. Out on the sidewalk, shivering in the chill air, he was sorry he had left his jacket in his backpack. Eamon and his family had disappeared, perhaps had already shut themselves inside their home in the small cluster of the village.

Carter would never learn what the man had done. But whatever it was—some crime or sin or stupid error—it would always matter. People like Nick wouldn't ever let him forget. And Eamon would never leave this village; he would stay in constant humiliation. What good would it do for him to leave? He would always be haunted. He would live out his life in this insignificant place where he had committed an act of great consequence.

Carter turned back toward the main street, wondering if he would recognize the house where he had rented a room for the night, then realized that he didn't want to find it, that he didn't want to be here.

He would retrieve his backpack in the morning. Now he went out into the darkness. Away from the village, back on the path he had walked at sunset, Carter sensed that he was following the maimed footsteps of the man led by his ancient mother, out in a ritual of aimless exercise, not even knowing where he was or why he was.

Riding West

When Peter turned the corner and found Denise waiting at the curb with three suitcases, he leaned out the window, not sure whether to be amused or annoyed. "Hey! It's only two weeks." His own few changes of clothes were rolled up inside an old duffle bag thrown in the trunk.

"You never can tell?" she said. "What you're going to need. Where you'll end up."

He couldn't figure out why she was wearing stockings, high heels, a red sleeveless dress, carrying a small white purse. They could have been going across town to a party, not setting off for four long days on the interstate, heading west in an old Escort with a deep gouge rusting down the passenger's door. He glanced in the rearview mirror and caught an edge of his unshaven jaw, then glanced down at his tee shirt, jeans, and flapping sandals. What a mismatched pair they'd make sitting side by side for hundreds of miles.

Peter got out to load two of her suitcases into the trunk. The biggest had to slide onto the back seat; he strained to lift it but didn't ask what she had inside. Then she sat in the car and waited for him to shut her door.

If he'd kept his mouth shut, this wouldn't be happening, Peter thought—traveling across the country with a stranger to a place he wasn't sure he wanted to see again. But one night after work when everybody was pouring from pitchers of beer and talking about vacations, someone asked Peter about his plans. Usually he just sat back and listened to the others. Answering was his mistake, nervously blurting intentions for a trip he had planned in detail but never expected to take: drive west for several days in a town on the Coast he had lived in once, visit familiar places, perhaps look up a few people.

That was what he told them, through he was sure it would never happen despite the hours he had wasted in daydreaming.

As Peter was speaking, Denise arrived from her job a few blocks away,
taking the empty chair across the table from him next to Glenn, her husband. "I've been thinking of a trip west myself. I'll ride with you," she said,
not asking, just stating a fact. "Split the gas and the driving. It'll save us
time and money." "What about you?" Peter looked at Glenn, hoping he
would be going too, but Glenn shrugged. "Not a good time for me." Peter
felt his scalp prickling. "It's an old car that's been having problems," he
told Denise. "The cylinder head, I think." She had smiled, bright lip gloss
flecked on her teeth. "I'll take my chances."

So here they were. Peter concentrated on the driving, maneuvering through the thick traffic in the center of town, taking a
shortcut through the industrial park, and coming out to the highway. He started to apologize for the condition of the Escort—the
back floor littered with empty grocery bags, crushed cans, tattered
sneakers—then changed his mind. Denise didn't said a word, looking out at the local scenery as if she were a tourist. This was the
first time Peter had ever been alone with her.

He and Glenn did data entry in the same office. The work called
for concentration and left little time for small talk. Some days they ate
lunch together or went for a beer; Denise joined them now and then,
part of a group chattering over sports or the weather or government
stupidities. He knew nothing about their lives.

Glenn was okay, Peter thought all along, but he'd never had a
reaction to Denise until they were sitting next to each other one
evening at a big round table and she pressed her leg against his,
tight from calf to thigh. He reached across for a pitcher of beer to
break the contact, but she shifted with him. Peter wouldn't meet
her eyes, didn't know what to do next. He suspected that if he
dropped his hand to her knee, she would seize it, rub it up and
down. Then what? He realized that he didn't want to know.

Her look didn't appeal to him—round olive face, flat features,
thick lips, dark lidded eyes, heavy calves. But she carried herself
like a femme fatale, and he could see men responding, as if to
an invitation of a secret smoldering, a promise of unimagined de-

lights. For him, he knew, even if Glenn wasn't a real friend, there'd only be disappointment. That evening he had stood up and moved to the men's room just to wash his hands, then slipped out to the parking lot without rejoining the table. Denise never sat next to him again, not until they were in his car now, she leaning against the passenger door, hands folded in her lap.

"Why are you all dolled up?" Peter asked her when they stopped for a red light.

She pulled the dress down over her knees. "I always like to make a good impression."

Though she was staring straight ahead, mouth fixed, he sensed that she was smirking. "We'll be driving from dawn till midnight," he said. "You won't meet anybody but gas jockeys, and you'll be too tired to show yourself off."

"Then you'll have to be the one to appreciate me."

"Why don't you pretend you've fixed yourself up for Glenn?"

"It wouldn't do me any good." She laughed. "Glenn knows all my secrets."

On the interstate, every time Peter pushed the Escort past seventy, he felt a hesitation, a surging in the engine, the car starting to vibrate, probably from bad alignment.

"Shit."

Denise looked up as if startled from a reverie. "Did you say something?"

"I said, shit. It's the goddamn car. We won't be able to go past 65."

"So?"

"We'll lose time."

"Does that matter?"

"We've only got two weeks. I don't want to waste most of it on the road."

"Who says we can't stay longer? As long as we like?"

"We have jobs. Remember?"

"Pull off at any exit and there are other jobs. No worse than what we're doing now."

"But our lives are back home." Peter found himself agitated, as if this were a real discussion and he had a point to prove.

"And what kind of life do you have there?" "Not much. But it's the only one I've got."

"See? There's nothing to lose."

"But you have Glenn." Peter pictured Glenn pounding at his terminal, lanky, red-cheeked, fair-haired, with large knobby joints, as if he had been snapped together. He was always earnest, intent on doing a good job.

"With Glenn," she said, "two weeks or two months or two years is no big deal."

"How do you mean?"

"I'd walk in the door, and he'd say, 'Oh, it's you.'"

"Tell me something," Peter asked her. "Were you really planning a trip before you heard about mine?"

Denise studied her fingers, bit at a split nail. "Of course not. But I have enough sense to seize an opportunity."

"What opportunity is that?"

"We have one car, and I can't afford air fare."

"You both work."

"Money never lasts with us."

For a second, Peter was about to ask her why, then suspected he wouldn't want to know the reason. Instead he said, "What will you do once we get there?" The plan was for him to drop her off at the rapid transit station in his old town, and she'd head into San Francisco, eventually get in touch with him to make arrangements for the drive back.

"Indulge my whims."

"Do you have friends there?"

"I have friends everywhere. It's very easy to make friends. Try it sometimes."

"I know enough people," he said.

Midday they stopped fifteen minutes for sandwiches, gas, and a toilet break, then back on the road that barely changed for hours, a straight line of macadam cut through contoured fields out to the horizon, a blur of farmhouses and silos, acres of dried corn stalks, every now and then a town in the distance. Peter told Denise to turn on the radio, but all they could get were commodities quotes and ranting call-in shows. They listened to the slap of tires and the groan of the engine. At dusk Denise took over the driving for the first time, spending several minutes adjusting the seat, making faces when she pulled back onto the highway. "Jesus, Peter, this transmission feels like tar."

"Sorry I couldn't offer more style."

"No matter. I'm a very flexible woman, able to shift my own gears."

When night fell and headlights cut into the darkness, Denise said, "What about sleeping?"

Peter held his watch to the dashboard. "We've got hours till midnight."

"I didn't mean that. What arrangements? One room or two."

He couldn't see the expression on her face. "Two, I suppose."

"There was a night a few months ago," she said, "when you could-have gotten into my pants."

"I remember."

"But you weren't interested."

"No."

"You may have missed the window of opportunity." For a moment she was silent, then laughed out loud. Peter had never seen her so amused. "So," she continued, "your virtue is safe with me in one room. Besides, we'd save money."

"All right."

Later, after rehearsing the question in his mind for a half hour, the exact words to use, he asked her, "Why was the window unlocked that one time?"

"Curiosity. I wanted to find out if you're really as dull as you seem."

"All you had to do was ask. I'm probably the dullest person you know."

She laughed again. "Then think of all the effort we've saved ourselves. I got my answer without working up a sweat."

They pulled off the interstate the first exit they came to after midnight and found a motel right at the cloverleaf, a flat cinder block building with a neon sign thirty feet in the air. Peter paid for the room with his credit card, and Denise gave him cash for her half, counted out the bills before they left the car even though he told her there was no hurry. The room smelled of an earthy dampness, the walls slick to the touch.

Peter used the bathroom first, took a shower to be ready for a quick departure first thing in the morning. He was in and out in five minutes, then burrowed under the spread of one bed. But, tired as he was, he couldn't sleep, hearing Denise's sounds behind the bathroom door—clatterings on the glass shelf, the constant on and off of faucets, a flushing roar, something dropped on the tiles. It seemed she was in there for an hour.

When she came back into the room, Peter opened one eye from the pillow and saw her standing at the picture window in a long nightgown, her body outlined by the neon glow, the heavy shape of her legs, the contour of her small breasts. His arousal surprised him. It wasn't her, he told himself; it was being in a strange room with a strange woman. He rolled over and faced the wall, wanting no part of Denise.

When his alarm watched buzzed at 6 a.m., she was already dressed, in slacks and a fine knit sweater this time, heating water for the instant coffee left on a table by the door. He threw on his jeans and tee shirt, strapped the sandals. She pulled back the curtains to a grey morning, and they sat in plastic chairs drinking the thin, tepid coffee and eating stale rolls.

"Some fun," Denise said.

"I've been in worse places."

"With worse people?"

"I remember places better than people." "

You're kind of a place yourself."

"How do you mean?"

"A shape on the landscape. Something for the passersby to glance at and forget."

"Somebody who won't climb through a window if you opened it for him?"

"Exactly."

"Then it's a lucky thing you have Glenn."

"My luck is amazing."

The Escort wouldn't start, not after five minutes of Peter twisting the ignition key and grinding the starter. A few times the engine sputtered, but died as soon as he gave it gas. He beat fists on the steering wheel. "Goddamn it, goddamn it, goddamn it."

Denise covered his hand when he moved to turn the key again. "You'll wear down the battery. It's probably flooded. Let's just sit for a while."

He shook his head and winced. "What a goddamn way to live." "What way?"

"A car like this piece of shit."

"It's not good to get so emotional about a machine."

"Oh yeah? How else are you going to get to San Francisco?"

"Something else would have come along."

"What?"

She gave a small shrug. "I'm not like you. When an obstacle arises, I trust my luck."

He wrenched the key so hard he thought it would snap. But the engine roared, spewed out a surge of thick black exhaust.

Peter turned on the radio himself this time, dialed through the static crackle until he heard a voice, somebody reading from the Bible, a cadence filled with yeas and verilies. He left it on even when a preacher's voice urged people to cast off their sinful ways. "Maybe we should pay attention," he said.

"You and me?" Denise laughed. "We're two people who resisted temptation. Think of all the goodness points we earned last night."

"I didn't think you kept track."

"It's not a bad idea to have an ace in the hole."

He turned the volume down to a meaningless hum in the speakers. "I'd have thought Glenn had stored up enough points from both of you."

"We must know different Glenns," she said.

"The one I know plays by the rules."

"Mine is working off demerits." "From what?"

"He'll have to tell you that. One of my rules is never to talk about poor Glenn."

"Why are you here—off by yourself?"

"I didn't notice him stopping me."

"What kind of a marriage is that?"

"Ours."

At a gas station, they filled the tank and brought sandwiches and soda from a cooler, eating in the car, Denise driving now, touching a napkin to her lips after each bite and brushing crumbs from her sweater as soon as they fell. When a glob of mayonnaise dropped onto Peter's tee shirt, he saw her watching and deliberately left it there until she reached over and wiped it away.

"Your life needs a woman's touch," she said.

He looked at her and swallowed his anger, silently counting one to fifty, refusing to say anything.

"You've never been married." She continued as if he had responded. "You've probably never even asked anybody. You're the kind of person who lives in a room with all the shades pulled. Afraid you wouldn't know what to do if you saw something interesting out there. So it's better not to find out."

"No!" He snapped the denial.

Denise gave him a surprised look. "No what?"

"I asked somebody once." Peter felt his leg trembling and clamped both hands down on his knee.

"And?"

"She said yes."

"So?"

"It didn't work out." He stared out the window, far ahead, into a vague distance where he thought he saw the outline of mountains, darK shapes wavering out at the edge of his vision.

When he moved to turn the radio up, Denise pinched his fingers in hers and snapped it off.

"Time for you to tell me about your life," she told him.

"That's not something I talk about."

"It happened out where you're going, didn't it?"

He nodded.

"Are you trying to find her? Repair your past after years of regret?" Denise made her voice breathless: "Darling, it was all a terrible mistake."

"She's not there any more. I wouldn't be going back if she was."

"She broke your poor heart."

"I broke her jaw," he blurted, then reached out as if to snatch back the words.

"Whoa!" Denise let out a snort. "Silent Peter?"

"I got jealous. It's always been that way. Whenever there's a woman in my life, I get fierce with jealousy." He found it easy to speak now, as if finally revealing his shame had made it trivial, no worst than admitting he bit his nails.

"What happened?"

"We were at a party. Her friend's apartment. I got up for drinks and found her dancing with somebody else. All harmless, but I went wild. Dragged her outside, punched her, kept punching her until people pulled me away."

"Were you drunk?"

"No. I never get drunk. The way I am comes from inside me.

"What does?"

"Whenever I have anything, I get furious with myself because I expect to lose it."

Denise took her foot off the gas and turned toward Peter. "Would you hit me?"

"For what?"

"I don't know. Dancing with a stranger."

"Why would I? You're nobody to me."

By evening, the rock face of the mountains was closing in, as if just over the next rise of the foothills. But they drove another hour, Peter at the wheel, and didn't seem to get any nearer, through the inclines were steeper now. He was leaning forward on the seat, tensing his body, thinking the car would slide backwards if he relaxed.

"You're going to be this way for the rest of your life," Denise said. "Aren't you?"

"How's that?" He spoke through clenched teeth.

"Miserable."

They reached the crest and began an abrupt descent, picking up great speed, Peter taking his hands off the wheel, glancing at Denise for a reaction, waiting for her to cry out. But she sat with her hands folded, and he was the one to slam into a skid at the edge of a ditch.

Then uphill again, the Escort shuddered, sending jolts up through his legs. The metal seemed to be flapping with vibration, and their speed slowed no matter how hard he pressed the gas. He slammed the transmission into low gear and they crept upward, reaching the top just as a great rush of steam rushed from under the hood. "Fucking head gasket!" he cried.

Denise began laughing, first quietly, openmouthed, barely making a sound. Then she roared, arms wrapped around her middle, tears running down her face. "Oh, Peter! Nothing ever goes right for you!"

Ahead, as they coasted downhill, he saw the arch of a bridge, a great sweeping river that glittered in the sunset, and beyond a town, all white, a wonderland set against the mountains. He just steered, without power, moving from simple inertia, rumbling over the bridge onto the main street, where he turned against the curb before he lost all momentum.

They found the town's one hotel a block away, just four rooms on the second story over a bar. Denise took her smallest suitcase from the trunk and Peter his dufflebag. He left her in the room to walk to a garage, where the one attendant, a kid working the gas pumps, told him the mechanic was gone for the day. He'd have to wait till morning.

When Peter got back, he saw Denise at a table in the bar talking to two men leaning forward on their stools, both in tapered jeans and cowboy boots, one with a wide brimmed felt hat and a mustache. She introduced him to the men, and he sat at the table with her, reported what the kid had said.

"If it's a gasket," the one with the mustache, Curtis, said, "they'll have to order the part. Could take days."

"It looks like we may have to change our plans," Denise said. Peter saw that she was smiling, as if they were acting out an elaborate joke.

"Plenty to do around here," Curtis told them. His friend, Eddie, nodded. Curtis signaled the bartender for more beers, one for Peter, another vodka martini for Denise.

Eddie offered Denise a cigarette, and she took it, rolling the filter on her thick, glossed lips. Peter had never seen her smoke, not for two long days in the car, not back home when she was with Glenn. Curtis snapped a flame from a polished silver lighter, and she drew in deeply, exhaling a stream of smoke in their faces.

Both Curtis and Eddie hooked boot heels over the rungs of their stools, swiveling back and forth, hovering over the table. Denise was talking to both of them, rattling on about nothing, but Peter could see her watching him out of the corner of her eye, awaiting his reaction. She moved her fingers away from her face, her jaw only inches from the arm he propped on the tabletop.

Peter stood at once. "I'll be back."

He thought Denise shook her head, once, abruptly, like a spasm. But he went up to the room and stretched out on the double bed, her suitcase open on one side, soft silk garments draped over the sides. He wouldn't touch anything.

After a half hour, Peter got up, pushed his tee shirt under his belt, and ran a hand through his hair. He was certain Denise would be gone when he got downstairs, her other two suitcases missing from his useless car, already miles from this town with a stranger who was now her friend. He wondered which man he would find left at the bar, Curtis or Eddie, maybe neither.

For a moment he thought he might stay in this town. Forever. Or until something happened. But he knew when his car was finally fixed, he would turn around and go back home, spending the days on the road wondering what he and Glenn would talk about when he got there.

Islands

Fire Island

They walked most of the way to Ocean Beach on the packed wet sand at the water's edge, Mike holding Lucy's hand as the last foam of breakers curled around their ankles. Lucy laughed and skipped, settling on her toes like a dancer. Mike watched her feet, watched his own as they splashed impressions in the sand. He was nineteen and barefoot beneath the sun.

Mike slipped his hand from Lucy's and sprinted across the beach to the dunes, toppling backwards with outstretched arms and legs. Lucy ran after and threw herself beside him. He wrapped his arms around her and squeezed as hard as he could. She cried "Oomph!" and kissed his neck.

Then they just lay looking up at the deep blue sky, together watching the wisps of clouds poised far above them, listened to the rush of the sea, saw the gulls gliding in wide circles. He pressed his foot against hers, touched fingertips along her tanned arm.

"I never want to go back," Lucy said. "It's perfect here."

"Yes." The word caught in his throat and tears flooded his eyes. He could not express his emotion, reveal how much he had longed for this moment in this place. He kissed her lightly because he did not trust himself to kiss her hard even though the beach around them was empty. Lucy hopped to her feet, playful again, gripped his wrist and pulled him up. "Come on. We can't lie here all day and forget what we came for."

"Booze!" He gave a cheerleader's yell.

Lucy began chanting, "Booze, booze, booze," and he chanted along with her, the two of them marching lockstep over the dunes, up onto the paths by the cottages, until they reached the sidewalk of the village. The liquor store clerk, a student himself, crewcut and deeply tanned, wearing penny loafers and summer weight flannels that Mike admired, sold them a fifth of Canadian Club without asking for proof of age. They exchanged broad smiles of complicity as if they were people free from rules.

By the time Mike and Lucy walked the three miles back to the inn, the sun was setting brilliantly. He had never before paid attention to the beauty of sunsets. "Look," he cried and stepped back to see Lucy shimmering in a pink glow. "Look!" She reached out and squeezed his hand.

In his room Mike measured Canadian Club by eye into a tennis ball can, added ice, sugar, and lemon juice to shake up a batch of whisky sours. They drank from paper cup, touching the rims in celebration of being tanned and barefoot and together.

At nightfall, in deepening shadows, they undressed, quickly removing their few garments—shorts, tee shirts, underpants. When they stood naked, they gazed at each other, Mike at the untanned stripes around her breasts and loins, at her tiny nipples, the pubic patch. Lucy was a small girl, short but solid in an athletic way, her hair in tight curls, her nose dotted with freckles. As he enfolded her into his arms, he was sure he would love her forever.

Manhattan

Adrianne sprawled face down on the chaise lounge while Mike rubbed lotion into her back. He traced a double dose along the pink grooves etched by her now unsnapped bathing suit top, stole fingertips to press the soft white breasts. A thousand windows peered down from the apartment houses that rose above the three spindly trees of the yard, but Mike blanked them out of his awareness, pretended they were surrounded by nothing but sheer rock face.

He had been lucky to find a garden in the city, four steps up from his basement efficiency and shared with the tenants on the first floor of the brownstone, a forty-year-old bachelor named Teddy Keane and a hostile German shepherd named Tiger. Adrianne called the garden a treasure. She loved it.

It was a warm Sunday, sections of the *Times* scattered across the slate patio, the dog safely chained to a wrought iron railing. Although the time was past noon Teddy had not stirred. They had the garden to themselves.

Mike rubbed hard into the small of her back. Adrianne placed a hand on his thigh. "Oh, that's nice." Her engagement ring flashed in the sun, impressive, Mike once again satisfied with his choices—the ring and the girl. She had stayed all last night, sleeping beside him for the third time since their engagement, more relaxed each time, accepting the naturalness of the occasion but still shy with her sexuality.

She was so sweet and sensitive, so soft. It pleased Mike to comfort her with his embrace, wipe away tears of insecurity with a fingertip. Although firm-fleshed, she seemed fragile, afraid to make decisions, depending upon him for all important choices, stunning him during his first serious attempt at seduction by asking him what she should do. Adrianne sighed, her flesh yielding to the pressure of his fingertips, and Mike had a vision of his future with this young woman: no matter what he wanted, what he did, she would submit. When his hand brushed her cheek, Adrianne seized it and kissed his palm.

"We're invading your pleasure garden." Teddy called down to them from the back door of his apartment. Tiger barked and leaped at the end of his chain. Adrianne quickly fastened her suit top and sat up. "Who's we?" Mike asked as he capped the bottle of lotion.

"Teddy and friends."

Teddy opened the screen for two men and two women, made introductions, and immediately organized everyone into setting up folding tables to spread lox, bagels, cream cheese, and the makings for bloody marys. The two men were Teddy's age, both in seersucker jackets and tennis sneakers. One of the women, white haired and young faced, made herself very busy as server, rattling wrists jammed with bracelets. Only one of their names stuck with Mike, Susan, a girl no older than himself, only a few inches shorter, lovely and slender, immaculate in a gauzy dress on this glowing summer's day.

Tiger roamed free now, fetching a plastic bone each time Teddy tossed it, indifferent to the others. The dog became a subject of conversation, then the garden, the day, the joy of such a Sunday in the city.

When Adrianne went inside to change from her bathing suit, embarrassed to be so scantily dressed, Mike spoke alone with Susan in a corner of the garden. He gestured toward Teddy and the others. "I haven't gotten you all straight yet. Who's with you?"

"I'm with myself," she said.

"Is that a general condition?"

"As long as I choose."

By the time Adrianne returned he had asked Susan for her address. Whenever their eyes met through the rest of the afternoon, she smiled as if sharing a secret.

Mallorca

A path wound down through the olive groves from their cottage to the Mediterranean. The nights were cool; they slept under his down sleeping bag unzipped into a quilt. But the bright morning sun brought quick warmth. Each day Mike and Susan dressed directly into their bathing suits and carried a straw bag of bread, almond paste, and oranges to the rocks at the blue water's edge for their breakfast. The billy goat fettered beside the path clanked his bell and ignored them, the chickens ran fluttering form their steps. It was the same every morning: goat, chickens, bread, almond paste, oranges, and bright sun.

Before eating they lay on their backs on a rock twenty feet above the sea and let the sun penetrate them. The rock itself was hollow with a small opening in the surface near the spot where they rested their heads. Each splash of waves forced a whoosh of air through the hole, a sound like the murmur of a human voice. Mike and Susan called it the Whispering Rock and kept it a secret from their friends, the one thing on this island that belonged to them alone.

Mike was hungry. He hand touched the straw bag, but he did not want to sit up yet. He shielded his eyes with a forearm and watched Susan, her belly showing the first bulge of pregnancy above the bikini bottom.

He was sure he wanted a child; they had discussed the consequences endlessly during the first four years of marriage. But he regretted her pregnancy as if it were about to spoil something vital in her. Perhaps it was because he had admired her tall slender body so much, the absolute flatness of her stomach.

Susan sensed him looking and flipped back the brim of her sun hat. "What are you thinking?"

"Nothing," he said. "Just enjoying being here."

"I'm starting to show, aren't I?"

"A little."

"And you don't like it."

"I want this baby as much as you do."

"But you're scared."

"Of what?"

"The changes in me. The threat to your sex life. The uncertainty of knowing that in the future there'll never be just the two of us again." Mike shrugged and turned to face the sea, the dazzling ripple of reflected sun. It upset him that she always had to analyze and define. Even about the Whispering Rock she explained point by point why the secret was so important to their relationship. He let the dazzle stun his vision.

"You're annoyed with me, aren't you?" Susan said.

"I'm hungry." Mike blinked, sat up, and passed the bag to her.

She spread almond paste on two pieces of bread and handed him one. He nodded thanks and chewed it in two bites. After the bread they peeled oranges and spat the pits down to the sea. On an impulse Mike leaned forward to lick the juice that ran down her chin. She laughed and drew away as if his gesture had been a tease. Just then he heard chicken squawks and the crunch of footsteps on the path behind them.

It was Mary Chin, the Chinese girl. That's what Mike and Susan called her even though she had been born in Rapid City, South Dakota and spoke with a Midwestern twang. The one time they invited Mary for dinner she drank half a bottle of cognac and fell asleep on the sofa bed. Mike had to walk her home with a flashlight through the darkness, wrapping an arm around her shoulder to hold her steady. At the door of her house she collapsed against him with a long melting kiss. Mike responded, thinking all the time that she would not remember this in the morning.

He offered her bread despite the frown in Susan's eyes.

"I've seen you here before," Mary said. "It looked so pleasant I couldn't resist coming down. Do you mind?"

"Of course not," he said.

Mary stretched out to the left of Mike. She wore white shorts and a tank top. Her skin was bronzed from hours in the sun.

"What's that sound?" she asked.

"The rock," Mike said. "It talks."

"What does it say?"

"Whatever you want to hear."

The three of them lay there for half an hour, Susan deliberately silent Mike could tell, Mary chattering away about last night's party at Rafael's.

Finally Susan spoke. "I'm going back up to the cottage."

She stood longlegged in the bikini knotted on her hip bones. The slight bowing at her knees excited Mike, but he debated staying behind with Mary. He decided he had better stand beside his wife. Mary said she would go up too. She followed Susan on the path with Mike last. To he surprise in the thick of the olive trees Mary reached a hand behind her to squeeze his. He squeezed back as chickens fled and the goat clanked his bell.

Martha's Vineyard

Mike hadn't been on a bicycle for years, but renting one seemed de rigueur in Edgartown, the best way to explore the narrow streets lined with white houses each once owned by a whaling captain. Or so it seemed. They rented from a stand near the town's pier amid restaurants, fast seafood stalls, ice cream parlors, and gift shops, an area thick with tourists in madras and sandals.

It took Mike a few moments to get his balance and maneuver around the clusters of people. Susan adjusted at once, erect and striking on her seat, shifting through the gears as if it were something she had done every day of her life.

Mike lost sight of her at South Water Street. She was moving swiftly and easily. Cyclists had to obey the one-way signs, so he could not take a short cut in the direction he thought she had gone. He rode up and back on South Water, then turned onto Main and saw her ahead pausing to skim the menu outside a creperie. But by the time he reached the place she was gone. Five minutes later she waved to him at a residential corner and sprinted away.

"I'm not racing," he called even though she could not hear. "I quit." He wheeled around in the direction opposite hers and moved down back streets without caring about scenery, trying not to think, knowing that when he stopped he would have to make a decision.

He ended up at the far end of North Water Street in front of a large hotel of darkly weathered shingles. He crossed over to the beach and pushed the bicycle along the plank walkway to the lighthouse. Only a few people were on the sand, a fat old woman in a black swimsuit that seemed to come in layers, a lone young man fully dressed on a towel, three teenage girls flaunting ripe tanned bodies. Most of the bathers in Edgartown chose to ferry to Chappaquiddick. Across the water from where he stood, beyond gliding sailboats, Mike could see the bright beach tents, children splashing in the surf, dozens of people sprawled beneath the glowing sun. The brilliance made his eyes ache, and it struck him how far all these people were from his life.

They would be divorced. At least he accepted the certainly of it, glad the boys were hundreds of miles away at summer camp where their nearness could not confuse his emotions. When he found Susan at the inn, he would speak calmly, sure of her agreement. Then, perhaps, they could enjoy their vacation.

MYKONOS

"I envy you all the places you've been," Dolores said. "All my life I've dreamed of travel but never go anywhere."

"That's because you chose to have so many children," Mike said. "You can't build a nest and indulge wanderlust at the same time."

"But I want to do everything."

They sat at a corner table where the light was so dim he felt a grey film covered his eyes. Except for a few men on stools in the other room, the bar was empty. It always was on Monday nights when they met there, arriving in separate cars. Mike held Dolores' hand in both of his on the tabletop, pleased with his urge to lean across and kiss her.

"If you could pick any place in the world," he asked her, "where would you go first?"

"Mykonos." "What's that?"

"An island in the Aegean."

"Why?"

"It's so beautiful in pictures. I can't imagine how a place could be more beautiful. When life gets awful—through all the trouble with Tom—I bring out my pictures of Mykonos and keep my sanity."

"What's it like?"

"White houses on cliffs rising from the sea. A sky the bluest of blues. It's perfect. I dream that if I could go there everything would be all right."

This woman of forty, greying, skin puckering about her pale eyes, was more innocent than her three adolescent daughters. Mike tried to picture her standing on a cliff against the blue sky of Mykonos, youthful and radiant.

"I'll take you," he said.

She laughed, her face suddenly flushed. "Don't tease."

"It would be a bit of a rush to arrange things. But we can leave within the month."

Tears welled when she realized he was serious. She pressed his hands. He thought she might weep. "Oh Mike, I couldn't."

"Why not?"

She met his eyes, wavered, and then looked down. "I can't." Her denial was almost a sob.

"Are you afraid Mykonos will disappoint you?"

"No. It's just not possible." Now her tears flowed.

As they clutched each other's hands in the darkness, Mike knew they would never go to Mykonos together.

Ocracoke

"Where are all the goddamned ponies?" Lorraine said.

They had parked across the highway by the ocean and now stood on a wooden platform overlooking a strip of fenced off land on the sound side of the island.

"The sign promised wild ponies," she insisted.

"There." Mike pointed to a cluster several hundred yards away across grey sand and stiff beach grass.

"One, two, three . . . six." She counted with a finger. "You said hundreds."

He looked at Lorraine and shrugged. She was the kind of woman who had never appealed to him—too hefty, too loud, blonde hair puffed and brittle with spray; the bathroom of her apartment littered with dye packs, curling iron, rollers, spray cans; her conversation underlined with sarcasms. And yet they had taken this vacation together. And for months of Saturday nights they had crawled bleary-eyed into her unmade bed to clutch at each other's flesh.

"George Hoffman told me there were hundred of wild ponies here," he said.

"That was how long ago?"

"About twenty-five years. We worked together when I had my first job."

"Times change, Michael. You've never caught on."

"He'd talk about Ocracoke by the hour, made it seem like another world."

"Fifteen miles of sand and scrub grass. Terrific."

"The ponies descend from some of the first Spanish horses to be brought to America. They're absolutely pure bred."

"I count six, Michael. Six lousy horses."

"Since that time I've always wanted to come to Ocracoke."

"Congratulations. You've finally made it. Glorious Ocracoke." "I guess we might as well turn back."

"My thoughts exactly."

Lorraine's high heeled sandals wobbled on the sand path to the car. Mike lagged behind, then stopped to watch her pull away from him as if unaware that he was following. But when she kicked off her shoes and stood poised on a dune, silhouetted against the glowing orange sun, he ran ahead to fling an arm around her waist.

Oxfords

Twenty years ago, when they seemed on the verge of a friendship, Henry found Stuart Hartwick tolerable. That is, their wives got on well and Stuart's conversation amused despite his arcane obsessions.

A few years under thirty, Stuart bulked large and portly, formal even at leisure, his white shirts always crisp with starch, his trousers sharply creased, his black slip-on shoes gleaming. His speech, like the rest of him, resounded with precision, each word carefully chosen and articulated. His dark mustache was almost square, and red-veined jowls sagged over tight collars. Unlike Henry, whose brief adulthood had been pinched by academic poverty, he had traveled so widely, imparted such esoteric knowledge of Baltic ferries, Hapsburg palaces, rare wines, and fine silks that Henry found himself content to be an audience.

Their wives had met first, Henry's Elaine and Stuart's Winnie. Young mothers of eight-month-old babies, Joy and Stuart, Jr., nicknamed Tink by Winnie, the two women found immediate compatibility in talk of formulas, diaper services, and sudden fevers. But Henry couldn't imagine them exchanging a sentence before the babies. Winnie, slow and bland, seemed to have spent her life waiting for the identity that motherhood would bring. Elaine's dark eyes blazed with promise. In fifty years, when their grandchildren were parents, he still would be discovering her.

Henry and Elaine made their first formal visit to the Hartwicks on a Sunday afternoon in late September, maneuvering through a grid of hard- packed dirt roads miles from their university. Henry, enjoying a rare day away from the heaped books in his library carrel, sang out at the dark soil and rich green crops, Elaine laughing at his excitement.

Their car pitched over unseen railroad tracks camouflaged by a growth of thick weeds. "We're in the fertility belt," he cried, reaching back to squeeze Joy's small foot.

Stuart and Winnie rented a large white house overwhelmed by vines and sagging branches far from neighbors in a farming township called Oxford.

"I know it's rather isolated here," Stuart said to Henry in lieu of a greeting as they shook hands in the foyer, "but I've always wanted to live in Oxford."

His face suddenly reddened as deep chuckles rumbled from his middle. It was one of the few intentional jokes Henry ever heard Stuart make. "And it's just right for Stuart to do his research," Winnie added. "He needs absolute quiet." Every now and then she brightened with little outbursts of enthusiasm that Henry found attractive. Usually she was a plain woman with pallid skin and drab hair.

Inside the living room of overstuffed chairs and family antiques he had shipped from back East, Stuart sat, crossed his legs, and sipped sherry. Winnie poured from a decanter for Henry and Elaine, then put Joy in the playpen with Tink.

"She's so dainty," Winnie said. Even though the babies were only a week apart in birth dates, Tink was a head taller and ten pounds heavier. Joy, in pink tights and frilly white visiting dress, sucked on her pacifier while the boy hugged a stuffed panda and scowled.

The mothers took chairs near the playpen, and Henry found himself across the room with Stuart, glancing over at the babies, fascinated by his daughter's play. When Tink reached out a tentative hand and touched Joy's face, his blood surged. "Cute boy you have," he told Stuart, suddenly warming to the man

Stuart fell into a coughing fit.

Henry looked away through a doorway into a room filled with precisely shelved books, many leather bound, totally unlike his own shaggy paperbacks stuffed into orange crates. He envied the man that room, a sanctuary where for several hours each day he could be alone with his own mind, where neither wife nor child could interrupt the pleasure of contemplation, the thrill of insights.

Stuart stood and led him inside, announcing that he had done the fine binding himself, precisely summarizing the technique. He reached

to an upper shelf and slipped out several thin volumes in brown leather. "I'd like to show you my diaries."

Henry took the one offered and ran fingertips over the goldleafed
tooling, then opened into the unlined pages of immaculate italic lettering. The heading for each entry was written out in full: Friday, September the twenty-first, Nineteen hundred and eighty-three. Henry,
fascinated, closed his eyes to breathe in the leather scent, pressed a
palm against the fine rag paper. After turning a few pages, he realized
the pattern of the entries: first the exact time of Stuart's rising, a sentence or two on the weather, a summary of the day's activities, usually
something like "nine hours at my desk with Saint-Beuve," and finally
summaries of his insights.

Now Henry became curious. He took another volume from Stuart's hand, one that ended only a month before, and flipped through
in search of something truly personal, an emotion, a note of upset or
caring, a reference to Winnie or Tink. But Coleridge dominated. Stuart
had been watching him with close expectation. Henry returned the
diaries into his hands and said, truthfully, that they were beautiful
books.

II

When the Hartwicks made their return visit to the apartment Henry and Elaine rented in town, Elaine fussed for hours, dusting and re-
dusting, straightening the prints, stacking stray books, repositioning
chairs six inches this way or that.

"Would you like me to repaper the walls?" Henry asked.

"It's so tiny and cluttered here. This place wasn't meant for a baby."

"We'll sell Joy. Trade her in on a Chippendale end table."

"Winnie has such lovely things. China. A silver tea service."

"And Stuart is the most cultivated man I know." Henry paused to
smile. "He's got cultivation coming out of his ears."

"Like stuffing. He's the stuffiest man I've ever met."

"But we've got charm, wit, and winning ways. An afternoon with
us will make Stuart grovel with envy."

Just as he spoke the man's name, the door buzzer sounded, exactly
at the arranged time. Winnie carried a squirming Tink and a shoulder

bag of bottles and diapers. Stuart held only a tissue-wrapped gift Bordeaux and a marked volume in his other hand. "There's a passage I've been wanting to show you," he told Henry.

Elaine accepted the wine and Winnie looked about for a place to deposit Tink while she ran back to the car for his toys and blanket. She stood holding the baby at arm's length, Stuart deliberately avoiding her eyes, as if he had arrived alone. Embarrassed, but not sure for whom, Henry took Tink from her and at once sensed a presence quite different from Joy. The boy twisted in his arms; strands of fine hair tickled his chin.

"Be careful," Stuart said. "It might be wet."

Winnie came back in seconds, retrieving her son and exclaiming how cozy the apartment was.

Stuart announced that he had been considering Longinus recently and began presenting insights as if he had prepared his conversation like a formal lecture. Henry had trouble following the man's ideas, sensing that he had entered a complex chain of thought rather late along the way.

Tink hit Joy with a plastic locomotive, Joy began to cry, and Winnie— mortified—gave her son a light swat on his thick pad of diaper. Outraged, he howled even louder than Joy. Each woman quickly embraced her child.

"He's been so cranky today," Winnie said by way of apology. Elaine nodded. "Joy gets that way too."

The babies shrieked redfaced, mouth wide, gasping for breath.

"It's hard to imagine so much noise coming from such tiny creatures," Henry said to bridge the awkwardness.

But Stuart, pinpricks of sweat on his forehead, ignored him and spoke directly to Winnie. "If you can't control that child, get it out of this room!"

Elaine looked quickly to Henry and then down at the rug. "Maybe we can go into the bedroom," she said to Winnie, half whispering. Winnie nodded, and at once they disappeared with the babies.

The moment the door closed, Stuart resumed the bass drone of his discourse. Henry couldn't listen to a word of it. He sat shocked by the realization that this man scorned his own child.

III

For weeks the couples did not see each other, though Winnie called Elaine for long conversations several times every few days. "She's so lonely out there. When Stuart isn't using the car, he's closed off in his library."

Henry dreaded running into Stuart at the university, but he never did, until one afternoon the large man, his bulk buttoned into a blue blazer, approached him on the library steps. "I've been meaning to discuss a matter with you."

At once Henry assumed Stuart would explain his behavior toward his son. Instead he wanted to share thoughts about Lawrence Sterne, some elaborate thesis about the interplay between the temporal and the phenomenal and the atemporal and the noumenal. Henry tried to follow the argument, uncertain whether he was in the presence of genius or a bizarre form of madness.

"But Stuart," he could not help saying after ten minutes of anxious listening, "*Tristram Shandy* is a very funny book."

Stuart frowned, squashing his mustache. "I suppose it is," he said as if this were a new idea that must be digested very slowly.

Then he looked at his watch. "I didn't realize the time. I must be off to my Oxford." He gave one of his rare throat- clearing laughs. "My little center of learning."

"Regards to Winnie," he called after the man's broad back. Stuart grunted.

"And Tink." Silence.

IV

The next week, just one day after the doctor confirmed Elaine's suspicion that she was pregnant again, Winnie called while Elaine had Joy at the park. Henry, coat on and eager to spend the afternoon in his carrel, explained that she would be back in an hour.

"I know she's not home," Winnie said. "She told me this morning. I have to talk with you."

"Yes?" Henry sensed great import in her tone. He paused, expecting her to go on.

"Not on the phone." He realized she was whispering. "Stuart is letting me have the car for shopping. Can we meet in town?"

Henry agreed, even though it meant rearranging his day, taking time from his research, without the slightest idea of what she might want.

When Henry arrived, Winnie was waiting in the Sears parking lot, Tink asleep in a bassinet on the back seat of the ponderous station wagon.

"Would you like a cup of coffee?" Henry asked, not sure what they would do with the baby.

"Can we just talk in the car?"

"Fine." He got in beside her and met her eyes, noticing for the first time how vulnerable they were. Her hands rubbed the steering wheel. "What did you want to talk about?'

Winnie breathed deeply and looked away from him, straight out the windshield. "Tink was an accident."

He waited for more, something of significance, but finally said, "So was Joy. We'd planned to wait."

"I mean a real accident." Tears ran down the side of her nose. "Stuart never wanted children."

She was sobbing and Henry realized what he should have known weeks before. "Have you told Elaine?" he asked.

"I've been too ashamed to tell anyone. Then I saw you holding Tink. You're such a wonderful father."

She lifted his hand and pressed the knuckles to her burning cheek. Embarrassed, he let her tears fall onto his flesh and waited through the long silence until she finally released him.

He squeezed her hand. "Tink is a sweet, handsome boy. Stuart will come to love him."

Her sobs discomforted him, almost made him guilty for loving his own wife and child so much.

Before she drove away, as Henry was starting his car, Winnie called out to him. "Please promise me that you'll never say anything about today to Elaine. She's my best friend."

At home he found Elaine and Joy napping on the big double bed and lay down to pull them into his embrace. He placed his open hand on Elaine's stomach even though he knew signs of life were months away.

V

The invitation came in the mail, a gold embossed card with date and time entered in Stuart's italic hand.

"I'll call and claim morning sickness." Elaine slipped it into a stack of journals.

"I thought you liked Winnie," Henry said.

"She's sweet and sad. But I won't spend another afternoon watching Stuart treat that poor child like a creature turned up on a slimy log."

"I'll play with him. Practice for a boy."

"Stuart will seal you off in that library the second you come through the door. That's my idea of hell."

"But imagine his library in this apartment. A room that's not cluttered with racks of drying diapers where I could do my work in peace. No more cage of a carrel. My books and my family. Only having to open a door to get from one to the other."

"Is that your Oxford?"

"I don't need a magic city. My life can be perfect anywhere." He kissed her and pulled the bulge of her middle tight against him.

"Do we have to visit Stuart and Winnie?"

He nodded, annoyed by the burden of Winnie's secret.

VI

At twilight, Henry drove away from their second visit to the Hartwicks in Oxford, lulled himself into a delicious dream of his family in a house like that, he with his walls of books, Elaine with her crafts studio, Joy and the new baby in their nursery.

Joy, missing her nap, slept on Elaine's lap, her face rubbing against her mother's breast as the car bounced along the deserted country road. Henry prolonged the silence, unwilling to open a conversation that would unleash Elaine's dislike of Stuart. Of course the day had been a disaster, Stuart practically ripping Tink from Henry's arms when he tried to hold the boy, Winnie sniffling back tears the whole time. He'd wanted to punch Stuart, drive his fist into the man's puffed face. No more. He made a private vow never to go back. He'd stay out of other people's lives. He had his own family to care about.

The rich glow of the horizon dazzled his eyes. He blinked and noticed the wooden X of the crossing sign, recalling the surprising thump of tracks from the first time they drove the route. Elaine brushed Joy's fine curls with her lips and hummed. The sign's paint was weathered down to bare wood, a poorly tended relic, Henry thought, of long past travelers.

At the sudden thunder of engine noise, his mind hung suspended in indecision, as if it were an enormous weight balanced just inside the windshield. Then he yanked the wheel and swerved, but the impact blew off the driver's door and threw him out of the car, away from the mangled steel that crushed his wife and daughter.

VII

Henry lay in a coma three weeks and spent four months in a body cast. Both legs suffered compound breaks; three ribs were cracked, his skull fractured, a lung punctured.

When he was out of traction, several weeks before his release, Winnie came to visit.

"Tink is with a sitter," she told him as if that explanation were vital.

"Yes."

"I wanted to see you right away, but they weren't allowing visitors. And then when you were conscious again my life fell apart."

"Oh."

"Stuart left us." She caught her breath. "One day he collected all his things, all his books and papers, packed the station wagon, and drove back East. I stood there and screamed the whole time. Tink was screaming too, but I couldn't even pick him up."

"I'm sorry."

She stopped talking and went pale. "Oh my god! I'm the one who should be sorry."

"I'd rather not talk about it," he said. She nodded, again and again.

"Tell me about you," he said to make her stop.

"It's just Tink and me now. We moved to an apartment in town. I couldn't stay in that house in Oxford. Stuart's mother sends money. There's plenty of money. I try to believe that Tink will be better off away from a father who despises him."

"You're probably right."

Winnie put her hand next to his on the crisp white sheet, and it struck him how alive it was, that it could touch and feel. That it was the wrong hand. "What will you be doing now?" she asked. Her fingers seemed totremble.

He buried his hand beneath the blanket. "Go away. I wish I could find a place a million miles from here."

VIII

Through the endless immobile days, unable to read, unwilling to watch television, Henry had envisioned Stuart's library, the walls of shelves, the odor of handtooled bindings, the deep impression of print on creamy pages. He imagined the books so often they became transformed into his own possessions, a room he had never known before, four walls filled from floor to ceiling with thousands of leather volumes. No door, no window, just a thick wool rug and a carved wooden chair. A place where he could shut out all other thoughts.

But the day the doctor, always gravely polite, told him that he would be released, he let himself remember the apartment he had lived in with Elaine and Joy—the shabby graduate student furniture, the prints cut from art magazines, but most of all the paperbacks wedged into wooden crates. He would have torn those books apart, burned them in one great bonfire, sworn a pledge never to read again if that would have returned his wife and child.

When he moved, he abandoned all possessions, but a thousand miles away he accumulated new books and read for hours each day. He justified his life through research, as if each note he took were a small payment exacted by some terrible debt. At night, when he could not sleep, he lifted a volume from his night table and snapped on the reading light.

IX

Over the years, Henry slowly admitted the world into his life, first accepting invitations for dinner, then for weekend gatherings, finally traveling to new places, cataloguing views and vistas in his notes.

He lost his dread of women, eventually lived with one, then another, and for three years a nurse called Barbara. But she took a job a thousand miles away, weeping for the first time the morning of her leaving. "You're a kind, sweet man. But you never let me know you."

"If I ever loved anyone so much again," Henry told her, "I'd spend every moment of every day in terror."

X

Years later, on a leave in Oxford, Henry converted dollars to pounds at the Barclay's Bank branch on the High Street and walked toward Carfax. He noticed a large man in British tweeds and a six-foot scarf staring at him from the grey wall of Queen's College.

"I say," the man called to him. "Don't I know you?"

The bass voice made Henry look closer. Immediately, he felt a desperate sinking. It was Stuart Hartwick, thirty pounds heavier, the patch of mustache all grey now.

"It's Henry of course." Stuart gave a ceremonial wave. "I always assumed we would meet again."

Henry resisted the impulse to run. Instead he said, "I see you've finally gotten to the real Oxford."

"Quite." Stuart seemed to miss the allusion to his old joke. "I've followed your career with interest, Henry. Read your books and articles. They're not my way of seeing things of course. But apparently you've made a success for yourself."

"I'm afraid I don't keep up as much as I should.   "I'm afraid I don't keep up as much as I should. I've missed your work."

"I don't find it necessary to publish." Stuart cleared his throat. "Well, Henry, what brings you here?"

"A grant. And you?"

"Newman and the Oxford Movement, of course."

"Where are you teaching?"

"I don't teach." Stuart seemed offended. "I've never taught."

Henry took a long look at his watch, savoring each tick as if it held an eternity. "I'd better eat something before my appointment." He stepped away.

"Excellent. I'll join you."

Henry, ashamed at his helplessness, led Stuart to a pub in a 14th century courtyard off Cornmarket away from the midday bustle where he normally enjoyed the steak and kidney, the lukewarm bitter in quiet solitude. They sat at one corner of a crowded table, Henry on a stool, Stuart on the wall bench beside a tiny old lady with rouged cheeks and shopping bundles piled on her lap.

"It's rather awkward for me at this moment," Stuart said "In what way?"

"Stuart is here. In Oxford."

After a second Henry realized he meant his son, Tink. "At which college?"

Stuart snorted. "None. He came here two days ago to track me down."

"How is he?"

"I have no idea. I haven't seen him in years."

"But you said he's here."

"I've managed to avoid him so far. But he left a note at my bank."

"The bank?" Once again, Henry felt bewildered by one of Stuart's explanations.

"My address is a secret. I hope he won't recognize me on the street."

"Your son?"

"I've chosen to have no part of paternity."

The old lady set her mouth and clutched her packages. "But what does Winnie think of all this?"

"That," Stuart said as if suppressing great anger, "is another story."

He did not explain, silently slicing his gammon steak while Henry, with a sudden pang, recalled the long-forgotten warmth of babies in his arms.

XI

A pounding on the apartment door awoke Henry at 6 a.m. It was still dark outside. He sat up in bed and called, "What is it?" The pounding sounded louder. He rubbed his eyes, ran fingers through his hair, and realized he had to use the toilet. "Just a minute," he called. When he came back, he put on slippers and a pair of trousers.

A pudgy young man stood on his doorstep, dressed in rumpled blue denim, a rucksack strapped over his shoulders. A wispy beard grew on a red-rashed chin. Henry knew the soft brown eyes at once.

"Where's my father?" the boy demanded.

"I have no idea. How did you get this address?"

"He left it at his bank. In case of emergency. I spent the night finding the damn street. It's all crooked alleys in this town."

Henry's neck tensed, but he only sighed resignation. Still half asleep, he held the door wide. "Come inside, Tink."

The young man froze. "Where did you get that name?"

"I knew you when you were a baby." Henry gestured toward an armchair.

Tink let the rucksack slide off his shoulder and collapsed into the cushions. Only then did Henry recognize his exhaustion. He offered coffee, but Tink shook his head.

"How is your mother?" Henry saw a hand trembling on a white sheet.

"The same as always."

"What's does she do?"

"Nothing." Tink frowned. "Nobody is our family does anything. We all live off Grandma's money. My mother spends her days polishing the silver. She can count butter knives for hours."

"Why are you so angry with her?"

"She just gave up when my father walked out."

Henry's hand tingled with the sensation of her burning cheek, the touch of her tears on his knuckles. "She loved you so much."

Tink glared. "She treats me like a victim. Her poor abandoned baby."

He slouched in the chair, mouth drooping bleakly. Yet Henry studied him with rapt concentration, suddenly realizing that Tink was a long-awaited visitor. He spoke very slowly. "You used to play with my daughter."

Tink gave him a blank look.

"Her name was Joy," Henry said, wondering if Tink could sense the pain it cost him to speak it aloud after so many years.

XII

Tink dozed and Henry watched him, imagining what it would be like to search for Stuart in Oxford. He would try all the obvious places—the Bodleian, Blackwell's, up and down Broad Street and narrow Turl, the Ashmolean Museum, and finally some of the college chapels—Merton, Christ Church, Pembroke. Then it occurred to him that Newman's college had been Oriel. But he knew Stuart would no longer be in that library, the porter explaining how Mr. Hartwick had suddenly packed all his papers and rushed off.

Henry pictured catching Stuart at the train station, grabbing him by the lapels and shouting, "Your son is in my flat." And Stuart brushing away his hands. "That woman violated our agreement. No children. My work requires absolute freedom from the ordinary."

With a toe, Henry touched the bulging rucksack on his rug, pushed against the dead weight.

XIII

"What will you do now?" Henry asked Tink after he awoke, as they drank instant coffee and ate crackers.

"Go home. Look for a room. Find a job. I won't sponge off Grandma the rest of my life the way my father does."

"Why did you come here, Tink?"

Tink looked down at his shoes. "To make him admit he has a son."

"He doesn't know how to be a father, Tink."

"Most men do it every day."

"Yes. It's the most natural thing in the world."

Tink stood and gripped a canvas strap, ready to leave.

Henry stood with him and held his arm. "Did your mother ever tell you about me?" he asked urgently.

"About what?"

Henry scanned the room, overwhelmed by foreignness, the buckled wallpaper, the ancient fixtures, the scarred bookcases. He gripped the back of a loveseat. "The accident."

Tink shook his head, then blinked with surprise. "Were you the ones?"

"My family." Henry dug fingers into the upholstery as if a great forcewas about to blast him though the sealed walls that had been his safety.

"Whenever she tells that story, she ends up crying."

"I've never let myself cry." Henry clutched even tighter, pressed his feet down into the rug.

"She made my father invite you."

"I accepted it."

"To be with them? Why?"

For you. But Henry did not speak aloud, amazed at the memory of his motive, at the strangeness of having this grown man standing before him, at all the years separating him from his own life. "I'm glad you came," Henry finally said.

Tink hoisted the rucksack onto his shoulders.

Henry saw himself taking Winnie's hand in the hospital. The idea had seemed preposterous then, awful in a grief so absolute it numbed his soul. If not Winnie, some other woman, some other child. "It didn't have to be this way," he said, looking back at a stranger's bookcases.

"What?"

"Forget about him, about her. Choose your own life."

He watched closely as Tink descended the stairs, each worn step thumping under his weight. When the front door closed, he crossed to the window and saw Tink in the street, pausing briefly and then swept off in the morning flow of the waking city—clerks with thick briefcases, old women on bicycles, undergraduates trailing long striped scarves, schoolchildren skipping beside stone walls.

A glowing sunrise dazzled the soaring spires. Tink stepped with the others toward the bright rays and then turned a corner. Henry imagined him walking all day, never looking back, suddenly discovering something new that would change his life.

He swung the windows wide and felt the breeze on his face, heard human voices rise from the street around him, the laughter of the children. With an ache of longing, he reached his arms toward all the life of Oxford.

Homemaking

HAROLD TALKED THEM INTO MOVING. He was Steve and Debra's succssful friend, full of advice for Steve since they were college freshman a dozen years ago. But Steve, bored and broke, had dropped out as a first semester sophomore, didn't even bother to buy textbooks, relieved to find a job servicing machines in a shipping department. Harold went on to a business degree, a career as a marketing manger, and a four-bedroom colonial in an upscale subdivision. So at first Steve and Debra didn't take him seriously when he argued that they should rent a house. Of course, they agreed the apartment was much too small, cramped, just two rooms. But how could they afford a bigger place?

A brown metal unit with a two-burner stove, sink, and cube refrigerator took up the back wall of the room where they ate and watched TV from a sagging sofa wedged against a playpen piled with toys and stuffed animals. In the other room, a plaid spread on a clothesline separated their bed from Molly's crib. Half their clothes wouldn't fit into the one narrow closet and had to be stored in cardboard boxes crammed under the box spring. When Harold pointed at the clutter and shook his head, Steve just sighed.

Though they lived at opposite ends of the same town, Harold didn't contact them for months at a time, then all of a sudden would be around constantly, he and his wife, Cheryl, coming by several times a week with bottles of French wine, sometimes calling first, sometimes just showing up. Harold was a big man, freckled and red faced, curly haired, overweight, noisily enthusiastic, half shouting when he spoke. Cheryl, small and taut, sharp nosed, said very little, her eyes intense, as if keeping secrets.

Steve just wanted to chew over old times when they visited — boom boxes blasting from the dorm roof, water balloons dropped from windows, the night they raced cars on the stadium track. But Harold went on and on about the apartment, pointing out the ironing board leaning against a corner, the pots hanging from a wall, the chipped enamel table, the coats heaped on the rack by the door. "This is no way for you and Debra to live. Not with a kid." He said it every time, pointing to Molly's crib with his eyes raised, though—childless himself—he never picked her up. Debra would look to Cheryl with a silent appeal, but Cheryl seemed oblivious, savoring a juice glass of Bordeaux, her gaze fixed on the lights reflected in the window.

Certainly, Debra would tell Harold, they wanted to move, desperately, but money was the problem. They were barely breaking even. Still, the more Harold went on, the more Steve wavered, half believing he could figure out a way to manage a higher rent. But Debra would say, "We can't afford it," each time after Harold left, fingers trembling as she calculated and recalculated their budget, copying rows of numbers onto a small lined pad.

Then Debra became pregnant again, probably the Saturday Harold and Cheryl stayed till 3 and left an open bottle for her and Steve to finish. They had fallen into a groggy lovemaking, too bleary-eyed in the morning to remember if they had taken precautions. They hadn't, and now Steve could imagine no logistical possibilities for coping with another baby in the two rooms. Debra suggested putting their bed in the living area and getting rid of the sofa; the springs were dragging on the floor anyway. But when he said, "Do you really want to live like that?" she shook her head and wept.

So they house hunted, Steve mostly, following up listings Harold tore from the newspaper, ragged-edged slips of paper he would stuff into Steve's shirt pocket. When Steve found one he liked, he went back with Debra, who toted year-old Molly in a back pouch and fingered the calculator in her purse, convincing him that the rent was hundreds too much.

"Maybe I can get a better job," Steve said.

"In this town?" Debra gave a hopeless shrug. "In this world? What can you do?"

He knew she was right, but resented her saying it, as if the economy were his fault. "I'm good with my hands. When I quit college, I started off making good money."

"Hands don't matter any more. You should have stayed in school." Her words were flat, a statement of fact, not an accusation, but Steve felt his face burning. He tried to turn it into a joke. "Too muchpartying with Harold." "Harold graduated."

Steve looked away from her, unwilling to meet her eyes. "Harold's smart."

"He didn't stop you from dropping out." "It was me. I didn't want to be there."

"Why don't they ever invite us to their house?"

He'd never thought about it. Harold had always been like that, just showing up in his room the few nights he tried to study, looming in his doorway, oversized, too soft to be an athlete, suddenly challenging him to arm wrestle, always winning and then taking him out for beer and pizza. "It saves us a sitter."

"Is that what he said?" "Harold's thoughtful."

"Then why doesn't he give you a job?"

Steve forced a laugh. "What can I do that he needs?"

Harold found them a house, bursting in with Cheryl while Steve and Debra were eating dinner, the apartment thick with hamburger sizzle. Harold looked very pleased with himself. On a whim, he told them, he had turned into a street that afternoon and saw the For Rent sign, wrote down the phone number of the real estate firm.

"And guess who the agent is?" Harold said.

Steve shook his head. He knew nothing about real estate. "Old Martha Selig."

Debra winced. "The lady the pigs attacked?" Cheryl nodded. Harold grinned. "The very one."

It seemed everyone in town knew the story, at least rumors about it. Steve remembered as Harold went on; he just hadn't associated the name. The attack happened many years ago, before he and Debra were even born. Now Martha Selig was a middle-aged woman. Then she had been a five-year-old feeding the pigs on her parents' farm several miles out in the country, dragging buckets of slops from the barn. The animals all knew her, crowding around grunting and snorting when she appeared in the afternoon. One day a sow just went berserk and set the others off. They swarmed Martha, trampled her with hooves, sank teeth into her flesh. She spent three months in the hospital, a year in bed, walked with a cane ever since. People said she had terrible scars, lived in constant pain.

"Do we have to get a house from somebody like that?" Debra asked.

The others looked at her. "Somebody like what?" Cheryl asked. "Maimed."

"You can't notice anything wrong with her except for the limp," Harold told her. "The pigs didn't get her face."

Debra sucked in her cheeks, as if fighting back morning sickness. Steve turned away.

Harold focused on Steve. "Listen. The rent isn't much more than this place. It's got two rooms downstairs and two up. You can afford it.""What's the catch?" Steve said.

"It's small and old and needs lots of fixing." "I think it's cute," Cheryl said.

"Would you want to live there?" Debra asked her. "Sure. If I had no other choice."

Debra insisted that Steve check out the house by himself. "I don't want to see that woman."

"It wasn't her fault," he said. "Blame the pigs." Debra shivered.

"You heard what Harold said. We can fix it up." "Why do you always let Harold tell you what to do?"

"If I listened to you, we'd rot in this place." He squeezed fists, stifling anger.

"Harold doesn't know everything." "He wants to help us."

"Who says we need it? Who says we need him?" Her eyes were moist, lips trembling. The pregnancy was growing, a swelling in the baggy jeans that made her look misshapen.

"It's not like we're doing so good on our own."

Steve met Martha Selig at her office and rode in her Buick to look at the house. She moved slowly and stiffly, emitted deep sighs getting in and out of the driver's seat; that was the only sign of her ordeal. But she wore dark slacks and long sleeves on a warm day, her top buttoned high on her neck. In the car Steve had expected the woman to feign good cheer and rattle on about the house. Instead she was dour and taciturn, as if annoyed that a client had disturbed her day.

Perhaps it was the property she was showing, a house with a rent that wouldn't bring her much of a commission. She took Steve out to a narrow half-paved street he hadn't known existed, where most of the homes were trailers packed one next to the other on bare cinder blocks. The house with the sign was the only two-story building on the block, very old, the flaked paint grey with soot, shutters missing, masking tape across cracks in the windows. An incongruous door in the middle of the second story opened out to a slanted porch roof too narrow to stand on. When asked about it, Martha, as if begrudging the information, told him the house was historical, one of the first in the town, built by early settlers, originally centered on acres of farmland. It had been designed for Indian raids, she said, so people could hide upstairs and the savages couldn't rush up the narrow stairway. The odd door allowed for hoisting furniture onto the second floor.

"How long has it been empty?"

"A year." She paused. "Maybe two."

Inside someone had started ripping wallpaper from the parlor, not working systematically, leaving swaths of bare plaster on all four walls, dried strips with faded flowers hanging loose where wall met ceiling. The warped floorboards of the two front rooms were coated with peeling brown paint, the kitchen linoleum worn down to patches of felt backing. The cabinet doors all hung open, the shelves lined with yellowed newspaper. Only the gas stove was new, gleaming white. The owner, Martha explained, got it on sale when he refurbished two of his other properties.

"Why didn't he fix this one up?" Steve wondered.

"It wouldn't be worth it. He'd have to charge the same rent as houses in the good part of town, and who'd want to live here if they could afford there?"

Back in the apartment, Steve wasn't sure. The more he described the house to Debra the more uncertain he became. "There's a narrow stairs to the second floor behind a door that looks like a coat closet. You have to duck your head and edge up sideways."

"It sounds," Debra said, biting her lips, drawing in her face, "much worse than here." He wanted to tell her to stop, that she was making herself ugly.

Then Harold showed up, eager, pushing a laundry basket aside as he sprawled on the sofa. "So what's it like inside?" He made Steve go through the details all over again. "Everything you're telling me is cosmetic. A scrubbing, a few panes of glass, a coat of paint. It's four rooms, a real kitchen, space for two kids. Debra's due in a couple of months." He pointed to the bulge of her pregnancy. "You'd be crazy not to take it."

"When am I supposed to get all this painting and fixing up done?"

"We'll find help," Harold promised, emphatic. "Get everybody we know to put in, say, two hours scraping and painting. One weekend and the place will be sparkling."

After Harold left, Debra buried her head in the sofa's padding and hugged her knees to her chest. "I don't want to move."

"You won't have to do a thing." Steve kicked aside the laundry and stood over her. "We'll take care of it all."

She gave him a bleary look, face ashen, than ran into the bathroom and dropped in front of the toilet.

Harold's weekend turned out to be closer to a month. Late in the evenings, working under dim ceiling bulbs, Steve hoped the need for a second coat wouldn't be so obvious after the paint dried. A few friends did help, mainly people Harold knew, at least the first days, then they ended up having other commitments. Even Harold kept having to work late, calling at the last minute to cancel, promising to make up the time.

One night when Steve was alone, standing in the middle of the floor and cursing at cracks too deep for spackle, a woman appeared, a shape in the darkness tapping at the warped screen door. Steve let her in, blushing, certain she had heard his obscenities.

"Harold sent me," she said when she introduced herself as Julia. Her head was covered by red bandana, her body wrapped in an over-size flannel shirt. "Lot's of work here," she said, then went up to the second floor with a paint can and a plastic drop cloth as if she knew exactly what had to be done. She painted so quietly that Steve shouted to ask if she was okay. "I'm great," she called down. When Julia left, he saw that she had finished a whole room.

The next night she arrived soon after Steve. He felt embarrassed that she was doing so much, a stranger putting aside her own life to help his. But she told him it gave her great enjoyment. "It's therapy. Taking part in a transformation. Helping to make something better."

At first, Steve found her a plain woman, long-faced and wide-hipped, too thin every place else. Then he came to like her energy, the snap of her dark eyes, the constant fluttering of her fingers when she talked. Working in the empty house, he spreading a broad path with the roller, Julia edging the trim with a narrow brush, her presence seemed a natural part of his day.

One evening Harold rushed in to check their progress, his car idling at the curb. He hurried from room to room and told them, "You two are doing a great job." He slapped Steve's shoulder, gave Julia a quick hug. Then he was gone. His visit couldn't have lasted more than two minutes.

Julia was laughing. "That's typical Harold."

"How well do you know him?"

"Oh, we're great friends."

"He never mentioned you before."

"He told me all about you." She reached out to touch his arm.

"College days?" He waited, apprehensive, realizing that he didn't want her to know what a fool he had been. "About now."

"Money's always been tough for me." "Harold wants you to be happy."

He set the roller down in the pan, wiped his hands across his shirt-front. "What about you? Does he want to make you happy too?" It struck him that he really cared to know.

"My life's fine. Ed's a good father. He takes care of our sons while I'm out with a paint brush trying to improve the world."

"When will I meet Ed?"

"Unlikely." Julia's smile surprised him. "We don't have the same friends."

"Not even Harold." She shook her head.

"Doesn't that complicate your lives?"

"It makes things interesting."

They had started from different ends of the room, but met in the same corner. Julia dabbed at the molding, Steve smeared the roller near a light switch. Their arms touched as they worked. He put the roller down and closed his hand over hers, guiding her strokes. Then they stood together looking at the wall. "We're doing good work," Julia said. He made himself step away from her.

Steve drove the rental truck for the move, uneasy at the wide yellow bulk behind him, the shrunken reflections in the side mirrors. Harold followed in his car with three friends Steve had never met before, all Harold's size, ex-athletes who had become beefy men, turning Steve's moving into a sport. Showing off their strength, they stood on the cab of the truck and single-handed hoisted chests and mattresses up through the door on the porch roof. Ignoring Steve, they swigged from six packs of beer and called out challenges to each other.

Harold gave directions, a beer can in one hand, a sandwich in the other, shouting at the men, telling them where to put things. He was as big as they were, but looser, flabby in the middle.

The whole time, Steve kept pausing to look for Julia, wondering if she would come, how he would introduce her to Debra, what the two women would say to each other.

"Did you invite her to help?" he finally asked Harold when they had a moment alone.

"That should be up to you by now," Harold told him.

Debra came with Molly in Cheryl's car after all the furniture was inside, bringing two suitcases of clothing and leftover food from the apartment's kitchen. Molly toddled to the middle of the living room to room and sat on the bare floor with an expression of distress.

After he returned from driving the other men back, Harold flopped on the sofa and closed his eyes, even though he had done little lifting. He told Steve where he could find the good wine in Cheryl's trunk.

When Steve came back into the house, Debra was embracing Cheryl, a head taller, hair tangled, her pregnancy a barrier between them. Molly clung to her Debra's leg, lips trembling at the edge of tears, as if imitating her mother. Steve could see Cheryl was uncomfortable with the hug.

"Debra thinks the house looks empty," she told him as she pulled away and smoothed her jacket.

Debra blew her nose and nodded. We don't have enough furniture."

"No problem," Harold said. "There's a farm auction next Saturday. Somebody died, left a house full of stuff."

When Debra told him she wouldn't go, that she had too much unpacking left, Steve didn't protest even though all she had done in the days since the move was sit at the kitchen table with a mug of coffee and stare at the stacked boxes. At work, on a break, he called Julia from a pay phone, swallowed when he heard her voice, then told her about the auction, adding that Harold would be there.

"It's always a treat to see Harold," she said and laughed as if sharing a joke.

The morning of the auction Steve and Harold met Julia in a downtown parking lot. She had borrowed her husband's van to bring back any furniture Steve was able to buy. Cheryl, Harold told them, had stayed behind to alter some of her old curtains for the downstairs windows.

Steve watched Harold and Julia closely, eager to see their interaction, wondering how they had ever become friends. But they said little to each other beyond polite greetings, Harold unusually quiet. He and Julia sat at opposite ends of the bench seat, Steve in the middle.

Even though farmland surrounded the town, Steve rarely went into the country. Any trips he took were on the interstate to the city several hours away, traveling so fast the view was a blur of corn stalks, cattle, and silos. But Julia knew the way right to the driveway of the farm having the auction. "I like to read maps," she explained, "to master new territory."

Implements were spread out on the gravel in front of the barn, domestic objects on metal folding tables close to the house — sets of mismatched china, table lamps, figurines, preserving jars with rubber seals, piles of old magazines, blankets heavy with mothballs.

"I wonder," Steve said, knowing the possibility was slight, "if this is the farm where the pigs mauled Martha Selig." Though the pens behind the barn were empty, he imagined the frantic stampede of the animals, mad squealing, grunts and snorts, a wild thrashing, teeth bared, the child's horrified shrieks. And for a moment he didn't want to own anything from this place.

"A different farm," Harold said, absolutely certain.

"What's wrong?" Julia asked Steve when Harold walked off to inspect a bureau.

"She must have thought feeding the pigs was routine. Then in a split second her world turned savage and nothing was ever the same again."

"Chance," Julia said. "If Harold hadn't turned a corner, you wouldn't have the house."

"Martha ended up with a life of pain, and we painted rooms together."

"Some of us turn out luckier than others." Julia touched his wrist with a fingertip.

Harold told Steve not to buy anything till late in the afternoon, when most people had left after spending their money and the bidding would go down. Some of the living room pieces, chairs and cabinets, were still available, and Steve owned them for a token payment, the auctioneer eager to end his day.

"So now you've got a full house," Harold slapped the side of the van when it was loaded. "Furniture, fresh paint, room to spread out."

"I told him some people have real luck." Julia smiled.

Back in town, Julia asked Harold to take over the driving and drop her by the stores. She had shopping to do. He could leave the van in the parking lot after they were finished. Let me stay with you, Steve wanted to ask her, then realized how impossible that would be.

Cheryl was gone when they reached the house, curtains in all the windows. Steve wondered what Harold would say if Debra asked where the van came from. But she just stood inside the doorway and watched them carry the furniture from the curb to the living room.

When Harold left, Debra told Steve that she didn't like having somebody else's belongings. "Why did those people sell?" she wanted to know.

"The old woman died," he explained. "A widow. There wasn't anyone left to take over the farm."

"Then all this"—she pointed at the chairs and cabinets and tables— "is like living with tombstones."

"That's crazy," he protested.

The baby was a boy, Timothy. The first snow of winter fell while Debra was in the hospital. Molly was staying with a friend of Cheryl, and Steve drove home in the evening seeing his moonlit house surrounded by a still whiteness. Alone in the silent rooms, all the lamps off, he sat among the dark shapes of unfamiliar possessions, unwilling to climb the stairs.

Soon after he set up a second crib and brought the baby home, the temperature dropped far below freezing. Harold came by to report predictions of an unusually cold winter. The bedrooms were chilly, the forced air system weak; the fan wasn't sending heat up to the second floor. The thermometer Steve bought for upstairs didn't rise above 45 degrees. Debra took Timothy into their bed and piled five blankets on Molly.

Before he went to work the third frigid morning, Steve dialed Martha Selig's office and started to explain the problem. But before he could finish Debra started shouting from across the room, "I have babies, a newborn. This house is a health hazard!" Then she stood in sudden silence, her hands at her mouth. "My wife is very upset," Steve said, and Martha, flat and abrupt, told him she would send a repairman that evening.

The man, Everett, appeared long past dark, standing on the front porch in a greasy wool jacket, heavy work gloves, and a cap with earflaps pulled low on his face. He gave off the odor of heating oil. Steve followed him down to the basement, where they had to stoop to walk. The walls were rough stone, the floor just packed earth, the furnace propped up on bricks in the middle under a dim bulb that dangled from a joist. Steve took a deep breath of mold and immediately erupted in loud sneezes.

Everett set down his tool kit with a clatter and squatted beside it. He lifted out a rubber flashlight that he stuck in his mouth, pointing it with his head as both hands fiddled with valves and tubing.

"Want me to hold the light?" Steve asked.

Everett shook his head, streaking the beam from one stone wall to the other.

After ten minutes of manipulation, he wiped his hands across his coat and set down the flashlight. "You've got a mighty old furnace here. Low on efficiency. That's why you're not getting much heat on the second floor."

"What can you do?"

"Nothing much. Except replace it. With Martha managing the property, I wouldn't hold my breath."

"What about electric heaters?"

Everett snorted. "This wiring would go up like a torch."

When Steve told Debra, she threw a pot across the kitchen, gashing a cabinet. "Damn that woman! I hate her! Damn her to hell!" In an instant of panic he pictured Julia, then realized she meant Martha Selig.

Steve got in his car and drove off toward town, desperate to talk to someone, intending to call Harold when he squeezed into the phone booth, but dialed Julia instead, trembling at the sound of ringing, afraid her husband would answer, realizing how much he missed their evenings together. He gulped when she answered, a sound like a sob. She agreed to meet him for a drink.

"It's like Martha Selig is responsible for everything that's wrong with her life," he said when they sat in a dim booth far from the TV set and the men at the bar who shouted at the ballplayers. "She's never even met the woman."

"Maybe it's easier to blame Martha," Julia said.

"Than who? Me? "

Julia shook her head. Steve realized that she had a new haircut, shorter, styled with a wave that accentuated her cheekbones. He wanted to tell her how good she looked. But when their eyes met, before he could say anything, she explained. "Than herself."

"For what? I'm the one who's supposed to provide. To make sure his kids don't freeze to death in their own house."

"Harold thinks Debra's the problem." "Harold said that?"

Julia nodded. She reached across the table to touch his hand, and he seized hers in both his, not daring to look at her, sure she would pull away. But she didn't. They sat with their fingers intertwined.

Julia went on. "She's not the wife he would have picked for you." Steve squeezed her hand, rubbed fingertips over the smooth knuckles, and stared at her with tear-blurred eyes. "Who would he have picked?"

"That never came up."

In the parking lot, he put an arm around her shoulder, the two of them leaning into the icy wind. At her car, he pulled her into him and bent to kiss her, but she turned the gesture into a hug and then brushed his face with her glove. He sat in his own car, watching the steam of her exhaust, the beams of her headlights, her car's slow movement across the snow-patched gravel, waiting long after she was gone before starting his own engine. Trembling, he touched his fingertips to his face and smelled the scent of her hair.

Harold appeared the next evening, stomping snow from his boots on the porch steps. Debra was in the kitchen staring at a water stain on the ceiling. When Steve let Harold in, she didn't come to the living room.

"I've got the perfect solution," Harold announced. "Move the kids downstairs where it's warm. Set up the cribs in the living room." He paused and smiled at Steve, as if expecting praise for his ingenuity.

But Steve only nodded. "Then it would be just like the apartment."

"Only for the winter. Hey, the year's full of months."

"How did you know about the heat problem?" Steve asked him. "News travels."

Steve followed Harold outside and leaned over him as he sat in his car. "Why did you send Julia to me?"

"I thought she'd be good for you." "In what way?"

"To give you perspective."

When Harold drove off, waving but facing straight ahead, Steve sensed it would be a long time before he saw him again.

Debra refused to help. She sat on a kitchen chair, tapping a pot against her toe. Steve put Timothy in Molly's crib so that he could disassemble his. The baby's sharp cries set off her much louder wailing. They wouldn't stop, one child echoing the other, the two of them so hysterical they quivered with breathless gasps.

Once Timothy's crib was set up in the living room, he moved both children downstairs and started on Molly's. The job took longer than he expected, bolting and unbolting, dragging frames and springs and mattresses down the narrow stairway.

"Come see," he told Debra when he finished. When she refused to move, he squeezed her wrists and tried to force her from the chair. She pushed him away and stared at the floor.

"I'm going out for beer," he announced. He slammed the door and tried to clear his windshield with the wipers, but the new snow was already too thick. He brushed it off with his bare hands, then had to suck his fingertips.

Before he went into the minimart, he called Julia. The phone rang a dozen times. Coming out, he tried again. This time a man answered, the voice rich and sure. "Wrong number," Steve muttered. He stood holding the phone, openmouthed, aching.

When he got back to the house, all the lights were out though it wasn't yet ten. In the living room, guided by moonlight, he saw the shapes of the babies swaddled in blankets. On the couch, surrounded by cribs, Debra huddled under all the comforters stripped from their bed, a dark lump. He watched the rise and fall of her breathing, suspecting she only pretended to sleep. Standing at the edge of the doorway, he turned from her to Molly and Timothy and back again. Shadows of crib bars fell across the bare floor. Still wearing his hat and jacket, Steve wrapped his arms around his chest and shuddered as if the chill would never leave him. He saw this woman and these children living in other rooms, in a home he would never know.

Awful Advice

RICHARD STILL COULDN'T KEEP HIS HANDS off Dolores after six months of eager caresses, even here in the waiting lounge at JFK Gate 37. Though they were in early middle age, parents of five between them, he clung to her as if touch were an addiction. Richard saw that strangers were embarrassed by his public desire. But he couldn't stop, didn't care. He pressed his mouth to the nape of her neck. "You're my queen and my empress," he whispered. "I'm going to honor you every night in London." When her fingers stroked his knee, he swallowed and closed his eyes.

"I see you've got a Nicholson's guide." Richard sensed a looming presence and looked up.

There stood a large flushed man with a midsection that overflowed stiff new jeans. A nest of slicked grey hair gleamed beneath the ceiling lights as he fixed them with a hooded stare.

"We also use Nicholson's London." The voice resounded from a nose that sprawled across the face like a mountain range.

Richard glanced down at the red paperback protruding from the man's carry-on. Dolores shifted away, slightly, leaving just a brush of contact.

"The travel agent recommended it," Richard said, trying to push his own copy deeper into a pocket.

"It's very useful." The man stepped closer, blocking the light. "It lists everything. Museums. Wine bars. Vegetarian restaurants. All night chemists. Shops where you can buy bespoke hats and family crests and custom-made umbrellas with secret swords. We have four copies. One for each of us."

He gestured toward the plastic bench across the aisle, at a heavy bosomed woman who appeared to be upholstered in tapestry, her mouth twisted as if she had just bitten into something rotten. Beside her sat two young women of about twenty in ballerina slippers and pink gossamer dresses, one with loose wispy hair a shade lighter than that piled atop her sister's head. Both gazed out like sleepwalkers.

"I'm sure the book will be be useful," Richard said.

"You'll probably find yourselves overwhelmed." The man leaned toward them and pointed a finger. "We visit London every summer. Don't be ashamed to ask for my help."

When he turned and strode away, Richard pulled Dolores close again and rolled his eyes. "What an awful man," she murmured, exciting him with the soft hum of her voice. "An awful family," he echoed.

In the plane while Dolores dozed with her head vibrating against his chest, Richard couldn't sleep, snapping awake at each bounce of an air pocket and forever opening his eyes to one of the Awfuls—a daughter floating down the aisle toward the toilets, Mrs. rattling seatbacks as she reached up to the overhead compartment for another sweater, Mr. Awful tapping shoulders to find someone who would listen to his analysis of the in- flight movie.

"Look!" Richard called. Dolores blinked and shielded her eyes from the glare of sunrise.

He pointed down at the shaded squares of green beneath them, here and there a glittering pond, the silver twisting of a river. "It's England!" He watched her face glow.

"Oh my God!" She squeezed his hand in both of hers. "It really is." "

A whole new country just for us."

"It's my dream."

He turned into her view and suddenly kissed her. Her mouth froze in surprise, then opened warmly.

She was even lovelier than the woman he had imagined in his years of midnight longings, since the summer day she appeared on his street, stepping long legs from a mud-splattered station wagon. And she had sensed his yearning for her all the time they were behaving like nothing more than neighbors, crying out in the moonlight, half laughing, half sobbing, when he finally took her in his arms.

She drew back from his kiss, smiling as she pushed him aside. "Let me look. I want to see everything." She gave a gasp of delight when the plane banked and revealed a vivid greenness spreading to the horizon. "You don't know how I longed for this moment. All those years with Ernie."

"I'd hardly have known England existed," he told her, "if it wasn't for you."

"If Ernie were beside me now, he'd only care about finding something down there to shoot."

Richard thought she was joking until he saw her tears. "Oh, love!" His heart swelled.

"My whole life I wanted beauty," she whispered, "and I spent fifteen years with a man who lined our walls with weapons."

Tears streamed down his face. "We'll love each other even more in London."

"It will be wonderful in London," she insisted.

Richard knew this trip was a risk, potential ammunition against them in divorce court. There would be custody battles when they got back home. Now Virginia wouldn't let him see the boys, dragged them to her mother every weekend, and Ernie called twice a week to curse Dolores as an unfit parent. But they had been desperate to get away from small-town scandal—the ringing phones, the stares in the supermarket, the sullen looks of his sons when they passed on the street, the betrayal on the faces of her children.

After they landed at Gatwick, jet-lagged, shuffling after the other passengers through a maze of ramps, stairways, and corridors, they watched Mr. Awful lead his family into the wrong line at Passport Control, waving his arms high above his head and calling "Follow me, follow me" into the cluster of British nationals. When a woman in a uniform blocked his path, he shouted, "It wasn't this way last year," and pushed his wife and daughters into the midst of the foreigners, just ahead of Richard and Dolores.

In the baggage area, while Dolores stood guard over the suitcase already retrieved from the carousel, Richard saw the sisters wrestling a luggage cart from a bearded man and Mr. Awful striding among the travelers dispensing advice on how to stack, pack, and carry. He lifted the nametag from Dolores' case and told her, "Never put down your home address. Thieves work in airports to find out who's left unguarded houses behind."

Most of the people from the plane headed for the express train to London, but Mr. Awful directed his family toward the taxis. "We've got too much planned to waste time here." His declaration rang out over the din in the terminal.

"Thank goodness they're gone," Dolores sighed.

Richard nodded agreement, breathing her perfume, nuzzling her earlobe.

Victoria Station was mobbed, the streets swarming, the taxi queue a hundred yards long. Richard's arms ached from the two heavy suitcases, but Dolores bubbled expectation. When a cab finally drove them off, she sat forward, pointing out glimpses of what seemed to be palaces and cathedrals as they twisted in and out a tangle of streets, through parks, around circuses.

For Richard everything seemed to be happening in fastforward—the flash of red buses, the figures scurrying on the sidewalks, the grey blur of buildings. He had expected grandeur and openness, not the sensation of being trapped inside a maze.

But Dolores's face was radiant. Richard turned from the city to lose himself in her fascination, following each of her gestures, every nuance of her expression, with a thrill of rediscovery.

She shifted back and forth on the seat, turning from window to window, laughing at her own frustration. "There's so much. I can't get a clear look at anything."

Throughout the long famine of marriage to Ernie, London had become the magic city of Dolores' dreams, kept vivid by glossy picture books she spread across Richard's lap as they planned their trip, pointing out domes, arches, gardens, and spires. "It's hard to believe," she would say, looking up from the book toward the bland streets outside her window, "that so much splendor really exists in the world."

If the choice had been his, Richard would have picked an island lush with dazzling colors, the two of them in a private paradise, making love beneath a brilliant sun on soft white sands. But eager to please her, he had cashed in an IRA despite the teller's warning that he would have to pay a penalty.

Their hotel, the Wellingham, that had appeared so elegant in the travel agent's brochure turned out to have minuscule rooms and no closet, just a hulking dark wardrobe whose door kept swinging open and two narrow single beds with crudely patched brown spreads.

"Do we have to stay here?" Dolores asked him.

"We've paid in advance," Richard said.

"But I wanted everything to be . . . beautiful."

When he thought she might cry, he whispered consolingly that she was tired, that everything would look better once she'd rested.

Richard beckoned her to his bed. Dolores insisted they stretch out for only a few minutes, keep themselves awake despite the jet lag and begin exploring right away. "I don't want to waste a second."

"Yes, yes," he said as he slid in beside her and led her into a lingering lovemaking. They slept deeply until late afternoon. Voices in the hallway woke them, Richard's arm stiff from the weight of her shoulder on the cramped mattress.

Dolores wanted tea. "Tea in London." She laughed as if the idea were beyond belief. Richard asked at the desk and was pointed toward the hotel's coffee shop down a corridor where floor boards creaked under threadbare carpeting.

The waitress brought two tepid pots and a plate of dry scones surrounded by little tins of jam. Richard, suddenly famished, spread a cherry paste on a scone that broke in his hand. He swallowed it in two sweet bites and licked the crumbs from his fingertips.

Dolores just sipped and nibbled. "Are you ok?" he asked.

"I'm fine."

"I don't want you to be disappointed."

She smiled and touched his hand. "We're going to see London the right way. All we have to do is know where we're looking, and we'll discover wonders around every corner." She slipped a hand inside his jacket and pulled out the Nicholson's. "We'll be guided by the experts."

For Richard, Buckingham Palace turned out to be a dull block of a building behind an acre of gravel, the guards ridiculous under the black puffs on their heads. Dolores stretched to tiptoe, trying to look over the people who blocked her view. When she braced a hand on his shoulder to raise herself up, he wrapped arms around her and lifted her into the air.

"Oh!" She cried out in surprise.

"What did you see?"

"Their uniforms are wonderful!" "Are they what you expected?" "Oh yes. Marvelous!"

Behind them taxis and double-decker buses rumbled past on the broad roadway, filling his head with diesel fumes.

At street corners, bewildered by the "Look Left," "Look Right" warning stamped into the pavement, Richard clung to Dolores. Cars bore down from unexpected directions. "Be careful," he urged, afraid to trust his instincts.

Dolores laughed. "Haven't you noticed? The drivers stop for pedestrians. People here are very polite."

Everywhere they went Dolores held the Nicholson's guide open, referring to it whenever a new view appeared. After a stroll along the Mall, they stood overlooking Trafalgar Square at twilight, the National Gallery spread behind them, stone lions crouched beside the fountain, Nelson's Column towering above. Pigeons swooped and fluttered, pecking crumbs at their feet.

"Wouldn't it be wonderful if we never had to go home?" Dolores said. He touched fingertips to her hair.

"I've never felt so excited!" She reached open arms toward the city. "There's so much. I can't decide what to do next. Let's find Westminster Abbey."

"Head straight down Whitehall," a voice behind them announced. "But it closed two hours ago."

Before he turned, Richard guessed what he would find. Mr. Awful in a safari jacket, Mrs. rotund in Burberry plaid, one daughter in what seemed to be harem pants, the other in a dirndl.

"Where are you staying?" Mr. Awful said.

"The Wellingham." Richard answered reluctantly.

Mr. Awful shook his head. "You should have asked us. The Wellingham isn't what it used to be. The last time we stayed there my daughter found stains on her sheet." He didn't indicate which daughter. "We checked out in the morning."

"Where are you?" Dolores asked.

"The Boughton."

"My husband is an expert on London hotels." Mrs. Awful said, conveying enthusiasm even though her face still seemed twisted into a wince.

"Have you chosen a restaurant for dinner?" Mr. Awful asked.

"We haven't thought about it," Richard said.

The daughters stared up at the column. They had inherited their father's somnolent eyes and their mother's pinched mouth.

"The Stratton has an excellent carving table. We eat there on every visit."

"Why don't you join us?" Mrs. Awful said.

"That's very kind," Richard said, "but we have other plans."

Mr. Awful tapped his wife. "Can't you see that these people don't want to be bothered with a family. They want to eat by candlelight and gaze into each other's eyes."

Dolores slipped her hand from Richard's, but he seized it and squeezed.

Dolores, maps fixed in her memory, insisted that they walk everywhere to really know the city, miles and miles each day: down Drury Lane to the Strand, beside the Embankment, across Westminster Bridge, along the South Bank, back over to Charing Cross, from the Marble Arch to Brompton Road. And everywhere Dolores recognized sights from her picture books. Some nights, she fell exhausted onto her bed, kicking off shoes, heaping clothing on the rug, within minutes deep in a heavy sleep.

Richard would prop himself up to watch her face in the moonlight that filtered through the drapes. It was a lovely face, the features finely formed, the brown hair soft around it. He longed to hold it in his hands, feel the shape of her lips.

In the morning, no matter how early Richard awoke, Dolores was already dressed, leafing through the guide, planning their itinerary, writing down lists, even calculating distances on the scale of miles.

But as much as they saw, as much as they did, Richard couldn't wait for the day to end so that he could draw her down beside him.

Wherever they went, there were always crowds—clustered around the Ming vases in the British Museum, pressing to glimpse the jewels in the Tower, queuing for half-price theater tickets in Leicester Square, pawing through cashmere sweaters on Regent Street, sampling cheeses in Harrods' food halls.

Dolores bought a paisley-covered journal to note all that they saw, all that they did, on cool ivory pages.

Except for a brief sunset one evening, it had been grey through the days, the occasional drizzles so faint they hardly felt them. But one afternoon as they shopped along Oxford Street, a sudden rain pelted down, sharp and chill. All around them people popped open black umbrellas. Richard darted into a doorway, expecting Dolores to follow behind him. But she was standing in the middle of the sidewalk, arms spread, face turned upward into the stream of water.

As they crossed a cobblestone courtyard outside a tiny twelfth-century church, a carriage clattered through an entrance gate, drawn by four black horses in gleaming harnesses.

Dolores clutched Richard's arm. "I can't believe it."

A groom in livery leaped down to open the carriage door. Two men stepped out, wearing tails and stiff top hats, bright red flowers in their lapels. One was white-haired with a trim shaped beard, the other ruddy and mustached.

The bearded man reached inside the carriage and drew out a woman all in pink—pink dress, pink shoes and stockings, a pink hat with a brim that touched her shoulder. When she stepped to the cobblestone, a breeze caught the hat and she had to clutch it to her hair, throwing her head back in laughter. The men laughed too.

Then another woman emerged, layered in white lace, long blonde hair under a veil, her throat wrapped in strands of pearls.

"How beautiful," Dolores said, face aglow, happier that Richard had ever seen her. "She's going to marry one of those men in that church. What a life she'll have!"

Richard surged with anger because these strangers were giving her such joy. "It's all an act," he said.

"What?"

"The fancy clothes, the horse and carriage, this old church. It's nothing but a costume party. They're trying to pretend this crumbling stinking place is beautiful."

In their room, as soon as the door clicked shut, Richard folded Dolores into his embrace, slid a hand under her sweater. But she didn't seem to notice, her eyes fixed in thought. She pulled free of him and drifted toward the window, brushing her cheek against an edge of the drapes and looking out over the traffic, listening to the groans of heavy engines.

"What's wrong?" he said.

"You're spoiling it, Richard."

"Me! What have I done?"

"It's the way you feel."

He looked at himself in the mirror, the back of her head reflected behind him, and knew he shouldn't speak. But he couldn't stop the words.

"I'm so damn sick of the paintings and the porcelain, the gilded moldings and the inlaid tables. None of that stuff has anything to do with us. We don't need London."

They stumbled across the Awfuls in St. James Park, Mr. and Mrs. sprawled on canvas chairs alongside the pond, Mr. feeding crumbs to the herringbone ducks, Mrs. looking up at the domes of the government buildings.

"We have tickets for the opera for this evening," Mrs. Awful called before Richard could get away.

"We were there yesterday," Richard told her.

Mrs. Awful squinted up suspiciously and gestured toward the two girls batting a balloon back and forth on the other side of the pond. "My daughters saw you in Parliament Square."

"It must have been someone else," he insisted.

Mr. Awful showed an empty hand to the ducks. "You're both in the midst of a divorce, aren't you?"

"How did you know?" Richard stood rigid, gripping Dolores' wrist in a cold clutching.

"My husband is a student of human character," Mrs. Awful said.

Dolores smiled at the woman. "Then he must know that I'm running away from home."

"May I give you some advice?" he said.

Dolores nodded, expectant, Richard pulling at her arm. "London isn't a city for passion."

Richard shuddered with an urge to tip over the man's chair and kick him into the pond. "You don't know anything!" he shouted. Then in the sudden silence he felt the eyes of the others on him, Dolores nodding along with the Awfuls even though none of them was moving a muscle. He stomped through a brilliant flower bed into thick green shrubs and hoped she would follow.

"I was twenty when I met Ernie," Dolores said. It was long past midnight and they lay on separate beds staring up into the darkness. "He kept telling me how wonderful I was, how much he loved me. I let myself believe I was a special person."

"You are special. You're perfect. It's him. He didn't realize how lucky he was."

She stayed silent for so long he thought she had forgotten his presence. Then she asked, "Didn't you love Virginia once?"

"I thought I did. I didn't know what love was until I met you."

"She has a sweet face. But she's thirty pounds overweight. The first time I saw her I thought, what a dumpy woman. I've stayed slim, Richard. Maybe what you really love is my waistline." She reached out to touch his arm.

He twisted away from her soothing. "It was a mistake to come here."

Richard closed his eyes while Dolores brushed her teeth. When she stepped out of the bathroom, he heard the creak of her mattress and then gazed over at the dark hump of her blanket.

Without a word he crawled in beside her and fixed her mouth with a kiss that drove her head into the pillow. He twisted her gown up above her waist and winced at the abrasive dryness, the whole time thinking, love me, love me.

He stayed beside her on the narrow bed all night, wondering if she were sleeping as little as he, but not daring to speak, afraid of what she might say. When daylight glowed around the edge of the drapes he tried to be tender, caressing her shoulders, brushing light kisses across her forehead, down her cheeks. She lay inert under his touch until he rolled away. Then she kicked her legs from under the blanket and stepped toward the bathroom.

"It's not just passion," he called to the closed door. "I need you." The shower blasted spray against the plastic curtain.

Their flight back home was very crowded. Richard heard someone say it was the time of year, the end of the vacation season. Although they arrived two hours before departure time, they couldn't get a seat together.

Richard protested, raising his voice to make the clerk understand how vital it was that they return home side by side. But the clerk, a freckled woman with a clipped accent, stayed cool. The computer offered no options; perhaps they could make an exchange on the plane. Dolores told her it was all right.

Their rows, five apart, got the first call to board. They merged into the line still deciding who would carry which hand baggage. He ended up with the presents for his sons, she with those for her children. They would sort out the others after landing.

On the plane, Richard turned, trying for glimpses of her, but the seatback blocked his view. Dolores had a window, squeezed in beside two shapeless women with blonde-dyed curls who cradled duty free bags on their laps and argued about which stores they had purchased their sweaters in.

Richard sat in the middle seat. At the window a boy in shiny black shirt and trousers was already plugged into earphones, jerking his shoulders to a rhythm Richard could not hear. He peered over the boy to watch the ground crew, men in orange coveralls making last minute checks of the wing flaps. Richard tried to imagine how it would feel to crash, whether he would experience a terrible pain or just lose consciousness.

The aisle seat beside him thumped heavily. But Richard would not turn his head.

"Tell me where you've been since we met in the park," the man said. "What you saw."

Without looking at him, Richard recited lists, speaking through the taxiing and the takeoff, the force of climbing that pained his ears, repeating Dolores' itineraries. In his mind the sound of her voice echoed like a distant memory.

"But you've missed so much," Mr. Awful said.

Richard's eyes flooded. "I didn't know where to look."

"You should have asked me. I know what's important."

Among the Gaytys

For most of the trip from the airport the helicopter seemed to float above the mountain peaks. Dwight felt the vibrations of the rotor blades as he looked down at jagged dark stone and icy crags. But when the pilot dropped into the layer of cloud, he closed his eyes at the sensation that he would be swallowed in a soft gray. When he looked out again, they were circling over a barren plain, nothing in sight but brown dirt and rock outcrop.

Dwight had been told he would be dropped off one mile from the village because the people the authorities called Gaytys were hostile to any aircraft. As old and primitive as their rifles were, they would shoot rounds and rounds. The government had agreed their airspace was not to be violated, amused through the negotiation, as if playing a game with children.

An anthropologist in the capital had prepared Dwight with a file of documents, photographs, and a brief video of the Gaytys in their gaudy orange and purple garb, their bodies stomping to a chant in some sort of ungainly ritual. No one understood these ceremonies or why they wore such clothing. That's why Dwight was there, gathering material for his dissertation and perhaps a book, supported by a small grant from the government.

But he hadn't expected to be abandoned in such desolation. The helicopter didn't set down, just hovered, and Dwight had to jump to the ground. The pilot shoved his backpack after him and took off without even a gesture of parting.

Dwight tightened the laces of his boots, slung the rigid frame of the pack over his shoulders, and began walking east across the rocky field in the direction of the outline of domed huts and smoke drifting upward against mountains. The pack held a year's possessions, the time he would be among the Gaytys. Exactly one year from this day a helicopter would return for him. Dwight had been told there would be no notification because there was no way to get messages to the village. He would have to count days and mark his calendar very carefully because the Gaytys possessed only a crude sense of time, guided by the moon and the state of their crops. On the final day, he would rise at dawn to walk back to that spot on the plain, where he would await the trip back to civilization.

He had been apprehensive about making this journey, the sensation that a hand was pushing at his back, forcing him to be here. In his dreams it had been his advisor, a drawn man with a skimpy beard who mumbled, but whose words seemed a warning. Go to the Gaytys or else.

The reason the man gave Dwight for choosing him was his facility for odd languages. No one else had come close to mastering the combination of grunts, glottal stops, and seeming throat clearings that comprised the limited expressions of the Gaytys. They had no future tense, no past. Everything was present. Dwight tried to explain that his ability was rudimentary. When he listened to speakers on old tapes with a hissing background, most of his understanding was guesswork. But no one else knew anything.

Dwight wasn't good with people. Being in a room with others made him want to bolt. He could engage in a conversation with one person at a time, but only if it were about a subject he knew. All he wanted was to be in a lab with artifacts, examining every detail, making notes, cataloguing. That's how he first became familiar that such a people as the Gaytys existed. He was presented with a case of crockery, knives, and swords. One long sword in a hide scabbard drew his attention immediately. When he drew it out, he hadn't expected the sharpness of his blade, making a deep slice in his thumb that took weeks to heal.

His advisor praised his analyses of the objects, all that he was able to surmise about the habits of these unseen people—the foods they ate, the steps of preparations, the rituals behind their dining, the animals they raised, the crops they planted. Then came the audio tapes and grainy film, just momentary snatches taken years ago.

The film had been converted to a video that he had watched over and over, the men in baggy bright orange pantaloons with animal skin vests over their bare chests, in round headgear of woven twigs. The women seemed wrapped in yards of bright purple cloth, as if someone else had held one end and the wearer had spun in circle and after circle until the cloth could be fixed with what looked like a bone pin. All the Gaytys had wide copper foreheads, high sharp cheekbones, cramped teeth, and pointed chins.

The film showed some sort of ritual dance, but not like the rhythmic, organized examples of other peoples. The Gaytys just milled about as if stalking, then individuals lurched forward in uncoordinated pounces, some slashing at nothing with long swords like the one that had cut Dwight, others shaking ancient rifles over their heads, then pretending to aim at others in the group. The meaning, if there was one, eluded Dwight, as much as the studied the films.

In one scene that greatly disturbed him, a white goat was tied to a carved and painted pole, ropes about the animal's bound ankles and chest so that it stood upright. Both men and women took turns rushing forward and thrusting swords as the goat's middle, but stopping just an inch away, until finally one man ran from the back of the crowd and slashed through the flesh, dragging out innards with the point of the sword. Even though the film was silent, Dwight could in his mind hear the animal's agonized bleats. He watched that scene only once.

Dwight found himself tiring under the weight of his backpack, his legs aching with strain, his feet stinging from the constant stepping on sharp stones despite his thick-soled books. He wondered if the Gaytys had been given word of his coming.

Someone in the capital had told him a message would be sent but didn't say when or how.

As he walked, his steps getting slower and slower, he spoke aloud, rehearsing the way he would greet the people and introduce himself. Reaching deep in his throat to make some sounds led him to cough up phlegm. He spit onto the dry dirt and wondered what would happen if he couldn't communicate, if the Gaytys found his gropings with their language an insult.

He had been advised to reveal as little as possible about his visit, not that he wanted to document their way of life, just that he admired them very much and wanted to spend time. His advisor warned him never to take photographs without explaining why, the man's mouth so grim Dwight couldn't make himself ask for a reason. But he did add that the film had been clandestine, the Gaytys unaware.

Just a few hundred yards ahead he saw the village, the round structures of stones gathered from the mountains and brought to the village in carts drawn by teams of some lean animals with loose tan skin and sweeping horns. He had seen these igloo-like structures in the film and was comforted by their familiarity. Thin wisps of smoke drifted from holes in the center of the curved roofs.

Dwight had to jump over a deep stone-filled pit to enter the village. He hadn't noticed it until he was right against the drop, unsure whether the backpack would pull him backward and plunge him down. But he made it, one boot catching on a lip of the pit and dropping him to his knees. He expected mocking laughter but, when he looked up, saw not a soul, as if the village were a deserted place.

Then people appeared from the stone huts, slowly, one at a time, and they wore nothing like the garb he had seen in the films. The men had on worn jeans cut off and ragged at the knees and faded tee shirts inside out. He could make out the reverse lettering—Old Navy, Hollister, Aeropostale. How did such clothing get to this place so far from everything? The women, instead of being wrapped in cloth, wore what looked like gray sweat suits. All, men and women, were barefoot, with long knobbed toes. It struck Dwight that their toes were shaped like their bodies, tall and lean, no fat on them, bones prominent.

Dwight spoke what he had learned as the Gaytys' greeting, first hesitant and then, after he cleared his throat, loud. But no one acknowledged the sound, not even turning to look at him, no curiosity about the presence of a pudgy blond man with thick glasses, wearing black boots, a safari jacket with stuffed pockets, and tan pants of a special rip-proof material, also with bulging pockets. He couldn't believe that they had ever seen anyone like him. Yet all they did was begin hacking at the dirt with rusty metal implements. Then the animals appeared, herded from a place behind the huts, creatures much like chickens, plumb and furry mammals, the horned cattle, and some sort of very large goat.

I should be writing this down, Dwight thought. But all he did was stand rooted, waiting from something to happen, with the strange notion that they would plant crops around him, thick vines that would grow quickly until he was tangled in a trap and smothered. Then he wondered what he should do, where he should step. He hadn't expected to be ignored. His mentor hadn't warned him.

In desperation he moved closer to a group of people squatting in a circle and digging with trowel-like tools. He spoke the greeting again, this time smiling and waving in a friendly gesture.

"Haw-lo," he heard, swerving his head toward the source. The sound was high-pitched, barely human. But from behind a high pile of rocks emerged a small person dressed in a black cassock. Dwight's first reaction was that this was a priest, though he couln't tell if it were a man or a woman the hair a dark tangle, the tiny feet bare.

The person stood directly in front of Dwight and still no one else seemed aware. It came up to Dwight's chin, but Dwight knew it wasn't a child from the creases around the wide, dark eyes. It reached out a finger to touch its chest and then point toward Dwight. "I—U."

"Yes." Dwight awaited more, some sort of explanation, but the person just repeated, "I—U" and did not return Dwight's forced smile.

Dwight tried some Gaytys, the grunts that meant, who are you?

"I eengrlish spyk," the person said, sounds like a squeak. "A lertle." "Name U." This time Dwight was the one to point, almost touching thecassock with his fingertip.

When the person spoke, Dwight heard something that sounded like Gryx, and he repeated it back, expecting that he was making a mistake, that the person would be offended and walk off in anger.

Instead it stabbed a finger at its breastbone. Dwight took it to be an affirmation and wondered why these people didn't nod or make facial gestures. From now on this person would be Gryx. Dwight said it again and awaited a response, but the finger did not stab again.

Gryx gestured Dwight to follow as they twisted through irregular rows of stone huts until Gryx and pointed to one. Dwight assumed that was where he was meant to live. He pointed toward the opening and then to himself. Gryx turned and walked away. Dwight pushed his backpack inside and wondered how he would ever find this hut again if he left it. He got down on hands and knees to crawl through the opening.

Once inside Dwight needed several minutes to become accustomed to the dim light that filtered through the holes in the roof and the front. The stone glinted specks of what seemed to be mica. A thin layer of straw covered with a pied animal skin would be his bed and two crude woven baskets storage for his belongings. He saw no way to block the opening and realized he could use his backpack. A circle of dark ash in the center of the clay floor indicated a place for a fire, the source of the smoke coming from the other huts. He assumed he would have to gather his own wood. If it rained, the water would come through the roof opening, and he would have to huddle against one stone wall. Dwight meant to unpack into the baskets but found himself exhausted from the trip. He stretched out on the animal skin and collapsed into a deep sleep.

When Dwight woke it was still light outside, and he felt a great hunger, remembering that he hadn't eaten for many hours, before boarding the helicopter in the capital. One pocket of his backpack was stuffed with protein bars, but he understood he had to rational them for the time that lay ahead. He knew the Gaytys word for food, thought he did, but didn't know who and how to ask, who might even respond.

For a long time he wrapped his arms around his middle and rocked back and forth, thinking he might get sick and wretch up phlegm. Then he saw bare feet outside the hut's open and the hem of a cassock. Gryx crawled through, pushing a crockery bowl ahead of him. An acrid odor filled the hut. Gryx set the bowl in front of Dwight and mimed eating with his fingers.

Dwight gestured that Gryx should sit and share the food. He wanted to ask questions, so many questions about how he should act here, what he should do, how he would gather information. But Gryx only stared at him with wide expressionless eyes and backed out onto the path.

Despite the strange smells, Dwight dug his fingers into the bowl and stuffed his mouth. The taste was very bitter, the chopped up pieces hard to chew. He sensed a mixture of roots, tough leaves, and chunks of stringy animal flesh. He expected this was what the Gaytys ate day after day, meal after meal, and he would have to accept it for the months ahead.

In the morning, the sun bright, Dwight found another bowl of food in his hut's opening and assumed Gryx had brought it. He ate only half and tried to lick his fingers clean. His innards began to cramp. He needed a toilet, badly, and realized he didn't know where to find one.

Before leaving his hut, Dwight thought to fix a tee shirt to the stones to identify where he lived, then walked on the paths, still wearing his boots, until he saw a people clustered outside two stone structures larger than the living huts far from the edge of the village, men and women apart. From the smell of human waste, he knew he had located a communal latrine.

When he neared, both men and women moved away, the men growling sounds as others hurried out of the structure, some pulling up their jeans as they fled. Dwight was alone inside, quickly sitting above an opening on a stone bench, evacuating loudly, his own smell overpowering the stench in the building, and he was ashamed of himself, of the foulness in him.

A fresh leaves piled on the dirt floor were the way he would wipe himself. He felt unclean, in need of a bath. When he left the structure, the men and women became to appear from behind huts, slowly reassembling. Dwight tried to mime water, gestures of washing himself. As he had assumed before he even tried, they ignored him, looked away.

On instinct he walked away from the village toward a sparse grove of spindly trees, turning to the right when he heard a rush of water, then came upon a stream. Gaytys' voices resounded from a distance, the splashes of people bathing. He found it impossible to distinguish male from female sounds.

Dwight removed his boots and socks, jacket and shirt, bare-chested but leaving on his trousers. He stood at the edge of the stream feet in water up past his ankles and reached down with cupped hands, spilling water over his hair, rubbing his arms and torso, reaching in under his briefs to cleanse his scrotum. It felt so good. He opened his arms to the sun as if in prayer and suspected this would be the only happiness of his days among the Gaytys.

And these were his days. After the ritual of the morning meal, the solo evacuation, and the washing, he would walk about the huts with his notebook trying to observe the behaviors of the people. Unlike their withdrawal at the latrines, they did not avoid him, only ignored. The men and male children tended the animals, scattering feed, brushing creatures with fur, lathering the cattle, cleaning the feathers of the fowl. The creatures seems to like the touching, pressing into the human hands. The large goat, Dwight noted, had a special importance, only a group of older men—village elders he assumed—permitted to enter its pen apart from the other animals and touch it. This seemed to be reverence, and he couldn't imagine them slaughtering the creature.

The women, young girls, and little boys and girls, devoted their hours to the crops, those planted amid the huts and those in plots at one edge of the village. They dug to plant seeds, weeded, plucked off dry leaves, carried clay pots of water from the stream.

All worked from morning to nightfall, stopping for the meals prepared by specialist cooks in a large hut in the center of the village and distributed by children using the same crocks served to Dwight. He alone had his brought to his hut by Gryx, whom he sometimes saw but usually not. The people also had break times where they would sit in circles and speak in mutterings Dwight could barely hear let alone try to interpret.

It stuck him that he never heard the Gaytys laugh or smile or show signs of distress or anger. Beyond the very small children running after each other, they played no games. Dwight looked for signs of worship but found no structure that could serve as a temple, not anywhere that a large group could gather. They never appeared to show individual reverence, nor did anyone look or act like a holy figure. After his initial reaction to Gryx's cassock, he stopped wondering if the person were a priest. The others did not treat Gryx with any difference, and Gryx seemed to have no role other than serving Dwight. When the men were tending animals and the women tending crops, Gryx just sat outside a hut, though occasionally a small child would approach and make sounds. The two of them—Gryx and the child—would look into each other's eyes, expressionless, for a long time, until the child turned and ran off.

When Dwight looked at his notebooks, he had not filled many

pages. Once he made his initial observations of the Gaytys and noted what he saw, their lives were nothing but repetition, without a hint of variation. Although they had no timepieces, they lived by a precise clockwork. He, with a watch, found that their meals and their breaks took place at the same period all the time. They had no recreation, no ceremonies, no day that differed from all the others.

Although he lacked a device to view them, Dwight replayed the old film in his mind, the flamboyant costumes, the aggressive stomping, swords that slashed the air, rifles that seemed to challenge the sky. Although the people and the village looked the same, he wondered if the camera had been in another place, capturing another people, some relatives of the Gaytys, alter egos.

Dwight had brought books to read, primarily other anthropological studies of remote peoples that he had hoped to emulate. But they had so many subjects to discuss, long chapters on the rites of worship and the rituals of death. Dwight never saw a Gaytys death or even an illness. Perhaps something would happen, but not yet. After reading these books and the few paperback novels again and again, he did not pick them up. As soon as he opened the cover, a full memory of the pages formed in his mind. They offered nothing new.

Much more, much worse than being bored, Dwight was lonely. Though he never had real friends—not at home, not at the university—and though he was ill at ease in the company of others, he realized that all his life he had lived in environments where people would engage with him—nod, smile, participate in brief exchanges. Even if they did not warm to him, recognizing that he did not seek closeness, they acknowledged his existence. The Gaytys did not. Other than their behavior at the latrines, they ignored him, not an overt denial, but just as if he were no more a presence than the air around them, nothing to regard.

Alone in his hut, in the darkness of night, Dwight found himself weeping, until he shuddered with sobs. He couldn't recall ever in his life crying before.

During the days he walked about the huts and the groups of people at their work, knowing they would not respond to his greetings or questions. He thought of all the hours he had devoted to learning the strange Gaytys language and hoped he would hear the people speaking among themselves so that he could try to understand. Perhaps that would give him some new information for his notes. But whenever others sensed him near their exchanges ceased or quieted to whispers.

He knew better than to try to talk with Gryx when he passed the person poised outside a hut, almost never moving, legs folded under the hem of the cassock. Dwight must have walked by a dozen times a day, no longer hoping that something would happen. Their relationship was nothing beyond the silent servings of food.

But one afternoon, though he was not looking at Gryx, he felt eyes upon him, attuned to his every step, but Dwight was reluctant to turn to be sure. It happened the next time he took the path next to the house and again. Finally, Dwight glanced back and found Gryz starting directly into his eyes, Gryx's dark and unblinking.

Dwight stared back, wondering what would happen, if Gryx would turn away. But the eyes locked.

Day after day their eyes kept meeting, but Dwight never stopped to speak or change his route to seek out Gryx more often, as if any alteration from a pattern would rouse suspicion, though he had no idea for what. What was Gryx in the village? Why was he so different from the other Gaytys?

Daylight shortened, and the delivery of the evening meal began to take place in twilight, then soon darkness. One night after hours of debating whether he should, Dwight touched Gryx's hand on the bowl of food and softly spoke the Gaytys words for "Come inside." To Dwight's surprise, Gryx did, then sat in the same position as outside the hut, the food between them.

Gryx said something that sounded like "It," and Dwight realized that he was being asked to eat. "It-U," he told Gryz with a gesture that he would eat too, that they should share the meal. Gryx scooted back, just inches. A signal of denial. Dwight dipped two fingers into the bowl and brought the food to his mouth, unable to open, to eat alone in front of this other person. He reached out toward Gryx and found a cupped hand. He dropped the food from his fingers. The two of them ate, taking turns at the bowl, all the time looking into each other's eyes, the hut illuminated only by faint moonlight entering through the top. When the bowl was empty, Gryx turned and crawled out the hut's opening on hands and knees.

They repeated this pattern every night for the next two weeks, Dwight marking the days on his calendar with a special symbol different from the X's of all the months before. Then alone he lay in darkness, listening to the wind and the clucks and calls of the animals, wondering what it meant. Was Gryx acting on instructions or was he violating some code? Dwight wrote nothing about this in his notebook even though he was sure no one among the Gaytys could read English or decipher his handwriting if they could. He didn't think if he would tell about these meals when he left the village, not ever in his life.

One night when the moon was gone and darkness total, when he had no sense of Gryx's eyes, when his fingers had to grope the dirt floor to find the bowl, Dwight brushed against Gryx's hand and, on a sudden impulse, gripped it, first wrapping around it and then interlacing fingers, his so much larger, as if the other were a child. After a moment Gryx pressed back, and Dwight had sensed that would happen, that Gryx would not flinch away.

He pulled Gryx toward him, first just by the hand but then reaching out with his other arm to wrap it around Gryx's waist. The sat in the center of the hut, Gryx pressed against Dwight, accepting his embrace, the two of them breathing in the darkness, neither speaking or making any sound beyond their breath. Dwight stroked Gryx's tangled hair. Eventually, Dwight shifted to lay on his side, pulling Gryx down with him, Gryx's body against his, the warmth of another person in the chill night.

When Dwight awoke the next morning, Gryx was gone, the food bowl too.

And that was how they lived for the next months, Gryx coming in the evening, disappeared in morning, the two of them embraced in sleeping through the night. And in all that time, all those weeks, Dwight never felt a sexual instinct, never a quiver in his loins, just a fullness in his heart. He could easily have moved a hand to Gryx's chest, a slight brushing to see if Gryx had breasts, to determine if Gryx were a man or a woman. But Dwight kept his hands away. He didn't want to know.

After a time Dwight came down to the final page of his calendar with just a few rows of days to check off with the symbol that meant Gryx and much more that he could not make himself comprehend, something he probably would ponder the rest of his life. And he had no idea what that life would be. He knew that once he left the Gaytys he would be alone again, always alone.

He did not, could not, express any of this to Gryx, their ability to exchange words too limited, his Gaytys too crude, Gryx's English just a scattering of mispronounced words. But they did try to communicate, Dwight occasionally laughing while they fumbled, Gryx never making a sound that resembled laughter, not even smiling. Dwight did succeed in teaching Gryx "friend," "fryn" as Gryx spoke it.

Dwight never showed Gryx the dwindling number of unmarked days on the calendar, though he gazed at them for hours at a time in the mornings and afternoons when Gryx was not in the hut.

On their final night together, he pulled Gryx closer than ever before, his tears falling on the soft flesh of Gryx's cheek, wiping them away with a fingertip. Gryx just lay still without any indication of an emotion. Unable to remember the Gaytys words that could close to his meaning, Dwight whispered in English, "I'll miss you." Gryx echoed, "miss," and Dwight never knew, as often as he replayed the sound in his memory, whether it indicated agreement or bewilderment.

During his final night Dwight slept not at all, wide awake when Gryx crawled out of the hut at dawn, stopping to turn his head and glance behind. Their eyes met for an instant, and Gryx was gone.

The backpack zippers stuck because they hadn't been opened in a year.

Dwight had the tug at them in frustration. But they came loose so that he could stuff in his belongings, just wadding his clothing. The last item on the hut's floor was his notebook. He held it in two hands, flipped the pages, knowing that he had made no new entries in months. About to shove it into a backpack pocket, he changed his mind and tossed it against an edge of stone, into the shadows.

Dwight tightened his bootstraps and left the hut, dragging the backpack until he stood and slipped his arms under the straps of the frame. He began the walk through the village out to the rocky plain to await the helicopter.

To his surprise the villagers stopped their planting and weeding and tending of animals to follow his movement. They stood to watch, silent, faces measuring his steps. He would not look at Gryx's hut, unwilling to make public their relationship, unsure what he would do it he saw Gryx among the other Gaytys. But he could think of nothing but Gryx and wondered if Gryx were thinking of him.

Dwight kept his eyes focused on the ground, first the dirt paths, and then he crossed the pit that surrounded the village, the rocky surface, his legs unsteady, trying not to stumble. When he finally did look up, he saw the mountains all around him and the village lost in the distance, just a few wisps of smoke dissipating in the air.

He had a long wait for the helicopter, standing all the time and wondering if he had gotten the day wrong, what he would do if he had. He couldn't make himself go back to the Gaytys, to Gryx. He would just stay on the plain until someone came for him.

The helicopter did arrive. He saw it appear over a mountaintop and slowly land, the rotor blades churning up thick brown dust. Dwight lifted his backpack, and the pilot grabbed it by a strap. Then he reached out to grip Dwight's wrist and pull him onboard. The pilot smiled and spoke a greeting in the language of his country, words that came back to Dwight as soon as he heard them. He gave the traditional reply but did not return the smile.

As the helicopter lifted off the plain, on an impulse, Dwight asked the pilot if he would fly over the village, certain the rifles were a mistaken legend. The pilot nodded and tilted back in the direction Dwight had walked. As they neared, Dwight realized he didn't want to see but couldn't tell the pilot to stop. They were too close.

As the helicopter hovered, Dwight was stunned to see the Gaytys all dressed in the garb they had worn in the film, the men in skin vests and purple pantaloons, heads covered by woven twigs, the women wrapped in orange cloth. The men carried long swords and rifles, twirling and passing back and forth. And they were milling in what must have been some traditional dance, an uncoordinated group, seemingly confused, their chant like the grinding of gravel. No rhythm to their movements or their sounds. But on a barren spot in the midst of them, Gryx sat, cassock pulled over knees, head bowed, faced pressed into the cloth. Now and then one of the others would lunge forward, extending a sword or a rifle toward Gryx, then backing into the group. It made no sense to Dwight, what it all meant, whether Gryx were a special being or a pariah.

He wanted to see what would happen, how the ritual would end. He remembered the goat in the film, shocked by a rush of fear. But the pilot signaled to him, touched a fingertip to his watch, and began to lift the helicopter. Dwight cried out, "Wait!" He saw the Gaytys below suddenly stop, some pointing rifles at the helicopter, though no one fired.

Then the helicopter rose into a thick dark cloud. The village had vanished.

Dwight looked out in all directions and saw nothing.

Missing Venice

A few minutes out of Padua, David dozed into a nightmare that they had missed Venice and, after hours of barely creeping, were suddenly hurtling toward the Adriatic. He felt himself grabbing at suitcases, struggling with the compartment door, desperate to jump from the train and pull Virginia after him, certain that if they did not escape at once, they would plummet into oblivion.

But at a metallic shriek he opened his eyes to iron pipe intestines, the thumping percussion of factories, smokestack fires that seared the darkness. The train lay at a dead stop in Mestre, stalled, as if it would never cross the last kilometers to Venice.

And it wasn't Virginia beside him despite all their months of anticipation, but Donny instead, his son, an oversized fourteen-year-old slouched on the seat, scowling at the flames in the window, kicking unlaced sneakers against a metal panel. The boy hadn't said a word the entire thirteen hours of the trip, through the excruciating pace, the endless delays. He didn't speak; he didn't read; he didn't even listen to his iPod; he just shoved hands deep into his pockets and oozed hostility.

But Maria hadn't shut up since they left the Stazione Termini in Rome. Plump and pockmarked, her shape reminded David of a miniature Donny, through she was a woman in her thirties, an absolute stranger until the middle of that day.

Heavy-lidded, David rubbed hard at his face, fighting off sleep. Maria grinned at his return to consciousness without a hitch in the story she was droning to his son, even though the boy gave no sign of paying attention, something about panic in Tangier, her passport sliding down behind her suitcase lining.

She had stumbled into the compartment, hours ago, just as the train was building momentum to leave Rome, huffing, grinning, baggage spewing from under her arms, off her shoulders.

The trip had begun extremely late, David fuming in his confusion, Donny lagging like dead weight. They stood on a platform for hours, David peering down the empty track, pacing among the heaped suitcases trying to get someone in the crowd of shrugging Italians to explain what had happened to the 8 a.m. Venice express, while Donny muttered curses and stuffed his mouth with candy bars. At 11 a train appeared and David scrambled aboard, dragging his baggage and his son after him, only to sit for another hour until the creaking start and Maria's breathless arrival.

She was the one to tell them about the one-day railway workers' strike. "We're all victims of a slowdown": the first words out of her mouth, then a non-stop rush, all the time the train inched over countryside, in and out of cities, across a barren brown landscape. Despite her chatter, David sensed that she was as miserable as the boy, her animation a desperate thrashing against a flood of gloom. All day he had felt the compartment sinking, as if the two of them were pulling him under.

To save himself, he gripped the armrest, imagined he was holding Virginia's hand, stroking the soft flesh, blood surging at her warmth. His fantasy of their being alone in a compartment, reaching over to draw a darkening shade and touching his lips to a smooth tanned shoulder. His wife at last, his new life finally begun. For months they had dreamed of being dazzled by the sunset on the Grand Canal, never considering that they could be an ocean apart, her tickets transferred to a son he barely knew.

"We're in Mestre," Maria said as David blinked his way back to comprehension. "It has a population of 75,000 and manufactures chemicals and heavy metals." Her head was a guidebook. "Pollution from Mestre is a serious problem for Venice. It's in the air, eating into the stucco."

David sighed, long and deep, almost a groan. The last thing he needed on this train was a pathetic lab technician from Santiago compelled to render every detail of every place she had visited during a two-month round-the-world once-in-a-lifetime holiday: the goiter of the woman who rented rooms in Macao, the cockroach found in a cafeteria meal on the Boul' Mich'. Short, squat, fatfaced. He couldn't imagine any man fantasizing about her in a locked compartment.

While David watched his son's eyelids droop and his head slump against the seatback, Maria renewed her outrage about the price of single rooms. "Some hotels charge me for a double even though I only use one bed. Can you believe that?" Her English jarred, with long vowels and trilled r's.

"It must be a problem travelling alone." David swallowed a yawn.

"I live alone. I'm alone most of the time."

The train stirred with a vibration that sent a tremor through the compartment. In his chest David felt the engine strain to break the inertia. He grunted as they lurched forward. Donny turned his face into the cushion and smacked a fist against the metal wall.

"Your son is exhausted," Maria said, then asked, "Do you have other children?" one of the rare moments she did not talk about herself.

David shook his head.

"Will his mother be waiting for you in Venice?"

"His mother is having a baby."

Her mouth dropped.

"His mother is not my wife. Not now. Not for years." David glanced at Donny to see if he was listening, but the boy had an arm around his head, fingers twisted in the hacked ends of a haircut he had given himself.

"I'm married to someone else now." David summoned up a picture of Virginia, soft and slim, lovely in summer dresses. It gave him great pleasure just to watch her move. But he couldn't shut out the memory of the anger that twisted her face: "The reservations are paid for. Non-refundable. He's your son. Just take him and go."

"And she's in Venice," Maria said, half statement, half question.

"She's back home too."

Maria knotted her brow.

"Look," he said, exasperated. "It's not a big deal. His mother asked me to watch after him for while. She's going to have to adjust to a baby. It's a tough time for everybody."

It had been hell, a night of phones ringing long past midnight, Lucy ranting long distance, Virginia weeping bitterly in the living room, irate women in both his ears. "You bailed out ten years ago,"

Lucy kept screaming. "Now you see him once a year and stuff him with ice cream. He's infantile. He destroys things. He wants to ruin my marriage. My life! He says he hates my baby! I want him out of here!"

All this three days before their flight, Virginia's suitcase spread open in the guest room, half packed with new clothes, guidebooks and brochures scattered across the carpet. And now beside him a son from half a continent away materialized at an airport gate, off one plane and hauled onto another, a sloppy kid with a smeared chin in a filthy outgrown sweatsuit. Instead of a greeting, he had glared at David and said, "The bitch can shove that baby back where it came from."

"It's nice that you're such a good father," Maria said, and the train lurched.

Finally, at 1:17 a.m. on the station clock, they arrived in Venice. David stirred himself to unfold two chrome luggage carts and strap down suitcases. Maria collected an assortment of canvas bags. Every time she grabbed one, she seemed to drop another. When David offered help, she grinned thanks and let him pick up after her.

For weeks he had anticipated sharing Virginia's awed reaction to discovering Venice. He deliberately had planned their schedule to arrive in early evening in time to change, stroll to an outdoor meal in the Piazza San Marco, and await the sunset. Now it was the middle of the night, Maria squealing at Donny to catch her umbrella.

They emerged from the station into a grey night under a cloud-covered quarter moon. The area was dingy, a row of tiny hotels with faint signs and loiterers slouching in the shadows. They had to wait for a vaporetto in a white shed bobbing at the water's edge. David rolled the two suitcases down a wooden walkway, Maria's heaviest duffle bag over his shoulder. Donny sank onto one of the slat benches, eyes puffed with fatigue.

Whichever direction David looked, up or down the canal, the view was drab, except for the small gold-domed church directly across a slice of water. Maria, seated beside him on the bench, already had her green Michelin guide open. "Fondamente Saint Simeon Piccolo," she said. "There are 190 churches in Venice, nearly all interesting. But I can't find any details about this one." Under a weak bulb she squinted at the page with disappointment.

Aside from two grizzle-faced vaporetto employees smoking cigarettes down to their fingertips, the only others in the waiting shed were three young people, a muscular male in a black turtleneck and faded overalls and two women, one curly headed and round, the other tall and dark, with pitch black hair, drawn cheeks, and stark facial bones. She wore a tanktop, long dark legs emerging from cutoff shorts. The night was chilly enough for David to button his sweater. But she did not shiver once.

All three were either drunk or stoned, with arms wrapped around each other, breaking out into snatches of songs, their speech chanted in a language he had trouble placing. It might have been Italian, but with harsh Germanic intonations. The dark woman's loud hoarse voice dominated, as she orchestrated each sound with an angular hand gesture. Every minute or so, at her lead, the three wailed, "Oh mama!"

Maria grinned at their antics, nudged Donny to make him look, as if the three were putting on a show just for them. But he turned away and spit at the water. David imagined the male suddenly stomping across the planks and knocking Donny into the canal, the boy flailing in a ridiculous splash, then sinking like a stone. A shadow fell across the man's face like a scar, and David swallowed.

When the plump woman gave her the edge of a smile, Maria took that as an excuse to approach and admire the jagged bronze pendant the dark woman wore against her breastbone. The three stared blankly at her English. She tried again in Spanish. After a silence, when the smoking workers halted their conversation to stare, the dark woman glared and did a jerky, arm-flapping dance step that forced Maria backwards. She slunk to the bench and looked to David for solace. But he pretended he had not seen a thing. He caught Donny glancing at him, face screwed in a smirk.

It was another ten minutes before the vaporetto came. By then Maria had located the stop for David's hotel, Campo Santa Maria del Giglio, in her guidebook. His travel agent had made reservations at what she called "a congenial but inexpensive little place" called the Villa Giorgione. He and Virginia had saved for a year; then Lucy's lawyer sent the bill for Donny's therapy, and Virginia had urged him to cancel. But David had insisted that they owed this trip to themselves; he wasn't going to let the son of a failed marriage ruin their future.

And now on a chill night at the fringe of Venice he could taste the folly of his decision.

David loaded Maria's suitcases on board and gave her his hand as she stepped down onto the deck. Donny waved off his help. The three young people, without luggage, waited until the boat started to pull away and jumped on with screaming leaps. Maria shrank against David each time a pair of feet pounded the deck.

When the boat began to move, churning out a white wake on the empty canal, she was smiling again, guessing the names of the palaces on the water's edge as if she had memorized the map. Palazzo Grimani, Palazzo Rezzonio, Palazzo Grassi.

David saw only facades and doorways, silhouettes of roofs and domes, low grey shapes of moored motor launches. He turned and realized that Donny had slipped inside the cabin and collapsed onto a bench, eyes closed, mouth open, chin bouncing against his chest with the vibrations of the boat.

Maria startled him with a nudge and a question. "What is your boy's mother's name?"

"Lucy." It felt odd to be speaking that name here, on a canal in Venice.

"Why did you leave her?"

"I didn't love her."

Her face took on its blank expression. "Is love so important?"

David squeezed his hands around the chill railing. "You wouldn't understand."

"And the boy?"

"He was a baby then."

"What is he now?"

"Listen! I didn't make him this way. He lives with his mother."

Maria looked toward the cabin and gasped. The three young people were hovering over Donny, rising on tiptoes, wriggling fingers. David couldn't hear over the engine noise, but he thought they were chanting.

When he rushed inside, they sprawled across the bench on the other side, arms folded and glaring. He shook Donny; the boy wouldn't open his eyes. "You okay?" David said.

"They're assholes," Donny muttered. David grasped his shoulders to make him move outside, away from them.

He heard Maria cry, "We're here!"

The vaporetto eased toward a pier marked with the name of their stop. David hoisted Donny and hurried to gather their suitcases, leaving Maria to fend for herself. The three young people shook open hands at them and called, "Oh mama!"

On the pier, luggage at her feet, Maria gazed helplessly and wondered if she could find a room at David's hotel. He shrugged and told her to try.

They moved through a narrow pathway between building fronts and found themselves on a cobblestone street. Maria consulted her map and pointed ahead. In a minute they moved through an open square deserted of people, the wheels of their luggage rattling over the stones.

The Hotel Giorgione was small and neat. Maria peered inside and said its lobby seemed very nice. When David pulled at the door, it was locked. He watch read past two a.m. He rapped on the glass until a clerk appeared, a bald man with a cardigan sweater under his suit jacket. He unlocked and held the door open a crack. David identified himself, and the clerk shrugged. "We have no rooms, signore."

"I made a reservation. I sent a deposit."

"I remember your name, signore. But your deposit never arrived. We could not hold the room without it."

David wanted to hit the man, slap his thick brown glasses across the lobby.

"Listen! It's the middle of the night. We're exhausted. I gave my travel agent a check six goddamn weeks ago!" Donny sat on the cobblestone and sprawled back against a suitcase. Maria just listened, as if storing away another anecdote.

"I can do nothing, signore." The clerk withdrew and quickly bolted the door, leaving them outside.

David had an urge to stand in the middle of the campo and roar frustration, bellow until he woke up every sleeping soul in Venice.

"I wonder what we'll do," Maria said, looking up at him with her thick face as if the three of them were a unit.

He tried to speak calmly. "Let's just find San Marco. There's got to be something there."

David made Donny drag one suitcase, Maria the other. He lugged her collection of bags, straps over both shoulders, handles in the crooks of his arms, up and down the steps of bridges that seemed to cross and re-cross the same winding canal. With no street lights, with the moon buried in cloud, the darkness swallowed them. He knew they were lost, wandering randomly in a city of strangers.

They finally saw other people, a couple, two young lovers hand in hand, sitting on church steps. In broken English, on a pocket map under a penlight, the couple traced a route back the way they had come, but when they moved away David couldn't remember any of it.

He decided to follow a single street wherever it led. In front of a small hotel with a polished wooden door a group of drunken men stopped their singing to swarm about Maria, crooning Italian endearments. One dropped to his knees and seized her hand, smacked a kiss on her knuckles. Another stroked her hair. She just stood in the middle of them grinning foolishly. Although his instinct was to abandon her, David pushed through, seized her arm, and pulled her away.

"Arrivederci," the men chanted after them, "Arrivederci," and dissolved into laughter. Donny started laughing too, just as loudly, the first amusement he had shown since David found him staring at a wall in the airport.

Maria dropped the suitcase and ran off, shoes pounding at the stones with heavy steps. At the first side street, no more than an alley, she swerved and disappeared.

Still burdened with her baggage, David seized Donny's shoulders and shook, suddenly furious. "You humiliated her."

"What about those guys?"

"All day she tried to be nice to you."

"She's an ugly pig."

David slapped him, felt the sting radiate up through his arm. The boy stared back, refusing to admit pain. Then David calmed. "You take both carts and follow me."

With Maria's bags bulging at his side, David could barely fit into the alley. He considered dropping them, then wondered if he'd been able to find his way back, if they would still be there.

It was a long passageway, windowless outer walls looming on both sides, warehouses perhaps or factories, built by people who didn't care about light. He turned back to made sure Donny was trudging behind with the carts. Their rumbling seemed muffled now.

He saw a sliver ahead, not really a light, just a shaft of grey glow less dense than the darkness. This is ugly, he kept thinking, bleak and ugly. On an ugly street on an ugly night seeking a ugly women followed by his ugly son.

And now he understood why he had made this trip—to take Donny far from Virginia, fleeing from fear that knowing his son would make her realize she would never find the life she had hoped for in him.

Then he stumbled over something soft, and the heft of the baggage toppled him forward until he sprawled across a tiny square at the end of the alley, a place barely wider than the length of his body. When he pulled himself up, he saw Maria huddled against a brick wall, her arms wrapped around her ankles, her face pressed deep between her knees. He had tripped over her.

In a few seconds he realized the strange yowling noise was her sobbing, a crying unlike any he had ever heard before, a terrible animal misery. "What's wrong?" he asked, though he was too exhausted to care.

"It's so awful." "What?"

"Everything." And she fell into an even louder wailing.

David began to reach out, as if there were no choice but to comfort her. But something stepped on his hand. He yelled and looked up at the thin bare leg of the woman from the vaporetto. She was wearing spiked heels. When he tried to pull his hand free, she shifted her weight and the jagged pendant dangled over him.

"Hey? What're you doing?"

She gestured back toward the darkness with her chin, and the others appeared, the round woman, the man in the turtleneck. Something glinted in his hand.

The round woman seized Maria's hair and pulled her head back, arching her neck, shouting something, a single harsh word over and over again.   David expected the man to swipe out and slash across her throat, blood to suddenly spurt over them all.

"Do you want money?" he made himself plead. "Credit cards?"

The man reached down and seized David by the back of the head and yanked him upward until they were face to face, grinding his nose into David's cheek. He reeked of a sweet aftershave like an ointment on his skin.

This is death, David thought, and the sensation of an absolute emptiness shuddered through him.

"Bastards! Goddamn fucking bastards!" Donny lunged toward them swinging a suitcase in a wide circle, thumping the man behind the knees, knocking his legs out from under him. The man tumbled atop David, then scrambled off into the alley. The two women backed against a wall, kicking and pointing at Donny, twisting their hands into some obscene gesture.

When the boy stood panting in the square, they screamed convulsively, the man too, next to them now, the three of them shaking their arms in the identical gesture. Then the tall woman did her jerky dance and spit at Maria. The three spun and ran into the darkness, roaring "Oh mama!" again and again.

Donny tried to hurl the luggage after them. It crashed on the cobblestones, splitting open and spewing clothing. David stared, trying to recognize each item, which of the twisted garments was his and which was his son's. When he turned, Donny was beside Maria, the two of them clasping each other, sobbing and clinging, as if their grief was endless.

Through the space between two buildings, past the tiled roofs, David could make out a narrow view, the glittering edge of a golden dome, a slice of distant sea. And he knew that whatever happened next, he was seeing as much of Venice as would ever matter to him. For months, Virginia had memorized a city from picture books—churches, squares, and palaces. But he had found another Venice, nothing like the one she had dreamed. He felt so sad for her that he wanted to weep.

Then he sensed the swelling of his hand. Something is broken, he thought. David touched the purple flesh with a fingertip and suddenly reeled. He cried out, blinded by the intensity of his pain. Through the tear blur he saw his son reaching up to him as if they were bound by a single hurt.

Baggage

HOWARD CAUGHT A LOCAL FROM PARIS TO LILLE to board the Lombardy Express to Rome there at five in the afternoon. With all his rushing to make connections he had not eaten anything all day but a breakfast croissant. Now he was hungry and annoyed with himself for bringing too much luggage for the trip: an overpacked black pullman case strapped onto a chrome pullcart, a matching one-suiter, and a carry-on shoulder bag weighted down with a camera, tape recorder, transistor radio, and voltage converter. All that paraphernalia for one solitary traveler. What a fool he was.

But he had expected to find a city where he could linger, slowly unpack his possessions into spacious drawers, stroll peacefully through empty streets, seek pictures that satisfied, record sounds that pleased. But each city disappointed. Crowds pushed him along sidewalks past hostile stares from the cafes. Every time he stopped to aim his camera, a blur of arm or head ruined the scene in the viewfinder. The oppression of strangers: bodies bumping against him, a din of harsh foreignness in his ears, a thousand shrugs in his face. Nowhere was there a smile for him alone.

Under his load Howard stumbled down the corridor with the lurching of the train, squeezing past the people standing at the windows until he located the compartment with his seat number. His stomach tightened when he saw the young man settled between the armrests. He produced his reservation card, held it out in front of him. But as he was about to speak, the young man met his gaze with soft brown eyes, and Howard could feel the stares of the others just beyond the edge of his vision. He sensed that they liked the young man, were ready to side with him against Howard's protest. But he would not give them the satisfaction. He just held his card and waited, refusing to look at anyone. The young man finally stood with muttered apologies, grabbed a small canvas bag, and hurried out the sliding door.

Howard found the compartment too crowded to disconnect the pullman case from its cart and fold the frame. So he hoisted it up over his head to the one empty spot on the luggage rack and forced his one-suiter atop it. The carry-on bag he kept on the floor under his seat.

He squirmed for comfort, felt a flush prickle his face, pretended to lose himself in the intricacies of resetting his watch because the others in the compartment were all studying him. Slowly, secretly, he looked back at them.

He sat in the middle across from a heavy old woman whose dress rode above her knees to expose rolled stocking tops. Closest to the door were two young girls, perhaps nineteen or twenty, one blonde and pink-cheeked with perfect white teeth, the other with piercing green eyes and thick auburn hair twisted into a severe knot. She was not as pretty as her friend. Both were as young as the daughters he had not seen in more than a year.

The other two people in the compartment, a man and a woman, took his attention. Sitting across from each other by the window, they looked so unlike. She was fair, plump, and freckled, her dress too tight, ovals of pale flesh showing where the buttonholes stretched across her middle. The man had a flowing black mustache and goatee that matched rich, wavy hair. He was dark and handsome, tightly muscled in expensive jeans and a black turtleneck. Howard watched for a time and saw that they did not acknowledge each other. She must have been alone.

But just as he considered smiling at her, the woman leaned forward, touched the man's knee, and whispered. The man responded with a burst of musical Italian, all eye rollings and hand gestures. She kissed her finger and reached it to his lips.

Howard turned away to the landscape rushing past the window. His clenched fists trembled with anger. He would not speak, he would not utter a sound during the entire trip to Rome. No matter what they said to him, no matter how they said it, he would feign ignorance of all languages and stay absolutely apart.

By the time the train reached Valenciennes, Howard was no longer a disruption to the compartment, just one more object in the clutter, familiar enough to be ignored in such close quarters. He felt relief that no one addressed him while he planned his incomprehension.

The old woman reached into her sack of a handbag to pull out a sandwich wrapped in white paper and a small bottle of red wine sealed with foil. She unfolded the paper in her lap and took a deep bite into the bread, tearing at meat and crust. Crumbs dropped onto the front of her dress and a spicy salami odor filled the compartment. The others did not pay attention to her, but Howard's stomach felt hollow with hunger and a weakness spread through his limbs. He tried to close his eyes.

When he opened them, he found the green-eyed girl looking right at him. Flustered, he made a gesture of cutting with a knife, brought an imaginary fork to his mouth, and pointed questioningly out at the corridor. He guessed the French for dining car would be wagon a manger or voiture a manger. But he tried neither, still resolved not to speak.

The girl glanced at her friend and shook her head. "Non," she said, "non." The others began to attempt explanations, the old woman with words that occasionally sounded French but had a guttural German pronunciation, the man in rapid Italian, finally the woman with him in crystal-clear British English: "I'm afraid there is no dining car on this train. There will be vendors at some of the stations in France. But other than those, you'll have to wait until we get to Italy in the morning and a food cart comes on board." Howard kept the understanding out of his eyes and screwed up his face at her.

"Perhaps he's Spanish," the pretty girl said in English to the woman, the z-like s's the only hint of her accent.

"He is not handsome enough," her friend said in a French simple enough for Howard to decipher.

The pretty girl giggled. "Le Scandinave?" The green-eyed girl shrugged indifference.

The English woman said something in Italian to the man, touching his knees again. It was obvious that she liked to touch him. The old woman just chewed on her sandwich.

The pretty girl began a conversation with the English woman. "Do you speak French as well as you speak Italian?"

"I'm afraid not. I studied Italian at university. My French is rather poor."

"I have been learning English since I was ten."

"You're quite good."

The girl nodded thanks. "How long will you be visiting Italy?"

"We're going home. We live there. Outside Bologna. In Budrio." " You and your husband?"

"He's not my husband." The man beamed a smile at the girl as she blushed. Her friend smirked.

Howard wanted to laugh, but he sat blankly, darting his eyes from face to face of the others in a show of confusion. Then he settled on the English woman, trying to decide if she were attractive.

She couldn't have been past her late twenties but dressed dowdily, with a grey sweater buttoned around her shoulder and squaretoed shoes. She was overweight, but her look was pleasant, the mouth a bit too wide, the lipstick too thick and too orange, the hair unflattering, not long enough for her round face.

She had several magazines wedged between her side and the compartment wall. Howard would like to have read them to fill the time but could not ask without exposing his English.

He stood, slung his carry-on bag over his shoulder, and stepped over the girls' feet to slide the door back and move out into the corridor. At the end of the car the young man who had been in his seat sat on the flap that folded out from the wall. He nodded as Howard passed him to enter the toilet, and it struck Howard that he must be a friend of the two girls, perhaps the lover of one, of the green-eyed girl.

A sign in four languages warned that the water was not suitable for drinking. Howard splashed it on his face but would not look in the mirror. Then he stepped on the flush pedal and watched the ground flash by under the hole until someone tapped on the door.

He opened it for the Italian and was surprised by how short the man was. Sitting he had looked tall. "Scusi," the man said. "Grazia."

When the Italian returned to the compartment and sat beside Howard, the English woman produced their food, fruit and cheese. Again Howardsuffered hunger pangs and wanted them to offer him something, so badly he might have responded to English. But he could see that they had barely enough for themselves.

Later, when the train was pulling in to Metz, the Italian nudged him and pointed to the vendor's cart on the platform. Howard ran to the door of the car while the train eased to a stop with a creak of brakes. By the time they came to rest the cart was far back. He jumped down and hurried to stand in line; but, just as his turn came, the train began to move. The vendor shouted, a conductor called. Howard grabbed a bottle of beer and shoved a twenty franc note into the vendor's hand. Clutching the beer, feeling like a fool, he leaped back on the train without his change. He had to walk through seven cars to get back to his compartment. The Italian gave him an opener for the beer. Although she did not make a sound, he was sure the green-eyed girl was laughing at him.

The old woman was digging through her handbag again, groping until she pulled out a ragged packet of rubber-banded papers. A brown passport slipped out with it and fluttered to the floor behind her shoe, unseen. She unfolded several sheets, read them closely, and returned the packet, finally realizing her passport was gone. She clasped hands beneath her chin and let out an exclamation of woe. The two girls, immediately solicitous, turned to her and listened to her fragmented explanation, the green-eyed one trying to keep her on track with questions.

They had her empty the handbag item by item, spreading across the seat an assortment of plastic cases, combs, medicine vials, a balled cloth that might have been a nightgown. The couple moved to help also, the man poking a hand behind the seat cushion, the woman scanning the floor. The old woman still obscured the passport with her shoe.

Howard knew all he had to do was point, reach out an arm, extend a finger. But he did not want to call attention to himself; he did not want to become one of them. Then the pretty girl bent down on her knees and saw behind the woman's foot. She held the passport in the air like a trophy. The old woman made a gesture as if to embrace her. The others grinned and the girl blushed happily.

By the time they left the stop in Strasbourg, it was dark outside, the six passengers reflected in the compartment window. Howard took the tape recorder from his carry-on bag and, through the earplug, listened to a tape he had made from his radio in Paris: static, the blur of tuning, music, a babble of voices in French, German, Spanish, Dutch, Italian, all cut off in midsentence as he had switched from station to station in search of something he could understand.

When the conductor came in to convert the compartment to couchette bunks, they had to step out into the corridor and take down their luggage from the racks. The Italian did most of the shifting, passing out the suitcases, the girls' nylon bags, and the old woman's cord-tied cardboard box to Howard and the conductor.

The conductor folded up the luggage racks, pulled a ladder from under the left seat, folded out the seatbacks to make the middle bunks, and swung down the top bunks from the wall. Howard would be in the middle. Before the conductor passed out sheet, pillows, and blankets, the Italian rearranged the luggage, stacked most of it in the space over the door on the ceiling of the corridor. The old woman's box and Howard's pullman had to stand in the middle of the floor. Howard brought has carry-on into his bunk.

The old woman would sleep across from him, the girls in the lower bunks, the English woman and the Italian man on top. Howard kept bumping into the old woman as they spread their sheets and blankets. The green- eyed girl looked up at him while he fumbled to make his bed. When the English woman climbed the ladder and swung her legs onto the bunk, Howard could see her white thighs above the tops of her stockings. She reached out to clasp the Italian's hand, and Howard was furious at his aloneness.

He could not sleep. The old woman fluted high-pitched snoring. His stomach twisted with hunger spasms. The train wheels slapped endlessly at the metal rails. He tossed and squirmed, shut in, claustrophobic. Because the curtains in the compartment were pulled to block all light, he could not see his watch and kept sliding the door open an inch or two to check the time.

At five-thirty, with the first glow of dawn, he contorted into his shoes and got up to use the toilet. Then he stood at the window in the corridor to look out at the Italian-Swiss Alps. Snow peaks and shadowed crags, a few cars far below on the highway, the lights of distant houses, and every now and then a village, unmoving and immaculately clean. The cleanliness of Switzerland made him feel scummy. His head itched; he had not brushed his teeth. He tugged down the window to let cold air blast his face.

Later, when the others were all up, the old woman and the girls standing in line for the toilet, the Italian restored the compartment from couchettes to riding seats. He replaced the luggage on the racks, stood on his toes to slide the old woman's box over the door. Only Howard's pullman would not fit easily into the new arrangement. The Italian left it on the floor and shrugged at him. But when the girls and the woman returned, there was not enough room for everyone's feet.

Howard pretended not to notice. But the green-eyed girl kicked his foot. He glared at her and quickly shoved his case onto the rack above the old woman while she looked up apprehensively. He wished she were not on the train, with her rolled stockings and her salami and her passport and her cardboard box. If she were gone, there would be enough room for the rest of them; he would not feel so crushed in with strangers.

They were in Italy now, stopping for a long time in Chaisso where Howard tripped against the green-eyed girl in his rush to get at the food cart being pushed down the corridor. He overpaid for a banana, a cup of lukewarm coffee, and a piece of stale raisin cake that still did not satisfy his hunger.

When the train passed Como and moved onto the open country-side of Lombardy, the French girls began to read paperbacks and the English woman and Italian man made eyes at each other, knowing— Howard was sure—that they were only a few hours from a bed.

The trip seemed bumpier now, Howard pitching from side to side in his seat, feeling vibrations through his shoes. He looked up to see his pullman case sliding loose from the rack above the old woman, rat-tling inch by inch across the dark crossbars, the wheels of the pullcart scraping against the ceiling. Two more inches and it would fall.

He knew he should shout to her to look out. But the sound lodged in his throat like an enormous mass. He tried to lift his hands, but they lay paralyzed in his lap.

The Italian saw and lunged forward with a cry. But he was too late. The case tumbled down, bounced off the old woman's knees, and struck her across the ankles with the chrome bar of the frame.

She let out a long wail of pain. The pretty girl burst into tears; her green-eyed friend pushed Howard's case off the woman, opening the doors and forcing it out into the corridor as if it were a vicious animal.

The English woman embraced the old woman, the Italian kneeling at her feet. Howard rubbed a hand at his throat, clutching against the sensation that he would choke on swallowed words.

The old woman's stockings were shredded, blood streaming from a deep ugly gash in her right instep. She moaned and wept and muttered a lament of pain. Both ankles swelled immediately, great purple bruises appearing through the holes in her stockings. The Italian unfolded a handkerchief and tied it around the gash.

The green-eyed girl disappeared into the corridor and came back with the young man who had been in Howard's seat. "L'etudiant en medicine," she announced. He pulled a first aid kit from his canvas bag, removed the handkerchief, cut away the stocking, cleaned the wound, and bandaged it. His work was quick and neat. He spoke soothingly to the old woman, who nodded and attempted to swallow her pain.

When the conductor finally came, the young man made a lengthy explanation, pointing to Howard, the rack, the pullman case in the corridor, while the conductor filled out a form.

"What will happen?" the English woman asked the green-eyed girl.

"We'll get off at Milan with her. The conductor is sending a radio message for an ambulance."

"Is her leg broken?"

"Jean doesn't think so. But it must be X-rayed."

At the central station in Milan the medical student and the Italian carried the woman off the train. The pretty girl took her suitcase and the green-eyed girl the cardboard box.

When they were all gone, Howard retrieved his pullman case from the corridor and placed it on the empty seat beside the English woman. He expected blood on the frame, but there was none. The four black wheels of the cart bounced on the cushion.

He thought of all his possessions inside, pictured them one by one in his head as he watched the bouncing. When he glanced up, he saw the English woman holding the handle with the identification tag that noted his American name and address.

She met his eyes and, barely moving her lips, spoke so softly Howard could not hear her curse.

The End of the Circle

SHEILA NOTICED THE FAMILY FIRST. "Look!" The father knelt beside a baby boy propped against a door of the National Theatre on Karl Johans Gate, trying to place a carved troll in his small hands. She made George stop.

George paused to watch, eager to move on, humoring her, aware that babies were her weakness. She had given up teasing their own children to make her a grandmother, after he convinced her that it was useless, with two divorced and the third more interested in her career than motherhood.

George couldn't see the father's face, just the top of his tan scalp, balding in the manner of young men with fine blond hair. His muscular arms accentuated the thinness of the child's pale legs protruding from a padded diaper. The boy opened his fingers and watched the troll drop to the sidewalk. The father picked it up slowly, and this time wrapped the boy's arms around it so that he would hug it to his chest. Then the man let go and backed away. He pulled a videocam from the nylon bag slung over his shoulder and focused on the boy, puffing his cheeks and fluttering his lips to make him laugh. But the boy just stared. The man motioned his wife to get closer to the child.

George looked to the mother, a slight woman, fair and freckled, with loose red hair fanned by the breeze. She was peering across the street where a line of people queued at a bus stop, as if searching the faces. George followed her gaze, curious to know what she sought. "Julia!" the man called. But before she could move, the boy began to toddle toward his father, holding out the troll as if to return it. The man swept him up in a hug.

When he realized that George and Sheila were staring at them, he turned abruptly. From the flash of the man's grey eyes, George expected anger, insults, an embarrassing confrontation. The man's open shirt exposed a thin gold chain against his broad chest, and George swallowed at a sensation of danger. But the man broke into a smile and pointed at the videocam. "Would you mind taping the three of us?" he said, the accent plainly American. "All you have to do is look in the lens and press this button."

George laughed out loud. "I thought you were Norwegians."

He shook his head. "Oh no, we're apple pie and Fourth of July. Aren't we, Julia?"

"Upstate New York." Her voice rose, as if the fact startled her.

"What's your boy's name?" Sheila asked.

"Timothy." The father separated the syllables. "A big name for a little guy. And I'm called Ronny."

George, amused now, introduced himself and Sheila, said that they were delighted to be meeting Americans, though half the people they ran into at the hotels in Copenhagen and Stockholm had been from California. He expected Sheila's poke; she didn't like him chatting with strangers. Instead she reached out and touched fingertips to the boy's soft hair.

Ronny handed George the videocam and moved beside Julia at the National Theatre entrance, hoisted Timothy to his shoulders, and grinned at the lens. For a moment, the boy looked terrified to be so high. Then he reached down and blocked his father's nose with the troll's squat body, the gnarled wood rising like a growth between the man's eyes.

George thought it made a cute picture.

"He's too thin," Sheila said when they left the family. "Who?"

"Timothy."

"Maybe he takes after Julia. She could use a few pounds herself."

"He's nothing like her."

George realized that the boy was dark, different from both parents— black hair, large brown eyes with long, thick lashes. "Then he's probably a finicky eater, the way Greg was at his age. Now look at our son."

"Greg was never that scrawny," she insisted.

Though he wanted to say, what is it to you, George took her hand, unwilling to let her anxiety ruin his mood. He was feeling happy, strolling on a wide promenade of under a brilliant sky.

"What a pleasant city Oslo is," he said. They moved onto a shaded path beside a circular fountain that sprayed a cool mist. George nodded at three elderly women on a bench eating ice cream. They saluted with their cones.

Later, when they crossed the road from the City Hall to the fjord, George saw the family sitting at an outdoor cafe on the water's edge. Ronny called out to them, lifted Timothy to his lap, and gestured at the two empty chairs. "Why not?" George said. He found himself eager for company, a diversion from the weeks of sightseeing. He gave Sheila a quick glance and guided her forward with a hand on her shoulder.

Ronny signaled the waiter and pointed to the sizzling plates of grilled shrimp at the next table. "That's what we're having."

George nodded. "Sounds great."

Julia's blue eyes gazed out across the fjord, but George saw only the glints of sunlight on the water. Sheila asked if she could hold Timothy, and Ronny passed the boy to her. In her arms he squirmed for a few seconds, whimpered once, and then lay still, face pressed into her shoulder. She brushed the top of his head with her lips. About to tell her to stop, it's not yours, George saw the urgency in her face and kept silent, uneasy at his own annoyance. He wondered if the others noticed. Her need bewildered him. They'd already raised a family.

When she returned the boy to his father, George looked away to study the rigging of a sailing ship moored at pier beside the cafe. Beyond it a fortress rose on a bluff that overlooked the fjord.

Ronny pointed at the stone walls. "What do Norwegians have to be afraid of?" Timothy sat on his lap and sucked juice from a bottle.

"Swedes once. Germans in the 20th century." Though Ronny's words had been teasing, Julia spoke with a gravity that surprised George. "It's called the Akershus Fortress, and the Nazis shot Resistance fighters there. After the war, it's where Quisling was executed."

Ronny sliced the edge of his hand across his throat and made a squishing sound. "Doesn't pay to be a traitor."

"How do you know so much?" Sheila asked Julia, almost an accusation.

"I read."

George found himself drawn toward her. Despite her ethereal look, Julia was a direct young woman, grieving over events that had taken place decades ago, long before she was born, back when he and Sheila were Timothy's age. Though he barely knew them, he had trouble matching her with Ronny, she so frail and serious, he so solid and breezy.

The waiter brought the plates of shrimp and, at Ronny's signal, another round of beers. A passenger ferry left its slip, churning a wake as it moved toward an arm of green land across the water. "Museums are over there." Julia pointed. "The Kon Tiki and the Viking ship."

"We should hire you as a guide," Sheila said. "How long have you been here?" George had been about to ask the same question.

"In Norway just days. In Europe three months."

George sighed, an exaggerated sound of regret. "I wish we could have done that at your age. We didn't make our first trip till we were forty. Couldn't afford it before."

"Neither can we." Ronny winked.

"But you're here," Sheila said.

"Ronny's between jobs." Julia leaned forward to dab Timothy's mouth with her napkin.

"Cleaned out all our savings. Poof." Ronny exploded his hands. "Bone dry. Five credit cards up to their limit."

George nodded, surprised that Julia would let him be so irresponsible. "Then what?" he asked. "When will you go back?"

"There's so much we haven't seen." Julia spoke quickly, as if to insert herself before Ronny could answer.

"I'm taking my son on the Grand Tour." He bounced Timothy on his knee, and the boy squeezed his eyes shut at the rough ride.

Although Ronny reached for his wallet, George insisted on paying for the meal, conscious that he had so much, eager to treat people living out what had once been his fantasy.

They crossed the road together and stood in awkward silence by the blank red brick of the City Hall, George glancing at Julia, hoping she would speak, trying to think of a way to continue the encounter, when Sheila asked, "What are your plans for the afternoon?" George was surprised that she too wanted to be with them, then understood that it was the child. He awaited their response, suddenly concerned that Ronny and Julia wouldn't want to waste the day with an aged couple.

"The Vigeland sculptures," Julia said.

"Us too," George said quickly. "They're supposed to be a highlight."

Ronny's face brightened. "Why don't we go together?"

George signaled for a cab and folded the stroller into the trunk while Ronny held Timothy. As soon as they set off, Ronny insisted on paying this time, slipping a crisp 100 kroner note from his wallet and rolling it into a tight tube as the driver maneuvered through the streets.

In Frogner Park, sunbathers sprawled on towels spread over the rolling grass, young people mainly, the women casually topless. For an instant George expected a comment from Ronny, a joking allusion to Julia's thin chest. But all the man did was throw his arms to the sky and say, "What a day!" George wondered how he could have had such a notion.

The first of the sculptures, bronze figures of men and women and infants, rose on columns from a bridge, then ahead large white shapes sat in a circle around a monolith. "The Wheel of Life," Julia told them.

When George got close, he realized the statues captured the cycle of human existence—mothers with babies, frolicking children, couples, families, friendships, finally old age and the moments before death. Though the figures were thick stone, almost crudely hewn, the faces indistinct, George found himself moved, struck by how close he and Sheila were to the end of the cycle. If the five of them made a circle in age from Timothy to himself, they could form their own wheel.

"I don't like this," Julia pointed at the monolith. Though it towered above the individual statues, George had not given it close attention. Now he recognized a mass of human forms, limbs linked, piled one atop the other. "It's supposed to show the continuum of humanity," Julia said, "but it reminds me of concentration camps." She did not look away.

George nodded, made uneasy by the tangle of bodies. He turned to Sheila for a reaction, but she was watching Timothy. When Ronny seated him atop a stone child and stepped back to tape, she moved close, as if to protect the boy from a fall. Ronny swung the videocam toward Julia and George by the monolith, focusing on them so long their smiles froze.

Standing next to Julia beneath sweeping green tree limbs, Sheila on a path helping Ronny lift Timothy into his stroller, George had an impulse to invite them to spend time with them, to share the cabin they had rented for a week on a farm in the hills above Lillehammer. He knew he should have consulted Sheila but hoped she wouldn't resent an opportunity to spend time with the boy. For him, it was Julia's quiet appeal, his sense that something very deep ran inside her. He cleared his throat and asked.

When Julia turned to Sheila to say they couldn't impose, George had a moment of panic, unsure what his wife would do. But when Sheila gave a faint smile, he relaxed and explained that the cabin had two bedrooms and that there would be plenty of space. He saw Ronny signal Julia and step in front of her. "All right. But we'll pay half."

"It's already paid for," George argued, "in advance. And it wouldn't cost us any less if you weren't there."

"Then you'll have to let us buy the groceries." Ronny shook his hand as if they were sealing a deal.

All evening George kept waiting for Sheila to speak about it, but she said nothing beyond commenting on the food at dinner and telling him how tired she felt. But she was still reading her book when he turned out the light on his side of the bed and rolled over.

Early the next morning, when they went down to their hotel lobby, George found the family waiting. Timothy was sleeping on a padded chair, mouth open, dried mucus clogging his nostrils. Julia had on the same flowered dress and Ronny the same blue shirt they had worn the previous day, his chain flashing in the artificial light.

George's plan was for them all to take a cab to Fornebu Airport, where he had reserved a Hertz Volvo, a station wagon with room for six. But Ronny cleared his throat. "We don't have all our stuff with us now." He and Julia carried only two small zippered bags

Sheila brushed a hand over the matched luggage set she and George had aligned on the lobby carpet. "Where is it?"

"At the Central Station. In a locker."

"We thought the car rental was there," Julia said. Sheila shook her head. "No, only at the airport."

"You all wait here," George said. "There's no sense in everybody going."

"I'll come with you," Ronny insisted. He rode with George in the taxi, apologizing several times for messing up their plans despite George's protests that it didn't matter, that they were on vacation and had open days ahead. "We've been taking public transportation for so long," Ronny explained, "that we've forgotten what it's like with a car."

Once they had the station wagon, George decided to retrieve the family's luggage before returning to the hotel for Sheila, Julia, and Timothy. "Then they can just pile in and we'll drive north." He hoped Sheila would soften toward Julia while the two of them were alone.

Ronny's key wouldn't turn in the oversized locker no matter how hard he twisted. George put on reading glasses to study the lock and saw that more coins were needed; he reached into his pocket and dropped several kroner into the slot while Ronny watched.

Ronny swung open the locker door and gripped the frame of a backpack, sliding it out and then bracing it on the floor before he hoisted it onto his shoulders. Thick rolls of nylon—bright yellow and blue—were strapped to both sides, two pairs of hiking boots tied to the bottom by their laces.

George slid a hand over the slick material. "What's this for?"

"A tent. Poles inside the pack. Sleeping out gets you close to nature.Saves money too."

"Last night?"

"No. We pooled pennies and found a room." "How long can you keep this up?"

"As long as I have to."

George expected Ronny's deep laugh, as if he had made a joke, but the man stared ahead.

Route E6 north narrowed to two lanes a few miles above the city.

Everyone rode with headlights on despite the brightness of the day. Julia explained that it was the law in the Scandinavian countries. "And they do obey the law here," Ronny said. "Never drink and drive, George. You'll spend the rest of your life in a Norwegian clink." His tone was teasing, but George sensed an edge of mockery.

"I'm grateful for the warning," he said. He tried to watch the scenery as he drove, the rolling green of the countryside, the glimpses of Lake Mjosa through the thick trees, but his eyes were drawn to the mirror where he could see Julia gripping an arm rest and Ronny hugging Timothy on his lap, smacking kisses on his forehead while the boy reached up to touch his father's unshaven jaw. Sheila reached back and stroked Timothy's cheek, mimicking his gesture.

"Is he always so good?" she asked.

"Timothy is a wonder." Ronny squeezed his son tight with a loud ooomph. Then he put on a stern face. "Don't you ever misbehave, boy. I don't want to lose you in a Norwegian jail."

Julia stared straight ahead as if mesmerized by the rhythm of the ride. When she sensed George watching her reflection, she forced a smile. Timothy closed a fist around his father's gold chain and tugged.

A dog began barking and leaping at its tether when George parked the Volvo outside the farmhouse. They had been twisting upward on a narrow road for fifteen minutes, ears popping as they climbed higher and higher. Timothy pressed fingers into his, mouth contorted as if he were about to cry. Ronny made calming sounds the whole time.

Mrs. Sundt, the farmer's wife, had limited English, memorized phrases about the electricity and the microwave, a few pleasantries. George saw that she seemed startled by the appearance of the family with them, seeking words to express her bewilderment.

"These are new friends," George tried to explain, speaking very slowly. "Jegg er venn." Julia read from her phrasebook, pointing to herself and then to Sheila and George.

"Ja. Ja." Mrs. Sundt furrowed her brow as if unconvinced while she led them up a path to a shingled cabin.

"It's perfect," George said when the woman unlocked the door and showed them inside, all lacquered white pine, walls, ceiling, and floor, the furniture pine, everything smelling fresh and new.

He and Ronny unloaded the station wagon and carried the luggage and the backpack to the bedrooms. After she and George arranged their clothing on the built-in shelves, Sheila volunteered to do the shopping in the village market at the bottom of the hill because George wouldn't know what to buy. Julia offered to help and motioned Ronny to slip her some cash. But he made a show of passing it to her, fluttering the bills from his fingertips.

When Sheila and Julia left, Ronny put Timothy down for a nap and opened the empty refrigerator. "I wish we had some beer."

"Now that they can't arrest us," George said.

"You never can tell when they'll come and get you."

"Not in Norway," George joked.

"You always have to watch your back."

They moved outside to take in the view from the front porch. A tin- roofed barn filled the foreground. George couldn't see any cattle but heard them lowing in their stalls. A blue tractor sat parked in a field of new sprouts. Across a wide still river dark green pines grew up the hillsides. The river twisted under a bridge and then disappeared behind a bend in the landscape. Thin layers of white clouds hung unmoving high in the sky.

"I could stay here forever." Ronny stretched both arms upwards and sighed.

"Have you considered living in Europe?" George asked him.

"Oh, I've considered everything."

"What does Julia say?"

"Julia, you may have noticed, is big on information, but not solutions."

"You're lucky in your wife," he said, resenting the tone of Ronny's voice. "Julia is very pleasant."

"More so when we started out. All this traveling hasn't done much for her disposition."

"Then why do you go on?"

"We do what we have to do."

George gave him a puzzled look, but Ronny's eyes were closed, his head tilted back in the chair as if he, like his son, were already asleep. George couldn't decide if his large, full features were handsome; they should have been, but something was a little off, not quite centered.

Sheila and Julia came up with sacks of groceries. They took turns showing off their purchases, one at a time, pleased with their choices. George smiled back at them both, glad that they were getting on so well, relieved at his wife's good mood.

"Wine. Bordeaux." Sheila held up two bottles. "Julia and Ronny's treat."

"Orange juice." Julia pulled out the container. "Milk for Timothy."

"Salad."

"Fresh fish."

"A feast," George said. "Who needs restaurants?"

Ronny came in from the porch, rubbing his eyes. "Let me do the preparations."

"Can he cook?" Sheila teased Julia.

"When he wants to," Julia said. "It's one of his talents."

"And what are the others?"

"Those," Ronny winked, "are confidential."

They ate at a picnic table at the side of the cottage, using juice glasses for the wine. Both Sheila and George praised Ronny's cooking and told him he should make a career as a chef, though George didn't really believe he was quite that good. But the food, the Bordeaux, and the long northern evening had made him expansive.

They exchanged tales of places they had visited, Julia and Ronny in recent weeks, Sheila and George over many years. Mountains, lakes, villages, cities. Wonderful experiences to share, George thought, delighting in his memories.

When the wine was gone, Ronny held an empty bottle in each hand and shook both over his glass. "Dead soldiers. Time for the aquavit." George saw Julia clutch at his knee under the table when he stood up to enter the cabin.

Back in seconds, standing over the others, Ronny poured the clear liquor into their wineglasses, Julia's turning pink from the leftover wine. Then he toasted. "Skol!" Sheila sipped and made a face. George sputtered when he tasted. "My God! This is strong." Ronny threw his head back and drained his, then gave an openmouthed sigh. "Another of my talents." He poured for himself again. Julia just swished her glass.

Timothy was playing on the grass, eyeing a grey cat at the edge of the crops, child and animal staring at each other, the cat darting away each time the boy lunged toward it. Near 11, when the darkness thickened, Ronny sprang from the table and swept up his son. "Time for beddy bye." The boy began shrieking, face suddenly red, mouth a wide circle. "Look who's having a tantrum," Ronny chanted.

"I'm so sorry." Julia apologized, her pale cheeks flushed.

"Don't be silly." Sheila said. "I raised three just like him. They do grow out of it. Eventually."

George said he would clean up and do the dishes. "You both take care of poor Timothy. Soothe his miseries."

Before he moved toward the bedroom, Ronny reached back for the aquavit, the bottle dangling from his fingertips as the boy thrashed against him. Julia hesitated in the hallway, then followed them inside and closed the door.

In bed, George cleared his throat, tried to speak softly. "Is this all right?"

"The boy. Timothy. He's not a happy child."

"The way his father dotes on him?"

"How often does he laugh?"

George realized she was right. "Is it important?"

"Were our children like that?"

"But she's fine," he said, hesitant. "I really like her."

"Can't you see how edgy she is?" Sheila spoke in a harsh whisper. "I can feel her nerves vibrating."

After a silence, he made himself ask, "Did I make a mistake?" Sheila twisted her head into the pillow and turned toward to sleep.

A sudden noise made them both sit up with a start. It was pitch black, the middle of the night. A thumping resounded from the other bedroom, at first a steady rhythm, then frenzied, stopping abruptly with a loud twang of bedsprings.

"My God!" Sheila said. "The child's with them."

"It's probably not the first time. They sleep in a tent."

"I expected better from her."

When the silence continued, they relaxed and pulled up the covers. George could tell Sheila was furious, but he decided not to speak of his own disappointment, not then, maybe some time in the future. He lay awake remembering the first years of their own marriage—passion in a car, under a tree, but never in front of the children, never as houseguests. He imagined Julia pinned under Ronny's thick body, his eyes squeezed shut, throat taut, mouth clenched, while she stared up at the darkness.

Later, from her breathing George could tell that Sheila had fallen asleep again. He had to use the toilet and tiptoed barefoot on the cool wooden floor, closing the door slowly, trying to muffle his sounds, hesitant to lift the plunger and disturb the cottage with the surge of flushing.

When the noise died, he stepped out to the living room and saw the door to the porch open, Julia at the railing outlined in the first glow of dawn, wearing a long nightgown, shivering in the chill.

George moved beside her. "Are you all right?"

He could see her tears when she turned to him. He touched her shoulder and she fell against him, shaking with sobs. He closed his arms around her, feeling the ridge of her spine, the ribs under her taut skin. There was nothing to her.

"We didn't do anything," she wept. "It wasn't sex. There hasn't been any sex in weeks."

"What then?"

"Ronny jumping up and down on the mattress, getting wilder and wilder."

"Was he drunk?"

"Ronny does crazy things. Everything's fine, and then he snaps." "But why?"

"It's the way we live." Her body wrenched in a spasm, shuddering in his arms.

George stoked her hair, wondering what would happen if he kissed her. It startled him that he wanted to kiss her, that he had so misunderstood the nature of his affection. As he pulled her closer, he heard the click of a door lock and sensed Ronny's eyes staring out at them from the dark cabin.

He eased his embrace but could not release her. "What can I do?"

She touched his face with a fingertip. "You're a nice man. You have a nice wife. You shouldn't worry about strangers." She pulled away and disappeared inside.

George finally dozed toward morning, and it seemed only minutes later that Sheila was shaking his arm. "Let's go for a walk," she said. "I need fresh air."

He needed coffee first, brewing the water while she dressed, then sitting on the couch with the hot cup listening for sounds from the other bedroom; but even Timothy was quiet. He wondered if Julia were awake too, as he had been, unable to sleep, lying rigidly with her arms fixed at her sides.

Out on the path behind the farm, they saw Mr. Sundt carrying great brown sacks from a shed to the barn. George repeated what Julia had told him.

"Why should he want to do that to us?"

He placed a hand on Sheila's shoulder to calm her. "There's something going on between them. We don't have anything to do with it. You were right. I hadn't realized how unhappy she is."

"I'm not overjoyed myself. This is supposed to be our vacation."

"We used to fight once. Remember?"

"Of course I do," she said. "And we were poor once. And we raised three children. And we're still putting up with the aftershock of two divorces."

"But you and me—we're ok."

"We're the best we can be, George." He wouldn't ask her what she meant.

When they got back to the cabin, Julia was in the shower. Water beat against the metal stall. Ronny fixed breakfast for his son, the boy naked beneath an undershirt, swollen belly and gaunt thighs. George could smell the diaper in the plastic garbage pail.

"I'll get rid of it," Ronny's tone was annoyed though neither one of them had complained.

"It's all right," George said. He had come in half expecting the man to curse him for embracing his wife, rise up and smash a fist into his soft middle. When nothing happened, he feared that Sheila would abuse Ronny for his deception.

"We had plans to go to a national park today," she said instead. "Rondale, up in the mountains. It may be too long a ride for Timothy."

"We'll go with you." Ronny spoke abruptly, surly. "There's nothing to do here. You don't know what it's like spending months trying to figure out how to fill the day."

"You've had all of Europe."

"Well, when you come down to it, Europe is just a place like any other."

George hadn't heard Julia enter the kitchen, looked up with surprise to see her standing there in jeans and a tee shirt, her damp red hair pulled back in a knot, accentuating the sharp bones of her face. She met his eyes. "Maybe you and Sheila would like to be by yourselves."

"No. That's all right." He didn't want to leave her alone with Ronny.

On the E6 at Ringebu, George saw signs pointing right for the stave church; but he didn't tell the others, unwilling to make a stop and go through the bother of tourist conversation. They all rode without speaking, the only sounds Timothy's whines as he twisted on his father's lap. Ronny kept shifting the boy's position to make him comfortable. In the mirror, he could see the man grit his teeth. Sheila was smoldering too, he knew, in another way, furious at him for offering no way out of this situation. George tensed himself, wondering what would happen if he reached over and shook her, demanded: what do you want me to do? Make them get out on the side of the road? But he clutched the wheel and said nothing.

Ronny was the one who broke the silence, snapping at the boy. "Goddamnit, Timothy. Stop fidgeting!"

Julia reached out. "Here. Let me hold him for a while."

"You? What good are you?"

Sheila turned in sudden anger. "She's his mother!"

Ronny poked Julia's shoulder, again and again, until she drew away from him. "Hear that. The lady thinks you're his mother."

Sheila glared at him. "Your wife then." Forced laughter rasped at his throat.

"I'm nothing." Julia closed both fists in her hair and pulled it loose, twisting it under her chin. "I'm not a mother and I'm not a wife."

Although she spoke quietly, George found himself roaring. "Just shut up! Everybody just shut up!"

Timothy began wailing. When Ronny ignored him, folded arms and stared out the window, Julia lifted the boy onto her lap and pulled him against her thin chest.

George considered turning around, then knew it wouldn't be any better at the cabin. So he drove ahead, following signs, turning onto a narrow, pitted road of sharp curves through the rock.

He saw few buildings, rare signs of human life, as the car climbed through miles of dense stunted pines. In the back seat, Julia pressed her face into Timothy's hair, eyes shut, tears squeezed from beneath the lashes. Ronny clenched both fists, the veins of his arms bulging, a sharp pulse in the tendons of his neck.

George missed the turn to the park, an arrow outside a brown building pointing up a long dirt path gouged with tire tracks. He slammed into reverse, clashed gears, then swerved forward.

The landscape was desolate, the ground nothing but rock and lichen, dust swirling across the windshield, dark snow-streaked peaks in the distance.

The road pitched them back and forth, deep ruts jarring them off their seats. George refused to slow down until heavy chains blocked the road ahead. He had to stop in a parking area among a few scattered cars and two large tour buses. They couldn't go any further.

"Who on earth would want to come here?" George said aloud, hoping they all could be tourists again. But no one answered him.

He opened the station wagon door to step out onto a path, but was stunned by a fierce, chill wind. He wasn't wearing a jacket; none of them were. He slammed the door shut. "It's freezing out there."

"Timothy does have a mother, and Ronny does have a wife," Julia said, as if to no one, and hugged the child tighter. "But it's not me."

"Maybe an ex-wife." Ronny sneered. "We left town before the divorce was final."

"Something's wrong, isn't it?" Sheila said. "You shouldn't be here."

Julia nodded. "We ran off before she got custody. And now we're afraid to go home."

"Did you love him so much?" Sheila asked.

"I did. I loved him desperately."

George wanted to shout: Stop talking! I don't want to hear! "

You can't go on this way." Sheila spoke calmly, very slowly.

"Ronny won't admit it."

"Goddamn you!" Ronny swung toward Julia to rip Timothy from her.

She locked the boy between her knees and slapped at him.

"Hey!" George turned and groped behind to separate them, Julia's swats stinging his arms, Ronny's fists pounding his shoulder. Julia twisted away and forced the boy between the front seats to Sheila. Then she dropped her hands to her sides, defenseless, waiting for Ronny's blows. The man was livid, face bloated with rage.

He'll kill her, George thought, tensed, ready to hurl himself into the back of the station wagon. Instead Ronny threw open the door and shouted at Sheila: "Keep the brat! I'm sick of him!" He tumbled out onto the gravel, trying to run down the road past the chain barrier. The force of wind knocked him backward. He crouched, covered his face with his hands, and plunged ahead, punching and clawing at the air. Hail began to fall, large pellets suddenly bouncing off the earth, clanging at the steel roof of the Volvo.

"Should I go after him?" George asked Julia.

"He'll come back. He always does."

"What next then?"

Her eyes were hollow, her lips so pinched she seemed to have no mouth. "Get rid of us. Get us out of your lives."

Timothy was wailing. Sheila held him close and began to rock, singing softly, his screams obliterating her soothing. George sensed that this child would never stop shrieking. He would shriek even when he was silent. And George wished he could flee, but his limbs felt like stone.

Little Life

Morning dew seeped into the knees of Sylvia's slacks as she crept under a rhododendron looking for Stephanie. She hadn't been up this early in years, awake most of the night for fear she'd miss the alarm. Maybe it was too early. Most mornings when she went down to turn on the coffeemaker Stephanie was meowing at the sun porch door, rubbing the frame when Sylvia opened it, yawning with hunger. But that was at seven. Now it was just six, the sun barely rising. But she had been nervous about not finding the cat on this day ever since the shelter finally called with news of an opening.

Alan had been sympathetic, knowing she would have loved to keep the cat, make a pet of it. But his allergy was terrible. The one time she forgot and touched him after stroking Stephanie, his face swelled and his eyes reddened with a sneezing fit. No way could they have a cat, and Sylvie decided it wasn't right to make the poor creature live outside even though she fed her twice a day. For the month after it appeared in their yard, the cat had fled every time Sylvia stepped outside and called, "Here, kitty, kitty." Eventually, the food did it, the certainty of regular meals. It even reached a point where Sylvia could pick her up, the cat almost weightless, purring loudly, desperate for affection. It deserved an indoors home with a family, pampered by children. But first she had to catch it and get it to the no-kill shelter.

If he had been here, not in Denver on a business trip, Alan would have helped her, wearing gloves, taking an antihistamine. But he couldn't pick the timing of his job.

"Stephanie," she whispered, made kissing sounds. "Please, Stephanie."

A noise made her look up, the slamming of a car door. Sylvia stared into the sunrise and saw a shape in the golden glow, large and square in the driveway. She scooted back around the bush to change her angle, touched a hand to her forehead to shade her eyes. It was Benny's van, the rusting gash the length of the passenger's side, the plastic sheet still taped up where the missing back window should be. But Benny was supposed to be seven hundred miles away, working. What hadn't he called? Why was he there? On this day when she had to catch a cat.

Instead of Benny, standing in the driveway was a tiny thing that looked like a child. The sun dazzling her, making her dizzy, Sylvia stood up and stepped closer. It wasn't a child but a very small woman in shorts and a sleeveless sweatshirt, her legs thick, her pale face like a flexed muscle, cheeks bloated, two small eyes peering out directly at Sylvia.

Before Sylvia could ask her who she was, Benny came running around the front of the van and swooped Sylvia off her feet, spinning her and planting wet kisses on her cheek. "Mom! Mom!"

He was stoned. She knew it immediately. When he got manic like this, he was stoned, sputtering meaningless sounds of excitement. What had happened to his therapy, the doses of Paxil and Wellbutrin? He'd been doing so well, promoted at work, engaged to Vicki. Benny was laughing as he hugged her, Sylvia moaning despair as he clutched her.

"Mom! Guess what!" Benny stepped back and seized her hands in his, turning a circle as he danced around her. "Guess what!" The way one shirt tail hung at his side, the way his pants dragged the dirt, she could tell he was getting fat again.

"I can't guess," she told him, her voice flat with an old weariness.

"I'm fucking married!"

"Married? Where's Vicki?"

"Not fucking Vicki. Daphne." He repeated it more loudly, with a sudden anger that she did not understand.

Benny rushed back to the girl in the driveway and dragged her toward Sylvia, pushed her against his mother. The girl just came up to her chest, hands at her side, looking out with glazed eyes. Although Benny had forced them tight against each other, they were not really touching.

Sylvia looked down on Daphne's head, the purple streak in the cropped brown hair. "Are you really married to my son?"

"Benny woke up the justice of the peace. Banged on the door. The man wasn't happy, but he did it." The girl spoke in a monotone, barely audible.

Sylvia pushed her away and clamped Benny's face in her hands. "What's going on here? What about Vicki? We've been planning a wedding. Her mother and I talk all the time."

"The fucker's cancelled."

She wanted to hit him but held herself still. "Benny, when did you stop taking your pills?" It had to have been abrupt. People couldn't just stop. They had to taper off. Stopping would make then crazy. Benny was crazy. Here first thought was to call Alan, then decided it wasn't fair. He had his meetings. What could he do so far away? He wasn't Benny's father, and he had done more than enough to help her through her son's episodes for the fifteen years of their marriage. He had been so happy about Vicki. He would be crying right now if he knew.

"We both stopped." He wrapped an arm around Daphne. "That shit's no good for you. Daphne read about it. We walked out of group therapy one night and threw those fucking pills into the sewer. And we haven't been apart every since. I said, 'Let's get fucking married, and we fucking did.'"

Benny threw his head back in laughter, rubbing wide circles on Daphne's back. The girl barely moved, almost comatose Sylvia thought. But she was the one who raised her arm and pointed toward the shrubs —"What's that?"—startled as if she had never seen a cat before.

It was Stephanie, black and white against the green bushes, meowing, looking at Sylvia with what Sylvia knew was longing. She wanted to be picked up and cradled. Sylvia reached down and spread her hands under the cat's soft middle, lifting it to her chest, bringing her chin down to the silken fur of its back, swaying back and forth. The cat purred and Sylvia's tears beaded on the top of its head.

"What the fuck is that?" Benny was laughing, shaking a finger as he pointed.

Sylvia saw a thick ring on his fourth finger, but it wasn't a wedding band. "This is Stephanie." She hugged the cat tighter as if her son was about to rip it away.

"So you're trying to kill Alan. Have him choke on an allergy attack." Benny forced gagging sounds, staggered in a swoon.

"I wish I could keep her." Sylvia's voice trembled with sorrow. But if she didn't deliver the cat to the shelter this morning, she would lose her place on the waiting list. She broke into sobs.

"Mom. It's just a fucking cat."

Tear-blinded, Sylvia saw that Daphne was staring at her. She expected the girl to say something too, words that would echo her son's. But all she did was stare.

When Sylvia stopped crying, she carried the cat to the shelter's cardboard carrier by the sun porch, knowing how much she would miss the little face waiting outside the glass door every morning, head cocked, tail straight up. A terrible sadness overwhelmed her. She couldn't blame Alan. The allergies weren't his fault, and he had cared for her enough to marry a woman with a troubled teenager, shared in the counseling sessions and the disciplining. Finally, they both believed they had succeeded, Benny clean, doing well in a good job, engaged to Vicki. But now. She wished there were a shelter that would take her.

With the cat in her arms, she couldn't unhook the tabs to open the box. "Help me," she called to Benny. He shook his head, still laughing. Daphne was the one, approaching slowly as if sleepwalking, saying something to Benny when she passed. Next to Sylvia, she dropped to her knees and spread the box top. Sylvia hesitated, not wanting to let go, but knelt to set Stephanie inside, surprised how docile the cat was, how it immediately curled and closed its eyes.

"Is it sick?" Daphne asked.

"Of course not. She's fine. She trusts me. That I won't let anything happen to her."

"That's nice." The girl rose and drifted back into the yard near Benny. He wrapped arms around her and lifted her off the grass, planting kisses on the top of her head.

Who was this girl? What was she doing here? Sylvia wanted her to vanish. Benny too. Both of them go back where they came from and let her think about the cat.

Without her realizing it, the day had become bright with morning light, lovely weather, a soft breeze, the scent of lilacs from the bush in the yard. When she looked toward the garage, she saw that Benny's van was blocking her in. She called to him and asked that he please move it.

"I'll drive you," he told her. "You're too upset. In no shape." That seemed to please him. "And what kind of shape are you in?"

His face darkened.

"I can fucking drive."

He put a hand against her back and guided her toward the van and slid open the gashed side door with a metallic creak. "Get inside." It was an order. He gave an abrupt wave to Daphne. "You too."

The girl opened the front passenger door and strained to reach a foot up to the frame and pull herself up. She was that short. Benny took the carrier from Sylvia and placed it on the back seat. "Do you want a boost?" Sylvia shook her head and climbed inside. He slammed the door shut.

He started the van with a roar, tromping on the gas pedal. Dark exhaust clouded the rear window, crackling though a hole in the muffler. He burned rubber backing out the drive, but Sylvia wouldn't tell him to slow down. That would make it even worse. She knew Benny. Oh God, did she know Benny.

"So where's this fucking shelter?"

She gave him directions. He knew the town, had lived there for years. He was speeding, swerving around corners, sending Sylvia and the carrier sliding across the seat. Her belt clamp was broken. She held the carrier, but the cat didn't make a sound. Sylvia tried to peek through one of the air holes but saw only a swatch of dark fur.

Sylvia's heart was pounding by the time they reached the shelter. Benny slammed brakes in the parking area, cinders beating against the bottom of the van. She took deep breaths before speaking.

"You two can wait here. I want to do this myself."

"No fucking way. I want to see what this place is all about. Come on, Daph."

Would they turn her away after one look at her son and this dwarfish girl? She'd beg. Please find a family for this cat.

The young woman at the reception desk had a pretty face but several layers of chin fat and loose flesh swaying on her arms. She checked a computer screen and smiled at Sylvia. "There you are. On our schedule for today." She pointed to the carrier in Sylvia's hand. "And I'll bet that's Stephanie. Can't wait to meet her."

Sylvia sighed. Everything was going to be all right.

"Did someone explain the procedure?" the young woman asked, and went on even though Sylvia nodded. "One of our vets will examine Stephanie's vitals, give her rabies and distemper shots, and that'll be it. We'll check her in. Home sweet home."

They had to wait for the vet. Sylvia and Daphne took seats in plastic chairs, but Benny leaned over the counter watching the young woman's fingers on the keyboard with a wide grin. "You're sure some typist."

She didn't smile back. "That's why they hired me."

"Benny, sit down," Sylvia told him, and to her surprise he did, flipping though pet magazines, waving covers in front of Daphne's face. "Here's one called fucking Cat Fancier. Can you believe this shit?"

Sylvia felt an urge to slap him, something she hadn't done since he was a toddler though she had wanted to do many times. One more word out of him, and day she might actually do it. She opened the carrier to look down at Stephanie. The cat lay in the same curled position it had been in for the first, the eyes closed. She had expected agitation at being taken to a new and strange place.

When the vet, a stooped man with thinning hair and a gray goatee, came down a hallway to call for her, Sylvia hoped Benny and Daphne would stay seated. But they followed at her heels, Benny pointing at the drawings of dogs and cats and rabbits that lined the walls as if he were seeing something very strange.

All of them crowded into the small treatment room, the vet spoke only to Sylvia, his tone businesslike. "Please put Stephanie on the table." She lifted the cat from the carrier. It lay limp in her arms, barely moved when she set it down on the stainless steel.

"You can see she's very docile. She'll be a wonderful pet."

The vet just pressed him lips tight and touched gloved fingers into the cat's abdomen, brought his stethoscope down to the rib cage, then examined each of the four limbs. The cat lifted its head and gave a soft meow. The vet touched his goatee with the back of his wrist and wouldn't look at Sylvia.

"I'm afraid you have a very sick animal here."

"Sick? I've been feeding her for weeks. She had a great appetite."

"Look here." He spread the fur on the right hind hip to expose two small red scabs. "Those are bite marks. She must have gotten into a fight."

"With another cat?"

"With some wild animal. A cat. A raccoon. An opossum. Hard to tell."

"But you can give her a shot. Antibiotics."

The vet shook his head. "Whatever bit her could be rabid."

"Then give her a test."

"It doesn't work that way. State law says the cat has to be quarantined for six months."

"Six fucking months!" Benny blurted what Sylvia was thinking.

"I'm afraid that's the law."

"Can she stay here?" Sylvia asked.

"Afraid not. We don't have the facility. And we can't risk exposing the other animals." "Then where."

"You could board the animal at a special place. But that would get very expensive. Or you could keep her at your home."

"In that fucking box!" Benny threw up his hands, shouting. Sylvia saw how agitated he was, on the verge of a real outburst. She held his arm, afraid he would throw her off. But he didn't. She knew it wasn't the cat that bothered him. It was rules, the threat of confinement. She looked back at Daphne with a pleading in her eyes. The girl stepped forward and stroked Benny's other arm.

"That's impossible," Sylvia said. "It would be so cruel."

The vet nodded. "I agree."

"Then what?"

"Euthanasia."

"Oh, my God." Her knees gave way, but Daphne held her up, surprisingly strong for someone so small.

"Can you do it?" the girl asked the vet, the first time she had spoken in that room, her voice soft and quiet.

"Yes. That's something we do."

"It's not right. It's not fair." Benny beat fists on the steel top of the treatment table, the sound ringing, but the vet ignored him and spoke to Sylvia.

"Some people like to be in the room. You have that choice."

Sylvia stood helpless. The day wasn't supposed to be this way. In bed, alone, to anxious to sleep, she had imagined Stephanie surrounded by children, stoked and purring, amid a family that truly cared.

It was Daphne who spoke again. "I don't think that's such a good idea."

The cat lay limp in the vet's arms. Benny opened the door for him and then slammed it closed.

Sylvia fell back against a wall, heaving with sobs. "I loved that cat. I never loved anything so much."

Daphne wrapped arms around her waist, pressed her head against Sylvia's chest, sighing, "Her poor little life."

Sylvia hugged her back and wept.

Saving Cimini

Cimini and Lukacs sat at a metal-topped table against the railing by the water's edge, Lukacs with his back to the lake, twisting a napkin around his middle finger, scuffing a heel against the cobblestones. Cimini, unmoving, gazed out at the boats gliding across the glistening surface and beyond them at the lush Swiss hills on the far shore.

"Where, exactly, do you suppose the border is? A line on the water. Italy here. Switzerland there." Cimini pointed first to one spot on the water, then another.

Lukacs would not follow his eyes. "What's the difference?"

"It could be a matter of life or death." Cimini broke into a grin.

"I've known you for years, Cimini. You don't have to put on a performance for me."

"Perhaps I'm trying to disguise great fear." He threw his head back as if to laugh but made no sound.

Lukacs noticed the young woman at the next table stealing looks at Cimini despite the fat baby squealing on her lap and the small girl clinging to her knees. She was dark and broadshouldered with thick lips slightly parted. Her legs were crossed, her short white shirt twisted up on her thighs, a loose sandal flapping against the sole of her foot as she flexed her toes. The husband, very thin, his gaunt face overwhelmed by round spectacles, didn't seem to realize his wife was coveting another man. Or perhaps, Lukacs thought, he was just pretending.

Women were always staring at Cimini's face and he never noticed. The shape of his head seemed cast in bronze—broad tanned cheekbones and a hawkish nose, dark curled hair and a rich mustache, a strong jaw, a powerful torso.

He awaited the woman's reaction when Cimini stood up and she looked at the scrawny legs and flat buttocks. Cimini was shaped as if he had once suffered a severe wasting disease in the lower half of his body. Each time Lukacs saw the man again—emerging from a crowd, stepping out of shadows on a narrow street—his stomach twisted at the sensation of something missing.

"I am grateful that you are willing to take me in your boat." Cimini's brown eyes overflowed sincerity. But Lukacs refused to meet them, to allow the man to drown him in mock gratitude.

"We have friends in common," he said.

Cimini pressed Lukacs's fist against the table top and spoke with an urgent hush. "Now, at this moment, I have no friend greater than you." Lukacs twisted his hand free. The man's intensity infuriated him, as if they were merely playing a game with no consequences. For his own sake, Lukacs knew he could not make a move that was not anchored in urgency. In two hours it would be over, and once again for as long as his luck held he would have Cimini out of his life.

Lukacs looked up and caught the woman's eyes fixed on Cimini's profile.

Startled by the contact, she quickly turned away to attend to her children. The girl was trying to climb on her lap with the baby. The woman spoke abruptly to her husband, and he stood to lift the girl into his arms. The child cried out and kicked her feet, almost knocking the tray of red wine bottles from the shoulder of the passing waitress. The waitress stumbled as she ducked away but regained her balance before the bottles fell. The father shook the child in rebuke and muttered apologies. The waitress frowned, a roughfaced woman with wirey yellow hair who stopped traffic with an outstretched arm each time she carried a tray across the town square between the restaurant's kitchen and the tables on the quay.

The three Frenchmen at a corner table above the lake nudged each other and smirked. The wine was for them, another serving.

"They're drunk," Lukacs said.

"Who?" Cimini turned his head and for the first time saw the family at the next table, the blushing mother, the scolding father, the sullen child struggling against his grasp. He gave a puzzled expression.

"Over there. The French." Lukacs gestured with his head. "Or they're very good actors."

The three, men in their thirties, barechested and newly sunburned under their sailing caps, tilted chairs back against the railing, their table top littered with plates and empty wine bottles. They had been eating and drinking when Cimini and Lukacs arrived, and now they were only drinking. "I envy their pleasure," Cimini said.

"They're ridiculous."

"Aren't you ever tempted by frivolity?" Cimini asked.

One of the Frenchmen lifted an empty bottle out high over his head and splashed it into the lake. The others laughed aloud.

"That's not happiness," Lukacs said. "It's idiocy."

A second Frenchman threw two bottles at the water, simultaneously, one from each hand, and the third turned crimson, sliding down in his chair until his face pressed the cool metal of the table's surface. They were once muscular men whose bulk was turning to flab, sweaty pink flesh hanging over the waists of their shorts. The first, seeing that the waitress was across the square inside the restaurant, began tossing silverware into the water a soup spoon, knives.

Two Italian policemen out on the pier noticed the Frenchmen. They stood together in discussion, gesturing their heads in the direction of the quay. Although they were only border guards, unarmed, stationed to check passports of people debarking the lake steamers, Lukacs spoke between his teeth.

"Police. Face me. Show them the back of your head."

Cimini shrugged. "Save your worry for later."

The waitress stood above them, so sudden Lukacs nearly knocked over his cup. She ignored him and spoke to Cimini. "Desert? A brandy?" Cimini shrugged. "Why not a brandy?"

"We have a long drive ahead," Lukacs told her, shaking his head.

"A brandy never hurts," she said. Cimini winked at her, and she patted his shoulder as she moved toward the traffic.

"That wasn't smart," Lukacs said.

Cimini ignored him and gestured out toward the square. "The border is only a few hundred yards into those trees, and yet Italy is another world from Switzerland. See how fast they drive here, in the middle of the town. And the waitress walks right in front of them." He smiled again. "Maybe that's true heroism. A mystery to us both."

Lukacs would not respond. "And no sidewalks," Cimini continued. "The road comes up right against the buildings. They forgot to make room for people to walk, only for cars to drive. But in Switzerland everything makes sense. Everything is orderly."

"Is that why you want to go there?" Lukacs asked, even though he knew the real reason had nothing to do with order.

Cimini sat silently gazing out toward the villages on the Swiss shore, the stone church on a hilltop high above the stuccoed houses, the white yachts aligned at their moorings.

The baby began to cry and the mother cradled it in her arms. The Frenchmen were laughing again. Lukacs heard another loud splash and glanced over at the policemen. They were still watching, in close conversation, as if debating whether destruction of dinnerware was their responsibility.

One of the Frenchmen brought a bottle to his lips and toasted Cimini. When Cimini returned the salute, Lukacs kicked his leg under the table. "Play the fool when you're alone," Lukacs told him. "When we're together I'm at risk too."

"Everyone is at risk." Cimini gestured out toward the tables and the lake and the green of Switzerland. "Do you think this is real life? The glowing sunlight, sails mirrored on a gentle lake, a family out for a Sunday excursion, young men having a drunken party? It's like a dream, a very pleasant dream."

"Are we more real?" Lukacs said. "Sitting here, waiting for darkness?"

"Have you ever lived in Germany?" Cimini suddenly asked.

"Of course."

"That's right. I've forgotten that you've lived everywhere."

Lukacs couldn't judge his tone. It wasn't like Cimini to be sarcastic. "During your time there, were you ever in a concentration camp?" he said.

"Of course not. That was decades ago." Lukacs had no idea what he was after.

"I tried to visit Dachau once."

"Yes?"

"I went on a Monday."

"So."

"They're turned the camp into a memorial. Like all the other public monuments, it's closed to visitors on Mondays." Cimini shook his head. "These days you can't get into Dachau on a Monday." He smiled broadly as if very amused.

"And?" Lukacs squeezed his fingers down on the edge of his chair, refusing to let the man see how furious he was.

"Some people want to pretend the whole world is Switzerland."

A Frenchman stood and lifted his chair, swinging it in a circle above his head. His friends thought he was hilarious; but he just dropped the chair back down under him and sat again, very pleased with his antics. Cimini was laughing too, the young woman smiling, though her husband pressed his mouth shut in a thin line.

A squat old man in baggy trousers staggered toward the Frenchmen, his face swollen with red veins. He braced hands on their table and spoke a slurred Italian. The Frenchmen leaned forward and stroked their chins. "He's telling them not to throw things in the lake," Cimini said.

"I know. I can hear."

When the old man turned and stumbled toward the waitress, one of the Frenchmen tossed a plate in the water, and the three put on innocent faces. The old man was trying to make the waitress understand what they were doing, pointing and waving his hands, clutching her arm and trying to pull her toward their table. She slapped him away and scolded. "Don't bother my customers. Get away from here, you old goat." Cimini lifted his hand as if to call the waitress.

"Idiot!" Lukacs whispered to make him stop.

"I don't like them mocking him. They're drunk too."

"Just today. He's drunk all the time."

The young woman parted her blouse to nurse the baby, its head deep in the folds of the cloth, and now the husband was looking from Lukacs to Cimini, openly watching their table. Lukacs tried to see if he was somehow signalling the Frenchmen. Around Cimini anything could have meaning, even a child at its mother's breast.

Cimini leaned forward, inches from Lukacs. "You don't believe in what I do. Why are you helping me?"

"I have a boat," Lukacs said. "I cross the lake very often. No one suspects me."

"But everyone suspects me, and here you sit exposed in the open with a suspected man."

"I was asked."

"And do you do everything you're asked?"

"When certain people do the asking. And I have no choice."

"They pay you very well for having no choice." Cimini displayed strong white teeth.

"Do you know how much I hate you?" Lukacs said.

Cimini nodded.

"I have no life. I spend my days expecting another message telling me to help you. The mail, the phone, a stranger on the street. Anything could be a signal about you."

"I don't think about you," Cimini said. "You are a man with a boat willing to take me to Switzerland. Nothing else is important just moving me from this shore to that shore."

"My life matters!" Furious, Lukacs slapped the table, the metal ringing out over the lake, then with a sudden fear looked out at the others. The Frenchmen were staring at Cimini as if following the father's eyes, the three of them with hands gripped on the railing. They had stopped laughing. A chill pierced Lukacs. Perhaps they weren't drunk at all, the bottles and silverware merely props in an act. They had been sitting here before Cimini and Lukacs chose this cafe, so they couldn't have been following; but others like them might be stationed throughout the town,

Cimini's face burned into their memories.

The Frenchmen slid back and stood to put on their shirts, fingers busy pushing buttons through button holes. One of them seemed to nod at the father. Lukacs was sure of it. He swung his head around and saw the mother and children were gone, she halfway across the cobblestone square hurrying toward the restaurant, the baby tucked under one arm, the little girl clinging to her other hand.

When father reached inside the plastic bag of baby supplies, Lukacs clutched his chair with both hands and tensed his knees. The Frenchmen were watching the father closely. Although the day remained brilliant, Lukacs felt his lungs burning, as if the oxygen had suddenly evaporated. He couldn't see the policemen; they were no longer on the pier. Cimini seemed to be calm, eyelids lowered, as if thinking of something far from these tables on the water. But his fingers were slowly creeping inside his jacket.

The Frenchmen moved forward in unison, then paused as if counting under their breaths. When the father began to withdraw his hand from the baby bag and they stepped toward Cimini, Lukacs kicked over his chair and bolted toward the square, colliding with the waitress, knocking her backwards against a car. The tray flew from her shoulder.

The detonations may have been gun shots or bursting glass. All sounds were jumbled in the din of crashing bottles and horn blasts and human shouts that jarred Lukacs' brain. He didn't look back, afraid that he would see Cimini standing on the quay, mocking him, his face alive with laughter.

Another Person

The summer after his mother died Philip took a job as a busboy at an island inn that catered to the wealthy. He had never in his 19 years known people who could spend weeks under beach umbrellas watching the roll of the surf. The job would help Philip earn tuition money needed for his sophomore year now that his father had so many medical debts. He had discovered the employment flyer on a dormitory bulletin board. After his application was accepted, it took him days before he could tell his father, certain he would be expected to spend the summer in a house shadowed with absence. But to Philip's relief the man just nodded and said it would be good for him to get away after all that had happened. And here he was, in a place he had never heard of, among people whose lives he would never have thought to imagine, his days devoted to gathering up their leavings while they pretended he didn't exist.

At college, though Philip had several friends for sharing meals and movies, he never told anyone his mother was dying, unable to think of a way to bring the fact into the conversation. The others just complained about roommates, mocked the professors, bragged how much sex they had and how little homework they did. How could he clear his throat and blurt, "My mother has terminal cancer"? A few times, very late, the hallway finally quiet, talking in whispers with people who had turned serious, admitting to fears of failing courses, of humiliating dates, of dismal futures, he had come close to speaking, then stopped, suddenly unsure that his mother was really ill, wondering if her cancer was something he had dreamt, not happening at all; that the next morning he would awake in shame and have to tell the others he had made it up.

Each day at the inn was the same: out of bed at 6 to serve breakfast, the sweet odor of the morning rolls already filling the dining room when the staff arrived; a break from 10 till noon; a buffet lunch on the deck; a few hours on the beach before dinner; then set the tables for the next morning and step out into an evening crisp with salt air. Philip lived in a cottage with the other busboys, across the path from the waitresses' cottage, the young women chaperoned by the sour woman who supervised housekeeping at the inn. A week into the summer Philip realized that none of the others really needed the money from their jobs, planning to spend all they earned on clothes or cars or electronic gear.

He roomed with someone called Terry and they got along well. Terry had a pleasant musical voice, offering continual anecdotes about life at his college, never telling the same story twice, always amusing, fun to listen to. When Terry started dating Theresa, Philip began taking long walks alone each evening, barefoot on the hard wet beach sand, moving far from the lights of the inn to a spot where stars glittered in an endless sky. He would think how slowly the days passed, how long this summer seemed, how he felt trapped in time.

For Philip living his life was like watching a movie he had entered late, unsure how much he had missed, bewildered by the plot, seeing the actors move and hearing them speak, but having no idea what any scene meant, how it related to what had gone before and led to what would happen next. Every time he caught his reflection in a window he would think, that's me, as if the image were another person, someone who ceaselessly followed him, annoying in his constant presence, near enough to touch but always elusive.

One afternoon when Terry asked him what he planned to major in, instead of saying that he didn't know, Philip found himself telling how his studies confused him. Everything was like the term paper he had written for freshman composition, the topic printed on a slip of paper literally pulled from the instructor's hat: General Gordon in Khartoum. He had spent hours in the library, retrieving dry books from grey metal shelves, taking notes, clumsily organizing the material, and receiving a C. All the time he kept thinking, why am I doing this? What does knowing about a useless general in a country that no one cares about have to do with being in college? The instructor was a fair young man with thin blond hair; the others ridiculed his pink scalp, and most plagiarized their papers. Terry shook his head and said they were fools; he was going to law school and you had to know how to do research.

Philip could talk to Theresa because she was Terry's girl friend, but he was shy with the other waitresses, especially with Lucy, even though she was less attractive than most, short with thick, muscular calves, wiry brown curls, and a broad pug nose. Of all the waitresses she seemed most attainable, the one who might be willing to go out with him. But when he moved his towel close to hers in the group on the beach, she didn't interrupt her conversation to acknowledge him, and he never asked her.

Terry told Philip that his older sister was a corporate lawyer, very successful, always flying to London and Rome and Zurich. It was past midnight, the two of them lying in the glow of a bright full moon that filled their room. She was his role model, Terry said, and he meant to do something important too, something that mattered in the world. He was very proud of his sister, and he wanted people to be proud of him. He was much younger than she, born when his mother was in her forties, his sister already a teenager. Philip started to remark on the coincidence; though he had no sister or brother, he too had an older mother. But before he spoke he realized that he would have to explain that his had just died. Instead he told Terry he was an only child.

"I wish you could meet my mom," Terry said. "All my friends think she's great. So do I. So full of life. So enthusiastic. They invite her to parties. They tell me how much they love her. But I let her know I love her the most."

Philip felt himself redden, embarrassed at the expression of emotion, even though it was coming from someone else. Near the end, when he stood over his mother's bed and tried to tell her that he loved her, the words caught in his throat. Her eyes had seemed so far away.

He pictured son and mother together, sharing the same broad

smile, the woman as outgoing and appealing as her son, and he suddenly envied Terry. "Yes," he nodded. "I'd like to know your mom."

For the final weeks of her life, Philip's mother had been discharged from the hospital because nothing more could be done for her. She lay between railings on a white metal bed installed in the large bedroom she had shared with his father, a plastic bag on a wire rack dripping clear fluid through a tube injected into a wasted arm, another tube collecting green bile from her nostrils. His father had moved into his room, and Philip, home from college for the holiday break, slept on the sofa; in fact, he spent all his time there, day and night, unwilling to turn on television, unable to read, hearing the visiting nurses speaking to his mother, their voices muffled from behind the door, more a blur of sound than words. He would like to have gone outside but didn't want to be seen by the neighbors and have to listen to their awkward sympathy. No one knew what to say to him, and he didn't know what to tell them.

Allen, Philip's best friend from high school, came to visit. Philip hadn't called him, but he showed up anyway, standing on the front porch with an arrangement of flowers in a plastic pot. It struck Philip as odd to see his friend holding flowers. "For your mother," Allen said. Philip rarely went into her room now, unwilling to see her so emaciated, jaundiced flesh drawn tight across the bones of her face. But he tapped lightly and opened the door to ask if she wanted to see Allen. Stretched flat in a darkened corner, she barely could nod yes. Philip stood back while Allen stepped toward the bed and told her that he had brought flowers, that he hoped she'd be well soon, his voice shrill, the sound of him overwhelming that still space. Then he turned and Philip saw the look of horror, the shock in his eyes, the mouth clenched as if he wanted to scream. Back in the hallway Allen touched Philip's arm once and was gone from the house, fleeing.

When his mother died, Philip was dozing on the sofa even though it was mid afternoon. He sat up at his father's shout, shocked awake. His father plunged down the stairway, wailing, a fierce lamentation, like cries of a wounded animal. He seized Philip, crushing his body against him, shaking with grief. Philip stared over his father's shoulder, gaze fixed on a stain in the wallpaper, eyes burning.

One evening Philip was the last one to leave the dining room, inserting the breakfast napkins into the juice glasses, their edges protruding like petals of a flower. When he closed the door to step from the inn, he could hear the whir of the refrigerator units and the rumble of the dishwashers; but outside the night was quiet. He moved to the front of the building, and when he saw no guests on the deck, sat in a web chair to watch the moonlight on the waves. Then he heard laughter, female voices —"He didn't!"—and more laughter. Theresa and Lucy moved across the deck, barefoot in shorts but wearing bulky cotton sweaters. Philip in shirt sleeves was shivering, trying to lean back into the shadows when they saw him. Theresa's greeting was friendly, and she sat in a chair across from his, Lucy beside her. Who did what? he wished he could ask, wondering what they would answer.

Theresa spoke first: "It's chilly tonight." Then Lucy said, "Aren't you cold?" He shrugged. "I'm all right." Theresa looked at her watch. "Oh my gosh. I told Terry I'd meet him." Then she was gone and Philip alone with Lucy, waiting for her to get up and leave too; but she did not move, and he didn't know what to say, the voice in his head cursing his silence.

"Do you like it here?" she finally said. "Sure. Why?" He couldn't see her eyes in the darkness. "You don't seem to be enjoying yourself." "I'm all right." He stared down at the boards of the deck, clamping both hands on his knee to stop his leg from trembling, a cool sweat spreading over his back; he clenched his teeth until she said goodnight and left.

The next morning when Philip awoke Terry was not in the room and his watch said almost 7. He had overslept, would be late, annoyed with Terry for not waking him. He threw on the clothing from last night and swished toothpaste in his mouth. When he reached the dining room, the others, the waitresses and busboys, seemed agitated, and he didn't see Terry. Bewildered, he moved to stand at his station although it would be ten minutes before the first guest arrived.

Through a window, out on a walkway, he noticed Terry carrying a suitcase, close to him, her arm over his shoulder, an attractive woman in dark glasses. His sister, Philip thought. Why was his sister here? A harsh wind from the ocean tangled their hair, rippled their clothing against their bodies. The two of them stood looking out at the sea, then turned and walked back toward the pier across the island.

In seconds, Theresa stood beside Philip, clutching his arm, her eyes glistening. "Don't you know what happened?"

Philip shook his head.

"Terry's mother died." She seized his hand, locking her fingers in his.

"When?" He felt numb, not sure this was really happening.

"Last night."

"When I went to sleep he was still out. He wasn't there this morning."

"His sister came in the middle of the night. They're leaving now."

Philip realized how much he liked the warmth of her, the touch of her body against his arm, and he blushed at his reaction but wouldn't pull away. "He never told me she was sick," he said.

"She wasn't. It was her heart. Absolutely sudden."

He imagined the woman sprawled on the floor, eyes staring, mouth agape, her son standing above her, crying out in his grief, and a sheet of blackness struck Philip like a blow. He staggered backwards, breaking free of Theresa, and ran through the dining room, down the steps to the employee toilet.

He slammed the door, fell against it, breathless, fingers trembling on the bolt until he could slide it tight. Then he turned and braced his hands on the cool white sink, his face wet from tears, his throat torn, his chest burning. When Philip looked into the mirror and saw the sorrow in his eyes, his body shook with sobs and, at last, he let himself mourn.

Habitat

Paul's mother and father chose the apartment on their first afternoon of visiting the newspaper rental listings. Father, bearing a certified check, went back the next morning to sign the lease with the landlord who lived in the apartment downstairs and told them to call him Mr. A. Father felt pleased with himself for talking Mr. A into a two-year term at a rent they could afford.

Grandma wanted to know all about the closets, Great Aunt Edna about the bathroom, older sister Martha about the southern exposure. They were all pleased by what they heard. The apartment sounded perfect, especially for so many people. Mother and Father would have the bedroom off the dining area, Grandma and Great Aunt Edna the master bedroom, Martha and little sister Grace the narrow bedroom over the stairwell, and Paul and his brother Robert what had been a storage pantry next to the kitchen.

With only space for a bunk bed, the brothers had to stack their clothing on built-in shelves that smelled of garlic, but they didn't object. In their last apartment they slept in the dining area on canvas Army cots that had to be set up each evening, while Martha and Grace used the sofa bed in the living room. Mother was always finding stray socks and undergarments behind the chairs and lamp tables but tried not to complain, even though Grandma was a compulsively neat woman.

Here in the new apartment they could, at least in pairs, shut a door and have a few hours privacy. Paul could hide his secret magazines on the highest of his shelves under winter sweaters. Great Aunt Edna could slip into the bathroom in the middle of the night without awakening half the family with her hollow old woman's noises.

On the first relaxed evening, after the week it took to unpack the boxes, hang the curtains, and lay the carpets, they lingered at the dinner table with extra cups of coffee and bottles of soda pop to debate which feature of the apartment was the very best. Great Aunt Edna claimed the water pressure, Robert the plexiglass shower door, Mother the self-cleaning oven, Grace the TV reception, Grandma the linen closet, Father the dimming light switches, Martha the strong sunlight that poured through the front windows, and Paul—embarrassed by the frivolity of his choice—the floral wallpaper. The competition was merely a game, good-natured, each pleased with the others' favorites.

Mr. A visited occasionally when they first moved in, always using the back stairs and rapping at the hallway door beside the linen closet. He was a small man with a large head, the cheeks and jaw even more disproportioned, as if swollen from a toothache. He wore starched white shirts with pointed collars and sleeves precisely folded to the elbows.His voice grated with hoarseness and he spoke slowly, as if English was not natural to him, yet revealed no sign of an accent.

The family members kept remarking to each other what a pleasant man he was, though Paul did not tell anyone, not even Robert, that it made him queasy to look at the man's bloated face, the grey pallor of his flesh. Mother invited Mr. A to bring his wife for a visit so that they all could meet her. He smiled so broadly they could see the clamps of his bridgework. "In time," he said. "In time."

Mr. A did not appear again for two weeks. Father waited past the first of the month expecting him to collect the rent check, but finally slipped it into the lower mailbox. Great Aunt Edna, just emerging from the bathroom, was the one who felt his footsteps vibrating on the back stairway. She hissed to Mother and Martha, and the family was already gathered around the door before he rapped.

He looked sheepish when Mother slipped the bolt and opened it. "I'm afraid I have to ask you for a favor," he said.

"Yes?"

"These houses were built before television, even before radio. Thesound carries terribly. Downstairs your programs seem to blast through the walls. In every room."

"We'll make it quieter," Father promised.

"But Great Aunt Edna is hard of hearing," Martha said, touching the old woman's shoulder.

"I'm afraid turning it down won't help," Mr. A said. "The last family tried that. The sound still penetrates."

"What do you want us to do?" Robert asked.

"Would you turn your set off at nine-thirty?"

"Do you and Mrs. A go to sleep that early?" Mother said.

"I'm afraid we do."

"But all the good programs are on then!" Grace wailed when he was gone.

Paul thought of a compromise that they tried for several nights. The television set had an earphone jack that bypassed the speaker. One of them would listen through the tiny ear button and whisper to the others a summary of what was being said. But the method became aggravating. Their comprehension lagged behind the action on the screen and Great Aunt Edna sulked because she could not hear the whispering. One night she got so angry she stood right in front of the set with her black skirt pulled wide, blocking the picture for everyone. Mother, who hated discord, stood up and said, "That's it. That's enough. The set goes off at nine-thirty."

They tried other activities—card games, puzzles, baking, sewing. But most of the family members began to drift off to separate rooms soon after the screen went blank.

A few days before the next month's rent was due, Mr. A rapped again. Paul let him in and felt chill at the grey expression on the man's face. The others were seated at the dining table, staring up over empty plates. Only Great Aunt Edna, who had not heard, scraped a spoon across the bottom of her pudding bowl. Mother offered a cup of coffee, but Mr. A declined.

"You've all been so cooperative," he said, cleaning his rimless glasses with the tip of his tie and not looking at any one of them. "I hate to ask for another favor."

"What is it?" Martha's hand clenched a teaspoon.

"You're all such early risers." Mr. A tried to smile but just stood over them with his lips parted.

"That's because there's nothing for us to stay up for," Grace said. Grandma pinched her arm.

"You're all up by five-thirty," Mr. A said.

"My sons have to leave for work by a quarter to seven," Mother told him. Paul and Robert supported the family. Grandma had social security and Father drew a small pension. Martha could never find a job where they appreciated her. But, of course, Mother revealed none of that to Mr. A. The family's finances were its own concern.

"I appreciate that they have to work," Mr. A said.

"Then what are you asking us to do?" Father said.

"The main problems are the footsteps and the showers. The floor squeaks and the ceiling thumps. And these pipes are so old the water pumping through them makes a terrible noise in the downstairs walls. Like cats screaming."

"Maybe you should replace the pipes," Martha said.

"Out of the question. It would mean a major renovation. I have two small requests. That you don't put on shoes until you are about to leave the house and that you take your showers in the evening."

Father traced his pinky about the edge of his saucer.

"My sons' showers are very important to them," Mother said.

"They might be even more refreshing after a hard day's work."

Mr. A rubbed his knuckles.

"I'm a bit confused," Martha told him despite Grandma's frowns.

"I thought you went to bed at nine-thirty. How can you sleep past six?"

Mr. A gave one of his infrequent grins. "I suppose we're not like you."

As soon as he closed the door, Grace ran to her room and threw herself on the bed in a tantrum. But Mother scolded her for such a childish reaction. "You just have to accept these things." Father, Grandma, and Great Aunt Edna nodded in unison.

Paul suggested that it would help matters if Mother got to know Mrs. A; they might even become friends. Mother brightened and pinched his cheek the way she had done when he was a child. The next few days, morning, afternoon, and evening, she called the A's number in hopes of introducing herself to the woman they still had not met. But Mr. A always answered the phone and said his wife couldn't speak at the moment.

Out of curiosity, Martha and Grace began to watch at the windows for Mrs. A, Martha in the front from the living room, Grace from the kitchen. For days they saw no one except Mr. A's arms reaching for the newspapers on the front steps. But Grace one day called out, "I just saw him! Dragging a big bundle into the garage."

Martha hurried into the kitchen, arriving at the window in time to-see Mr. A close the garage door. She quickly dialed his number in hope sof catching Mrs. A alone. But on the very first ring Mr. A answered. Grace began to cry. Mother comforted her with an embrace. "He must have an extension in the garage."

Soon afterwards, one night at ten, Grandma and Great Aunt Edna already asleep, Martha tweezing her eyebrows at the bathroom mirror, Paul and Robert sharing a peanut butter snack in the kitchen, Mr. A banged on the door with what sounded like both fists. Father answered, but—without a greeting—Mr. A demanded to see Mother. She came out of her room in a pink quilted robe and fuzzy pink slippers, her face white with cold cream. "What is it?"

"There are clothespins all over the yard." Mr. A glowered.

"We hang clothes from the kitchen window." Mother was speaking calmly although Paul could see her right hand trembling behind her back. "Sometimes the pins fall off the pulley line or slip out of my fingers."

"They must be picked up."

"I'll do it first thing in the morning."

"No. Now. At once!"

"It's pitch dark."

Mr. A pulled a very long, eight-battery flashlight from his jacket and shined it in her face.

By now Martha's head, red hair disheveled, appeared at the opening of the bathroom door. "Don't do it, Mother," she pleaded. But Mother shrugged toward Father, sighed, and followed Mr. A down the stairs.

Paul, Robert, and Father grouped at the window to watch Mother's hands reach into the circles cast by Mr. A's flashlight and gather the scattered clothespins. In the silence they heard Martha snap "Shut up!" at Great Aunt Edna but did not turn their heads.

Within a week the leaves fell from the two small trees in the yard and the cold weather set in. The radiators began hissing at once. "Well, at least he's giving us plenty of heat," Grandma said. But the next day they realized too much heat was coming up. The valves shrilled a continuous whistle and damp steam clouded the apartment. Robert brought home a thermometer that registered ninety-four degrees. Mother reminded them that they had promised in their lease not toopen the windows when the furnace was working. So the young people, even Father, walked around in shorts, their bodies slick with sweat. Butwhen Great Aunt Edna, a frail old woman, fainted, Robert threw open windows in all the rooms.

Five minutes later the phone rang. Father answered. Even before-he could say hello, Mr. A began ranting. "I pay good money to heat this house. And you think nothing of squandering it. I don't know why I should give people like you any heat at all." He spoke so loudly everyone in the family could hear.

"But it's like living in a steam bath," Father said.

"Heat rises. We must have it at least eighty-five down here."

"But we can't take it." Father's voice quavered and his face began to flush purple.

"I hate waste! Close the windows or you'll get no heat at all."

The family, which never disagreed, which rarely spoke in raised tones, argued loudly. Robert didn't care if they had any heat. Grandma feared the real cold of winter and thought it might not be so bad once the outside temperature fell. Martha screamed that she hated living there. Finally, Mother pounded her fist on the table and declared, "I won't stand for this!" She stomped from room to room slamming windows and snapping their locks.

The next day Robert set up fans in the living room and dining area,and the temperature dropped to eighty-seven on his thermom-eter. On Saturday evening Grace found a special delivery letter inthe mailbox. It was from Mr. A, notarized, announcing that, because they were wasting so much water and electricity, he was limiting their sup-ply. Water from eight till nine a.m. and six to seven p.m. Electricity the same hours, except for an evening extension from nine to nine-thirty.

"Why didn't he come up to tell us himself?" Grandma asked, clucking her tongue. "Or call?" Great Aunt Edna added.

"It's illegal!" Martha shouted. "I know that much about the law. Our lease says he supplies electricity and water." She had taken to reading the lease again and again through the day.

"Martha's right," Robert said. Paul nodded.

"What should we do?" Father asked.

"Go to the police," Robert suggested.

"Now!" Martha insisted.

"No. Wait until morning," Mother said. "Let's all get a goodnight's sleep to prepare ourselves."

Martha was dressed at six the next morning. But Robert wanted a shower before they went to the municipal building, and since the water did not come on until eight, was not ready until eight-thirty. When Martha, Robert, and Paul stepped toward the door, Mother blocked their path. "No! I've changed my mind. This family has never had doings with the police before. We've always taken care of our own problems."

"I hate that man!" Martha sank to the floor between Robert and Paul, shaking with sobs.

"But Mother," Robert pleaded. Paul turned at once to dial Mr. A's number, willing to beg for consideration. The phone rang twelve times before someone lifted it and immediately broke the connection. The same thing happened the next three times he called.

Martha stormed downstairs to slam her pocketbook against the A's door then kicked at the lower panel. She cursed and hobbled back up with a swollen toe, swearing it was broken.

"What if he makes us move?" Grandma said. "Where would we go?"

"It doesn't matter!" Martha cried. "This place is awful!"

"And what else could we afford? Tiny rooms? I'd rather be dead than live that way again. Wouldn't you, Edna?"

The old woman nodded over and over, gumming the flesh inside her cheeks.

"You're all cowards!" Martha rushed into the kitchen to hurl pots down against the floor, resounding sharp metal clanking throughout the house, ignoring Mother's demands that she stop.

Father shoved Robert toward her. "Grab your sister! Hold her arms!"

Paul found himself disagreeing. "Let her do it. It has to be done."

Father began punching him on the back. "I'm your father, damn you!"

Robert reached out toward Martha and she kicked at him, threatened with a skillet. Grace tried to throw herself between them. They were all shouting and shrieking, the whole family, even Great Aunt

Edna. At the phone's single ring they froze in silence.

"It's him," Paul said. But, when he stepped toward it, the ringing stopped. Martha broke from the kitchen, pulled Grace into their room, and slammed the door. Father twisted Paul's ear until his knees buckled from the pain. "See what you've done," Father hissed. But Paul had no idea what he meant. Mother passed alone into her room, Grandma into hers, Great Aunt Edna into the bathroom.

By the middle of the night Robert's thermometer read one hundred and six degrees. He had to light a match to see it with the electricity off. Paul whispered that he must get outside to breathe. But, after he groped through the darkness, he found both the front and back door locks jammed as if rusted solid. When Robert tried to push open the windows, they stuck after moving only a few inches. From behind Martha's door came a crashing of glass.

The others crowded into the hallway, bumping and shoving because they could not see. But Martha would not open for them, not even after Mother gave her a solemn order. Finally, they all curled on the floor and slept as best they could in the fierce heat.

When the first rays of sunrise broke the darkness, Paul found Great Aunt Edna slumped in her chair only inches from the blank TV screen, her head hanging over the seatback, her skin purple, eyes bulging, her upper plate dropped onto her bloated tongue.

As the rest of the family gathered, Paul expected them to become hysterical. Instead Grandma clucked annoyance: "Of all times for this to happen."

Mother retreated to the linen closet and came back with the family's worst sheet, the one with stains and frayed edges, to drape over the old woman. Father pointed a finger at each of them, muttering numbers under his breath. He head snapped back when he realized that Martha stood among them. Then he counted again and pointed a finger at her. "Where's Grace?" he demanded.

"I lowered her out the window last night. I sent her for help." Father slapped Martha so hard she tripped over Great Aunt Edna's rigid foot and jarred the false teeth onto the carpet.

"You fool!" Father roared. "We'll never see Grace again."

"I don't care," Grandma said. "I don't care about anything."

Mother threw a candlestick at the television screen and the room shook with the implosion. Father glared as if he would strike her too but instead opened his penknife and slashed great gashes across the back of the sofa, then pulled out handfuls of stuffing to rub into Grandma's hair. She yanked down the curtains and wrapped them around his neck. Martha, now in the kitchen, broke dishes, one at a time, sailing them out against the walls of the other rooms. Robert attacked the bathroom fixtures with the new wrench from his work tools, chipping porcelain across the tiles, shattering the lid of the commode, slivering the mirror.

Paul found himself in Mother and Father's room upending dresser drawers and ripping clothing from closet hangers. When he paused to look into their mirror, he saw that his mouth was wide open and recognized the sound that echoed from the walls as his own laughter. Then he stood at the window, about to smash the glass and toss Mother's jewelry box down to the garbage cans, when he heard the back doorbell. He stepped out into the hallway and saw that no one else noticed the long piercing ring. They were all grunting and heaving.

Father knocked Grandma to the floor and kneeled with a knee in her stomach as he fought to slip his knuckles under the knotted scarf she twisted against his windpipe.

Martha had found Paul's secret magazines and was tearing them apart. Mother stood over the pages as they fluttered to the floor, shoving her fingers in her mouth but still screaming at what she saw. Robert rushed behind Martha and hit her face until blood gushed from both nostrils.

The bell still screamed. Before Paul could reach the knob, the door swung open. There, centered on the fiber mat, sat a huge basket of fruit—luscious pears, gleaming red apples, oranges, bananas, plums, even mangos and pomegranates—all covered with bright yellow cellophane and topped with a satin bow. With great care, Paul opened the tiny envelope tucked against the straw and slid out the card. "From our family to yours," it said, "Welcome," signed "Mrs. A."

Under the Deck

What the people on the deck have in common?

The world. They had been all over the world, sharing experiences of places that most people had barely heard of, able to name a city a street a restaurant a hotel a lake a mountain and know that the others would envision the same memory. "Oh yes," someone would say. "The wine, the cobblestones, the church bells in the towers, the statues in the park, the buildings that seemed to grow out of the hillsides." Bungee jumping from a helicopter in New Zealand, enjoying string quartets in Aix en Provence, play reading in San Miguel Allende, boarding the TGV at Lausanne, climbing with a guide in Nepal, meeting for drinks on the Lido, booking a suite at the Imperial Hotel in Tokyo.

Where were they at that moment?

Sitting in cushioned chairs on the deck of a country home, drinking espresso, sipping Cointreau or Vin Santo and passing plates of airy sweets, watching the brilliant sunset over the lake, hearing the breeze rustling through the leaves, listening to the sudden trill of bird songs someone holding up a finger, cocking an ear to bring a pause to the conversation.

How did they feel?

Delightful. That was the word used by Valerie: "It's delightful here." She sighed, spread her arms, and looked up at the glow of the quarter moon. "Yes, it's wonderful," Arthur said. "Good food, good wine," Thomas added. "And good friends." Leslie raised her glass. "Hmmm," the others said as they joined her in a hum of pleasure.

How did they come to be together?

Several had been neighbors at one time. Others had met long ago through professional associations. Three were the children of the original group of friends, having gathered like this since they were toddlers, now out of college, beginning their own successes, at ease with each other, with their elders, speaking fondly of those who were not there this day, off to some distant place, storing adventures to share the next time they all came together.

Why were they here?

The occasion was purely social, an opportunity stimulated by a holiday weekend, a break from the long hours of their careers, organized by phone calls from the hosts, Andre and Eleanor. "We'll be at the lake," they had said, "and guess who else is coming," as if enticements were necessary with the promise of fine wines, excellent food, and fascinating people.

Whose holiday was it?

The nation's. It was a national holiday. That was part of their amusement, though no one spoke of it. But they knew what the others were thinking. For a number of them—couples, whole families, or just the husband or the wife—this was not their country. They had been born elsewhere: Edinburgh, Hong Kong, Lillehammer, Vancouver, Johannesburg. Yet they had lived here for years, owned homes, businesses and practices. None knew which of the others was or wasn't a citizen. The question never came up. They had raised a toast at dinner—"Happy Holiday"—smiled and touched glasses.

How many were gathered on the deck?

About a dozen of them. The number changed from one moment to the next, Andre and Eleanor moving back and forth into the house for another carafe of coffee, another bottle of liqueur, another plate of sweets, the young people coming and going, three there now, some already off to parties with other friends, more due to arrive, Annalise and Giancarlo, driving directly from the airport when their flight from Rome landed.

Where was Carl Muntz?

Under the deck, back against a wooden piling, hugging a brown paper bag to his chest, teeth chattering despite the mellow summer evening, limbs shivering in trousers still soaked from losing his foothold at the edge of the lake. He tried to hold himself absolutely still, pressing his lips together, aware of the rasping of his quick shallow breaths, freezing when the people above him paused to listen to the song of a bird, though he had no idea of the reason for the sudden quiet, certain it was he; that he had made a noise that would give him away, still unsure what would happen to his plan if one of them climbed down to the grass and crouched to look under the wooden platform, how he would react if a stranger's eyes locked on to his.

How had Carl Muntz gotten there?

By boat from across the lake, from the area where the bank was steep and the brambles grew thick, unsuitable for building, a tangle of reeds at the water's edge, heavy tree limbs dragging the surface.

Where did he find the boat?

He stole it from the yard of an empty cottage several hundred yards away, an old green rowboat that smelled of rot, upside down on two sawhorses and fixed to a tree by a rusted chain that he twisted until it snapped. Then he dragged the boat across the grass into the water, soaking his shoes for the first time, his trousers to the knees.

Why this lake?

For years he had come here to escape the town, to lie under the sun on the grassy bank and pretend he was the only human being in the world. That was before people like Andre and Eleanor built their vacation homes and spoiled his place. He had avoided the lake for three years, but this day could think of nowhere else to be.

How had he come to be under this deck?

By chance. When Carl Muntz rowed across to the south side of the lake, he slipped on a rock stepping out and plunged thigh deep into the water. He pushed the empty boat back toward the center and scanned the row of large houses set back on broad sweeping lawns. On an impulse he chose this one, lured by the sunset's jagged glare on the upper windows. When he reached the bank he ran, feeling the water squish in his shoes, panting openmouthed, tumbling onto his side and rolling under the deck.

Had he planned to stay there?

No. His intention had been to find a way into the house. But before he could gather himself together and seek an entrance, the French doors opened and people came outside, laughing, praising the evening's beauty, clinking cups and saucers, holding cognac glasses, their footsteps jarring the wood above his head.

Why was he there?

To ruin. To give pain. To obliterate these people and their house, wishing it could be all the people and all the houses on this side of the lake. To make them know what it was like to be him. In the brief seconds of their excruciating torment to feel the totality of his miserable years. From the moment he fled the motel that evening he had ached to spread his anguish.

How did he feel at that moment?

Frantic, agitated, his chest craving a cigarette, his muscles in spasm from the strain of holding himself still. He smelled his wrath like a rancid crust that coated his flesh, wondered how those above could be ignoring the stink of him.

Did he listen to their conversations?

Barely. He was much too busy revising his plan, trying to decide what to do next now that he had not gotten into the house. What he did hear confused him. City names that meant nothing to him, resorts and villages and hotels. For a moment he wondered how they could have seen so many places, but then remembered that this was the last place they would ever see. At the thought, his heart thumped like a huge drum beating in the night.

Where had Carl Muntz been in his life?

Nowhere was what he would have said, though, of course, he had been somewhere, though rarely very far from the town of his birth, not much farther than he could drive in an hour or two, always to places that looked little different from the one he had always known, the narrow row houses, the old cars lined at the curb, crowded into cinder driveways, the grey factories with smokestacks that billowed black clouds into the sky.

Was he impressed by the sophistication of the people on the deck?

He hated them. He had not known who he would find on this side of the lake, what the people who lived in these great vacation homes were like. But now that he heard their voices, their sounds of happiness, their soft laughter, he truly loathed them.

Did he know what these people did in their lives?

He couldn't have imagined that they were physicians and professors, artists and engineers, executives and investment bankers, bibliophiles and connoisseurs. All he knew was that their lives were totally unlike his.

What did Carl Muntz do?

Sit at a table in a tiny kitchen with his aged mother and smoke cigarettes down to butts that burned his fingertips, hear his father's TV blaring down through the ceiling, watch the old lady drink an unending cup of coffee, listen to her lament his terrible jobs, at least once a day exploding with anger at the unfairness of her accusations. He tried, he had always tried, but bosses ignored him; no matter how much he busted his ass they never gave him a chance. "People don't like me!" he would shout at his mother, beat on the table until her coffee spilled.

What was Carl Muntz carrying in the brown bag?

An incendiary device, a bomb. Homemade, a volatile liquid in a glass jar, one from the shelf that his mother used for canning. The liquid was acetone, a paint thinner from the hardware store, something anyone could buy. He had filled the jar halfway, having once heard that fumes were even more explosive; but first he had punched a hole in the lid with a awl and inserted a firecracker with a long wick. Although he had never made a bomb before, wouldn't have known where to look for instructions, he had been pleased with himself while concocting it, alone in the basement, speeding there straight from the motel and telling himself that he would build a bomb even though he had never before in his life thought about a bomb.

Why did Carl Muntz make the bomb?

Fury, hatred, desperation. In the basement, he stared up at the ceiling as if to look into the narrow parlor where his parents sat, too deaf to hear his clattering, old people, their flesh sagging, joints swollen, both of them groaning with the ache of movement. As he poured the acetone into the jar, he knew he would never see them again. But they would read about him, see his picture in the newspaper. A man with a bomb. A source of ruin. A bringer of great pain.

Why didn't he blow up his own house?

It wouldn't be enough. Not his house or his parents or every house on their street, the entire neighborhood. Who would care if he destroyed people like himself, people who didn't matter?

Why had he been at a motel?

He didn't want to think about the reason, even as he waited under the deck with nothing to do but try to plan what would come next and listen to the chatter from above. Every time the scene in the motel began to enter his memory, he made himself imagine what the bomb would be like when it detonated the earsplitting blast, the searing red flash of fire, the sizzle and stench of life consumed. If he could do what he had done in the motel, why not a bomb?

What stunned him from his reverie?

The chirp of a phone, cordless, on a table directly overhead, Andre's soft "Hello," and then his happy laughter. "Annalise, I knew it had to be you. Where are you? In the car. Coming soon. Wonderful. Wait. I'll give you your mother. Marta, it's Annalise. On the car phone." The others were laughing too. "It's Annalise," they all said, and one voice louder than the others, a woman, excited: "Darling, how was the flight? And Giancarlo? My love to Giancarlo." There was a murmur from the others. "Everyone's love to Giancarlo. See you soon."

Did Carl Muntz return to thoughts of the bomb when Annalise's mother hung up?

No. He pictured what Annalise would look like. Tall, thin, golden bracelets on long tanned arms, her dark hair in thick waves, her lips red and moist, her black eyes flashing. Like a woman in a magazine, a model, speeding toward them in a car that smelled of soft new leather and cost more than he would earn in a lifetime. He wished it had been Annalise in the motel. But if she had been there, would he have done what he did? Yes. He nodded to himself, a gesture of certainty. It would have been perfect if Annalise had been the one in the motel.

Who was the one in the motel?

A young woman named Sharon Fahy, half his age, probably the same as Annalise, but not someone whose picture would ever be in a magazine, skinny and drab, with a long face and crooked teeth, hollow cheeks and protruding ears. For the year they had been meeting, it made Carl Muntz sad each time he looked at her, each time he drove up to the QuickChek where she cashiered. Each time she opened the passenger's door of his rusting Plymouth, then sat silently with hands folded in her lap. Each time they headed directly to the same tattered motel for sex, she passive beneath his slack weight, he twisting frantically, hands groping at her fleshless frame, desperate for a reaction from her, some emotion that would give the act pleasure.

What were the people on the deck saying?

They spoke of Annalise. Julia, Valerie's daughter, told how they had met in Gstaad last winter for a ski break after Annalise's exhibit in Paris, both discovering that they disliked the town, the shops and cafes overflowing with overdressed people, women in fur jackets, men in leather, all glittering with jewelry and smelling of cologne. They packed up, checked out, and went to Chateau d'Oex, just ten minutes away on the train line, a town where the Swiss skied, where everyone was friendly and the food in the Cafe de la Gare, delicious, a tabby cat under the table winding between their legs. Then Giancarlo joined them from Milan, celebrating the completion of a major stage in his research, exuberant, dazzling in his skiing, people stopping to watch and admire.

Did Carl Muntz pay attention to her story?

To the last part, enough to imagine Giancarlo on skis, losing his balance, tripping, plunging over a ravine, landing head first on ice, his neck snapped, head twisted at a weird angle, lifeless eyes staring up at the people gathered above him.

How did he picture Giancarlo's face?

He didn't. The face he saw was Sharon's, eyes bulging, lip swollen, blood trickling down her chin, her front tooth chipped at a spiked angle.

Why did he see her that way?

It was how she looked when he realized she was dead, the instant he removed his hands from her throat and her body stood propped against the wall panel, before it slumped forward and sprawled onto the grey carpet.

What did he do then?

He tried to replace her clothes, the jeans and the sweatshirt, hands trembling too much to attempt her underwear, then ripping the cord from a table lamp and knotting one end around her wrists, the other around her ankles. He dragged her into the bathroom and hoisted the body into the tub, turning on the water and sealing the drain. When the water covered her head, her short wiry hair bobbing on the surface, he used his shirt to wipe down the room, erase his fingerprints, even though he knew the gesture was futile. They would know he had done it. He had signed the register; the clerk had seen him every week for a year.

Why did he kill her?

Because no matter what he did he could not make her respond to him, because that night he stopped in the middle of the act and shouted at her, "Why the fuck are we doing this?" "Because I'm so lonely," she told him and began weeping. He slapped her with the back of his left hand, then punched her with his right fist. The jagged edge of the broken tooth cut into his knuckle. When she just lay there, staring up at him, not making a sound, not a gesture of defense, he turned furious, locking his hands under her chin and lifting her from the bed, forcing her against the wall, beating her head against the dark brown paneling, feeling her windpipe collapse under his thumbs.

Did he mean to kill her?

Yes. At the moment he was doing it, he wanted her dead. But if, moments before, when they were still on the bed, she had reached out to embrace him, he would have told her he loved her.

Why did he cry out now?

Someone spilled steaming coffee on the deck. First he heard a muttered "Damn," then felt the hot liquid scalding his scalp. "Fuck!" he shouted and jumped up, banging his head against the bottom of a plank. "Who's there?" a man's voice called out, and then there was silence, until a woman spoke, slowly, hesitantly: "Come out, whoever you are."

What did Carl Muntz do?

He moved quickly, eager to be out from under the deck before people climbed down and surrounded him. As he twisted and rolled onto the grass, he held the bag with the bomb up with one hand and reached the other into his pocket for the cigarette lighter.

What did the people on the deck do?

They clustered at the railing, looking down at him, speaking excitedly to each other: "Who's that man?" "Do you know him?" "I've never seen him before." Finally, Andre, the host, called out, "Who are you? What are you doing here?"

How did Carl Muntz answer?

"I've got a bomb. Stay the fuck away from me." He flicked the lighter, shooting out an orange flame, but held it high above his head, away from the wick in the jar. He imagined the deck blown up, the bodies of these people heaped in fire, their silk tunics and plaid trousers and white cotton sweaters, their pearls and jeweled earrings ripped and twisted, smeared with blood and seared flesh.

What didn't he throw the bomb?

He wasn't sure it would destroy. If they had been inside the house, he would have gathered them together, collected their wallets and watches and jewelry, then blown up the room, watched the building burst into flames, all of these people coughing at thick black smoke, flailing their arms at the fire, shrieking terror as the walls collapsed. But here, outdoors, there was nothing to burn, only the wood under their feet. He thought to demand that they all go inside but knew he couldn't make them do it.

What idea suddenly struck him?

Escape. Their cars lined up in the driveway alongside the house. He would take one of their cars and flee. He flicked the lighter again and cocked the jar like a football, gesturing his intention to fling it onto the deck. "Throw me your car keys," he demanded. "All of them?" someone asked. For a second, he didn't know how to answer, then looked to see which was at the front of the drive, facing directly out to the street. "The brown one." "The BMW?" The fucking brown one!" "That's yours, Arthur." A gray-haired man nodded, reached into the pocket of a blue blazer, and tossed a key case down onto the grass.

Did Carl Muntz get away?

Carl Muntz scooped the case up in the hand that held the lighter and ran toward the parked cars. But before he reached the edge of the grass a little round sports car swung into the driveway, bright blue, loud music throbbing from four speakers, a young couple waving happily to the people on the deck, not noticing him, not realizing that this man with a bomb even existed. The woman, Annalise, was more lovely than Carl Muntz had imagined, blonde, not dark, not tan, still someone from a magazine. It was Giancarlo who was dark and tan, tall, muscular, handsome. "Stop that man!" someone called, and Giancarlo vaulted from the car and rushed toward Carl Muntz, who wheeled about and began running toward the lake. He dropped the key case, kicked it to one side, and then stopped. Giancarlo stopped too, wary, limbs tensed, ready to pounce. As he shot out a flame from the lighter, Carl Muntz heard a woman scream. It must have been Annalise. He touched the flame to the wick in the jar, made sure it caught, a small red glow at the tip of the black cord. Then he threw the bomb at Giancarlo.

Did the bomb explode?

Yes, but not on Giancarlo, instead the instant it left Carl Muntz's hand, the impact knocking him flat, the flaming acetone raining down on him, singeing his hair, burning his face, setting his shirt on fire.

What of Giancarlo?

Giancarlo, unhurt, having leapt behind the bushes before the blast, saved Carl Muntz's life, flinging himself on top of him, rolling him over onto the lawn to smother the flames, slapping at the fire in his hair with clumps of dewy grass. He called to Annalise for the blanket from his car, wrapped Carl Muntz from neck to ankles, pried open his mouth to secure his tongue, and then pulled off his shoes.

And what of Carl Muntz?

Convulsing, limbs twitching as if shocked with strong currents, he cursed Giancarlo, spit out choked obscenities until he screamed and fainted.

Did Carl Muntz recover?

His burns were quite severe, his face disfigured, third degree on his chest and back, in need of months of skin grafts that would leave his flesh crusted and mottled, one eye sightless, his nerve endings in perpetual pain.

How was it that Giancarlo knew exactly what to do?

He was a physician and, although he now devoted his time to research, had spent enough hours in clinics to be an expert in trauma medicine.

Where were the others during Giancarlo's heroics?

Crowded at the railing of the deck, scrutinizing every gesture, a memory as they watched, silently rehearsing the words they would use to recall this adventure the next time they gathered.

Structure

PATRICK WAS PATCHING THE VILLAGE STREET, picking out chunks of pavement from the potholes and ladling in steaming tar, when the car went by. Even though the village was on no main route, "dead center on the way to nowhere" as the people liked to say, he usually paid little attention to the occasional strange vehicles sealed tight in their sleek speed, from a world that had nothing to do with his. But this one was peculiar—old and bloated, of a make he did not recognize, dull green, wallowing on worn shocks and fat underinflated tires. It moved slowly, swinging wide to pass him. The driver, a man with a tanned bald head, looked closely at the small pile of pavement chunks Patrick had piled at the roadside as if counting them. Patrick touched the tip of his cap but couldn't tell if the man nodded back. When the car reached the end of the village, a loose muffler struck sparks off the surface of the creek bridge. Patrick stopped his work to watch it head out onto the treeless rock-strewn landscape and disappear around the bend past the sheep grazing at the pond. "Now who'd want to drive a thing like that?" he said aloud even though no one was near enough to hear.

He watched the dark clouds layered at the horizon, shifting smears of grey. There hadn't been a day of real sun in weeks. He thought about the stranger's glowing tan and wondered where the man had come from.

The tar pot hung from a metal stand over a black burner flame, the smell so thick Patrick could feel each breath clogging his lungs. He spoke out again: "Why do we do this?" Then continuing to himself: build roads, ride over them, make holes, patch them, make more holes. It was like that for the whole village, everybody doing the same thing again and again, the women cooking and cleaning, the men repairing the maze of penning walls, hauling stones from the fields in their wagons, moving the animals from one pen to another, shearing the sheep, milking the cows. And he forever mending something for somebody, fixing loose tiles in the roofs, deepening the wells, sealing pipes. "We never get anywhere," he said and tried to imagine where a car that odd could possibly take the man. Patrick pictured him at the end of the peninsula following the road out to the blue water's edge and sailing for a city where great towers soared toward the sun.

He worked for another hour, sitting cross-legged on the black-top, picking out chunks one at a time, spitting phlegm into each hole before he tipped the pot of tar. Then he saw the stranger walking in from the fields, not on the road, but taking a zigzag path back and forth among the scattering of large rocks, stepping from one to another as if playing a game in which his feet were not allowed to touch the earth. He wore baggy white coveralls and tan canvas shoes that laced up above the ankles. Over his shoulder was slung a cloth bag patterned with bright chalked designs. As the man came nearer, Patrick could hear tools clanging inside it.

"Car break down?" he said, disappointed that the man was not still traveling, farther and farther away from this place.

The man nodded, the bronzed skin of his head smooth and tight. For a moment Patrick thought he was very young, then saw the puckered flesh of his throat. "A car like that," the man said, "it was bound to happen."

The way he spoke surprised Patrick, soft and light, as if each word were a bubble that floated off the moment he let it loose. "Then why take it out there?" Patrick pointed toward a cluster of hills so distant they blurred into the clouds.

"That's how I discover where I should be."

Patrick blinked his puzzlement. "What?"

"Buy the cheapest car I can find that starts, point it in a direction, and drive until it won't run any more."

"Then?"

"I settle in where I am."

"For how long?"

"Until it's time to go someplace else."

"When's that?"

"When I get an idea about the way things should look here."

"It doesn't make sense," Patrick said, suddenly angry because he didn't understand and suspected the man was mocking him.

"I've come to make things different," the man said again as if that were an answer. He took a path behind the houses, and Patrick watched his loping strides until he was out of sight.

Patrick spent a long time cleaning the tar off his arms that evening, rubbing his skin with a kerosene rag and then lathering soap again and until his flesh stung. By the time he got to the tavern, it was crowded, the old men in black caps and suit coats lined on the bench against the wall watching the others with craggy, expressionless faces, the families sitting around the tables in the middle, children on their laps, the young lovers huddled in corners secretly touching each other.

As Patrick knew it would be, the conversation was about the stranger, and it struck him that was why he had delayed so long, because he didn't know what he would say. Everyone stopped when he entered the room. From behind the bar, Herbert slid him a glass already filled with brown liquid as if it had been waiting for him.

"We saw you talking to that man, Patrick," Edna Morris said, waving a cigarette, the little girl clinging to her shoulder, blonde and thin as her pale mother, staring wide-eyed at him as if he too had suddenly become a stranger. Long ago, before she married Arnie, Edna had sat tight against Patrick in those dark corners. He hadn't let himself remember in years, but now that she was staring right at him, he burned with blushing and quickly turned away.

"What did he tell you?" Arnie twisted his chair back and stood over him.

"He's going to stay here," Patrick blurted. "For a while, anyhow."

The others gave out a murmur of dismay. Even the old men on the bench were shaking their heads.

"Now why would anybody want to do that?" Herbert said, both his hands gripping a tap.

"There's nothing here for him," Arnie said.

"There's nothing here for any of us." Mrs. Collins laughed, shaking her plump red face, though nobody laughed with her, not even her wizened husband sitting shrunken on the stool next to her. She had been a dear friend of Patrick's mother when his mother was alive, and he always felt that she was disappointed with him for turning out to be who he was. In his mind Patrick rehearsed telling them: he buys old cars and drives them until they break down; that's his way of finding a place to make different. But he realized how foolish that would sound and worried that the others would blame him for saying something so ridiculous. "I don't like it," Arnie insisted, slapping a hand against the bar top. The others grunted agreement, shifting uneasily in their seats.

"Well, we can't make him leave," Mrs. Collins said. "People are free to do what they want."

Patrick looked down at the floor planks, unwilling to meet the other's eyes.

Where was the man now? What was he up to? Everyone was talking at once. When all the thick speculation in that small, tight room began to smother him, Patrick pushed out the door and stood in the street gasping the cold air. He expected someone to follow him, a hand reaching from behind to grip his shoulder. But no one came, and he turned toward the creek bridge as if to walk until he vanished into the rocks.

Just before the bend, he saw a rush of sparks explode against the night, and seconds later heard the sizzle of embers. The stranger must have stirred his fire. Patrick imagined the man resting his head on the bright cloth pack, searching the black sky for a glow of starlight. He would cover himself with straw, drink goat's milk, eat boiled roots. That was all a man like him would need.

Early in the morning, Patrick, usually the first one to begin working, took the shovel from his shed and stepped out onto the street. Narrow streaks of orange dawn glowed from behind the clouds, the closest sign of sunshine he could remember in days. But the wind swirled a chill dampness through his coat.

The stranger was already standing on the green triangle of grass where the street widened between Herbert's tavern and the Vances' store. Still in the white coveralls, the bright bag on the ground beside him, he paced from the center to an edge of the triangle with long even steps, then back to the center and out to another edge, as if measuring. When he noticed Patrick, he nodded. Patrick returned a quick wave of his hand, wondering how many people were watching from behind the curtained windows.

"Who owns this land?" the man asked.

"What land?" Patrick said, not sure if he meant the village or the fields.

"This." The man pointed down at his feet, and Patrick saw he was talking about the small triangle.

He shrugged. "Nobody. All of us, I suppose."

"Who do I have to ask for permission to use it?"

"For what?"

"I want to build something."

"There?" Patrick shook his head. "It's too small for anything."

"Not for what I want to build."

"I don't know about permission," Patrick said. "When somebody wants to build a house or a barn, they just do it." Then he realized he probably had told the man something he shouldn't have, that everyone would be furious with him.

"Then why don't I just start and if anybody doesn't like it they'll tell me to stop."

"Maybe that's not such a good idea," Patrick said.

"We'll have to find out." The man began forcing thin sticks into the soft earth, evenly spaced, as if he had used a ruler.

Patrick rushed directly to the field behind Susan Crane's vegetable garden, digging furiously at the shrubbery that grew around the rocks, hacking at roots with the shovel blade, unable to cut through, finally beating the shovel against the stone and stinging his hands with a shock of pain. He dropped the handle and squeezed both hands under his armpits. The sheep stopped to stare at him with their narrow black faces and quickly returned to nibbling at the grass. Now Patrick worked slowly and methodically, prying up the rocks one at a time and stacking them in a pile behind him, try to concentrate on guessing the crops Susan would plant in this new space. He didn't want to think what the stranger might be doing on the wedge of land. He was far enough from the village to see nothing or hear nothing. But he had forgotten to bring anything to eat or drink, and by the afternoon was so tired and thirsty he had to go back.

He took a roundabout path to his cottage that bypassed the village center, not wanting to see the changes the man had made, to have the others look at him as if he was to blame for the man's existence. Once inside he drank a quart of milk, then rubbed the cool glass across his face and down his neck. His first thought was to fall on the bed and sleep. But a clamor of voices rose from the center and he was drawn to the sound.

The people of the village were standing on both sides of the street, the Collinses, Herbert at the tavern door, the Vances by the front of their store, Edna Morris and her daughter with a group of the other small children huddled around them, three old men on a bench by the post office, people up and down the way, Arnie Morris apart from the rest, alone in the center of the road, face clenched and legs rooted.

Patrick looked for the stranger and finally saw him at the corner of the schoolhouse dragging a great rock behind him on a sheet of canvas, a thick rope tied through holes in the material and wrapped around his waist and shoulders. Patrick had never seen a canvas like that and wondered where the man had gotten it.

Dragging the rock was harsh work. Veins stood out on the man's bald head as he strained, and sweat poured down his face. The coveralls were filthy now, as if they had never been white. No one moved to help. Instead the people shrank back as he struggled past, grunting with each step he took. Eventually he came up to Arnie Morris and stopped, his chest heaving deep breaths. Arnie twisted his boot heels down at the pavement and would not move. Patrick was surprised at the size of Arnie; he had seen him every day of his life and never realized how big he was. Once when he was young, he had fantasized about fighting Arnie for Edna, and now he saw how foolish that would have been.

Arnie stared hard at the stranger and drew back an arm. Patrick could hear Edna gasp, but Arnie just brushed the hair back from his forehead and stepped aside. The man gave him a half smile and heaved at the canvas.

Patrick looked past him at the triangle and saw three other rocks just as large as the one the man was dragging. A dozen long metal pipes lay aligned on the grass. When the man got the canvas to the edge, he rolled the rock off beside the others, spread the canvas next to the pipes, and sprawled out full length, his chest heaving.

The people watched for a time until they saw that he was sleeping. One by one they looked at each other, turned, and went back into their houses. Patrick realized that he was the last one out on the street.

That evening he didn't go to the tavern, his body sorer than he could remember in years, as if he had been the one to move all those great rocks from the fields.

Patrick avoided the village the next morning even though he had promised Hilda Sayers to dig a trench and lay new pipes for drainage. Instead, still tired and aching despite a night of heavy sleep, he sat on a hillock among the sheep and studied the ewe Charlie Kimball had only half sheared the other day, irregular hanks of long hair alternating with patches of smooth white skin. It seemed unfair to the animal to make it look so freakish, half naked and vulnerable. In late afternoon when he made himself go back, he saw the stranger had spaced the rocks on the triangle, three in one row and another angled away from them in an arrangement that made Patrick sense a plan. Now the man was drilling into the rock with a gas-powered machine that made an uneven sputtering sound as the long bit ground into the stone and sprayed grey chips. The man wore goggles that covered most of his face. Wide black streaks stained the front of his coveralls.

Not many people were watching at this time of the day, besides the children who stayed far back, just the old men, the Vances, the Collinses, and Edna Morris. Patrick looked for Arnie but only saw his rusted van in the alley beside Herbert's tavern, curtains drawn across the windows.

When the holes were drilled, the man picked up a length of pipe and slipped it deep inside one of them, stepping back to study it and then tamping it down. He put a pipe in each rock, but at varying depths, so that the exposed ends rose up at different levels. Then he capped one pipe, the shortest, with an elbow joint, screwed in another length at a right angle parallel to the ground, and swung it sideways until it touched one of the other standing pipes. For his canvas bag he removed a blowtorch, lit a blue flame, and welded the two pipes. He worked deliberately, pausing to step back and measure with his eyes. Eventually the pipes in the rocks were all connected by crosspieces.

The stranger drew spots on two of the crosspieces and reached a new pipe from one to the other, but it rolled away from the marked spots. "Would somebody help me?" he said. Patrick felt Edna looking at him and made himself stare back at her. Their eyes locked as if each were daring the other to step forward. He could feel his muscles shuddering as if the decision to move would change his life. When Edna broke the contact, he saw Mrs. Collins already standing on the triangle holding an end of the pipe.

"Will it hurt?" She laughed boldly, but Patrick sensed that she was frightened. Her husband had gone into their house.

"It won't hurt and it won't feel good," the man said.

"Then I suppose I'm wasting my time," she said but pressed the pipe down onto his marking.

The stranger welded the other end firm and then the one Mrs. Collins had gripped. He picked up another length of pipe, and she helped him again until none remained loose on the ground. When he was finished, the four rocks were connected by a network of pipes that Patrick realized fanned out from the one apart to the row of three.

Arnie Morris appeared at the tavern door and shouted out, "What the hell's that supposed to be?"

"Not much as far as I can tell," Mrs. Collins shouted back.

The man gathered up his wrenches and drill, put the blowtorch back in the cloth bag, then walked out of the village. Patrick wondered what would happen if he followed but was unwilling to try.

That night Arnie, drunk in the tavern, tried to talk the others into storming out to the triangle and ripping those pipes apart. Edna wasn't there nor was Mrs. Collins and most of the women. The men cheered Arnie on, plotted strategy, but did nothing, and when Arnie collapsed openmouthed, his face flat against the damp bar top, slipped away with quiet good nights to Herbert.

Up at dawn, Patrick expected to see the stranger at work when he got to the street. But the man wasn't in the triangle. Curious, Patrick searched through the village, then gave up, wondering if the man had finished whatever he planned and left for good. He had just begun digging the trench for the Sayers when he spotted him walking past the pond with pieces of the green car hanging from ropes over his shoulder and tied to his waist—headlights, red lenses, a steering wheel, bumper guards, tail pipe. Over his head he carried the metal sheet of the hood. His coveralls were ripped now, split down the center of the back, exposing muscled flesh. Patrick thought he was less tan than he had been on the first day, already losing his color in the sunless climate.

Patrick couldn't help speaking. "What's all that for?"

The man gave him a thin smile. "I knew what I'd use the moment I saw that car."

He's crazy, Patrick thought and gave all his attention to his digging.

Later, when he went back to the village center, he found the hood fixed to one of the crosspipes pointing straight up into the air. The headlights were embedded in the rocks at either end of the row and the red lenses in the middle one. The steering wheel rose above the fourth rock at the end of the tailpipe. But Patrick's greatest surprise was seeing Edna Morris's daughter sitting on the man's shoulders turning the steering wheel and laughing gleefully.

The street was filled with people, and when he spotted Edna in the group, he expected to hear her scream. But she was beside the Cranes pointing to her daughter and laughing. Arnie stood back by his house with his arms folded across his chest.

Patrick went to Mrs. Collins. "What's going on here?"

"We're all wondering what he'll do next."

When darkness fell, Patrick sat outside his cottage on an old barrel and watched the shapes of the people moving along the paths and gathering in front of the tavern. They were talking, but the breeze swallowed the sounds. Only Mrs. Collins' laughter rang clear. He half wished she would come for him, reach out and lift him to his feet. It's over, she would say, forgotten, I forgive you. She had been so furious all those years ago, dragging him off the street into her living room the day after he had entered the tavern to find Arnie pressing Edna against the wall, she looking so young and fragile in the wrap of his broad arm. "Be someone!" Mrs. Collins had roared. "Do something!" "Look at me," he had told her, afraid he wouldn't be able to swallow his tears, stiff-armed, holding out palms as if to display the gangly awkwardness of his body, feeling the thick mat of hair tingling against his scalp. She had reached out and touched that hair. "Make yourself good enough, Patrick." He hadn't been able to let himself fall against her.

More people gathered, and the murmur of voices rose until it was as loud as the wind. They probably were talking about the stranger, perhaps planning something. Nobody would have cared if he joined them. But he chose to stand apart. Once he had believed they were all talking about him, the target of Arnie's gloating. But he never heard Arnie say a word about him, as if he had never done anything worth comment.

Though he usually rode his bicycle to cover great distances, Patrick walked, following the road away from the village, out toward the pond and beyond. Over his shoulder he carried the steel bar he used for prying loose roots and rocks and long rusted spikes, occasionally swinging it out at the shrub tops and then pushing against the pavement as if it were a walking stick. When he started the sky was a soft grey above the brown hills at the horizon; for the first time in a week he could see behind them to the green cleft of a valley that always made him think of a woman. But as he walked the clouds darkened until he couldn't make out anything past the flat sprawl of rock and scrub grass and grazing sheep.

He hadn't admitted to himself where he was going; but now, out of sight of the village, he said, "I want to see his car," and wondered when he would come upon the hoodless ruin, how far the man had gotten past the village on the first day. Patrick didn't know what he would do when he saw it, why he had gone into his tool shed for the steel bar.

The rain began, first just a spray like mist in the wind and then a steady pelting. It soaked his hair and ran down beneath his collar. He imagined finding the car and sitting inside, being lifted from the ground by the swirl of a great storm and then coming down somewhere totally new, a place different from any he had ever imagined.

Then Patrick heard laughter, an excited roar. He ran to a curve in the road and saw almost everyone he knew, practically the whole village, swarming around the remains of that faded green automobile. They had come in trucks and carts and motorbikes, their vehicles scattered on the grass along the roadside.

The stranger's car was propped up on rocks by its axles, the four wheels loose and flat on the ground. Scrawny Mr. Collins was wrestling with the back seat, all by himself trying to slide it out the door, his wife with her arms wrapped around herself, shaking with delight. The stranger was pointing down at the engine telling people what parts to remove, his coveralls tattered, the legs flapping in the wind and the top half hanging loose from his chest, sleeves knotted around his waist. Edna Morris stood close, listening, her arms pale white beside the golden flesh of his torso.

They all seemed oblivious of the rain, excited by their tasks. When Herbert saw Patrick, he shouted a greeting. "Just the man we need. Help me pry this door loose." He guided the steel rod between the hinge and the car frame, and the two of them heaved their weight against the lever until the metal snapped free. When all the parts he wanted were spread out on the ground, the stranger walked among them as if committing each to memory. Then he supervised the loading into the carts and truck beds.

A caravan rode back to the village. Patrick started off walking beside it until Edna waved him onto the seat of Arnie's van. He squeezed in beside two young boys, and Edna's daughter sat on his lap touching a finger to his ears and chin and nose as if they were playing a game. Edna drove and Patrick wondered where Arnie was.

In the village, they unloaded everything beside the triangle, and the stranger told them what to do. They wedged the back seat between two rocks, strung engine pieces to the crosspipes with wire—air filter, distributor, carburetor, spark plugs. When the man sliced the tires away, they stacked the wheels one atop the other and buried the four doors in the earth around them, so deep that only the windows showed. Someone had gone for Patrick's shovel. He did most of the digging, all the time thinking, what's this for? But at nightfall, when the rain slowed to a drizzle, he stopped to look at the others, everyone filthy with mud but working as eagerly as he was, and he didn't care.

The brightness glowed behind the morning haze, but a sheet of grey still blocked the sun. Before he went out Patrick gave himself a long wash, shaved closely, and put on clean clothes. The second he stepped into the street, he felt something was different and saw the thick wooden pole planted crooked in the triangle off to one side of the rocks, a sawed off scrub pine lashed to its top with hemp rope, tilting upward, above the green hood.

The others were rushing out of their houses with cries of surprise. From the way the stranger was standing in the center of the street looking up at the pole and shaking his head, Patrick knew at once he hadn't placed it there.

"It's wood," Mrs. Collins called out as if she had made a discovery. "Nothing else is wood."

"So what if it's wood?" Susan Crane yelled back.

"Is supposed to be rock and metal."

"There's no rules."

Patrick saw Arnie Morris leaning out of an upstairs window with a broad smile, as if he had just won a bet.

"Susan's right," Herbert said from the tavern door. "When you make something like that, you can do anything you want." The old men on the bench pinched their lips and nodded.

Two boys dragged a torn mattress across the street and leaned it against one of the rocks. The people cheered. Suddenly everybody was bringing something -- an old dresser with broken drawers, flowers in clay pots, a bed post, a man's suit propped up on sticks like a scarecrow, a cracked bathtub. Arnie Morris carried three cans of paint, and he and Herbert smeared streaks of bright red and blue and yellow up, down, and across the rocks. Children tied ribbons to the pipes. The whole village was swarming over the triangle of ground, each person adding something different.

Patrick couldn't decide what he should do. It occurred to him that he could pour pools of tar over the grass patches. But as he turned toward his shed, he realized that the stranger wasn't there with all the others. He rushed through the paths behind the houses, opening unlocked doors, searching the outbuildings, until he was absolutely certain.

Patrick ran back to the street, ready to plunge into the crowd, shake people by the shoulders and tell them. But at the edge of the triangle he stopped, unsure that he could make anyone listen. He beckoned to Edna, called her name when she would not stop wrapping lamp wire around a pipe. She came to him, annoyed at the interruption. "What's the matter now?"

"He's gone."

"Who?"

Patrick didn't know what to call him. "The man who did all this."

"I know," she said. "The fool bought Arnie's old van. A wreck of a thing that won't get him from here to there."

"But look what's happening with him gone. It's not the way he made it."

"What's that matter? It's ours now."

She turned away, and Patrick walked backwards one step at a time, trying to understand the din of activity. But it just bewildered him. "I liked it better," he said aloud, "when he was making it by himself."

Out in the field, away from the village, Patrick stood and faced the distant hills, picturing the open sea beyond, imagining that the stranger had already crossed to a someplace new on the other side.

He pushed a stone loose from the top of a wall. It thudded to the earth and the sheep skittered away. Then, as if discovering the fields he walked on each day of his life, he removed stones deliberately, one by one, spreading them on the ground. With at least a hundred scattered at his feet, he grouped the largest in a base and began to lock the others into a pyramid that had nothing to do with penning animals. When he had used up the loose stones, Patrick paused and saw that it wasn't finished. He sensed a promise just past the reach of his fingertips, and his face opened into a smile. He had no idea what he was making but knew these fields contained all the rocks he would ever need.

Roxanne's Ride

THE WOMAN BESIDE HER IN THE AISLE SEAT snored lightly, mouth open, glasses twisted halfway up her forehead, head bouncing on the high seatback. She had been silent for hours, hands clasped and lips tight, snapping a single word when Roxanne had asked her where she was going—"Home."

During the daylight, Roxanne had pretended to look out the windows behind her, really watching the other passengers: the red-faced man with the week's growth of grey beard, the plump woman in black laced shoes who reminded her of Mrs. Aumuck, her second grade teacher, the man in the plaid hat who winked at her and gestured with an eyebrow. She had laughed out loud and refused to turn in his direction for an hour although it killed her not to glance back.

She gave them names in her head—Greybeard, Old Lady Aumuck, Fruitloop, Twinkle, Stone Face for the woman next to her, Buzzard or the winking man—and made believe they were going to the same town, some boarded-up place in the desert they all would clean and paint and fix up new to live in forever. She would run the TV station, making up shows, singing, dancing, the way she did when she was six and her father laughed and clapped. When she walked down the street, everyone would call her name—Hey, Roxanne.

But now, staring out into the night, she couldn't help picturing her mother walking into the bedroom, kicking off her shoes and suddenly realizing that the top dresser drawer hung open, slips and bras spilled onto the floor, the lock broken on the hand-painted wooden Indian jewel box and the 428 dollars she had pinched together for a new refrigerator gone.

Even now, hours later, her mother still would be cursing her—her smoking, her stealing, her sty of a room, her scummy friends, cursing her name. "Goddamn you, Roxanne! I'm glad you're gone. Just stay away and stop screwing up my life."

She wanted a cigarette badly but swallowed hard and squeezed both fists, resolved to stop, to make herself good. All the others seemed to be asleep now, slumped in their seats, faces slack, breathing long and slow. The fools were missing everything, the promise of the night. How could people sleep when they were heading someplace new?

At dawn Roxanne still sat alert. When the bus lurched over a series of bumps, she could feel the vibrations in her teeth. Her ears prickled with the unending whoosh of ventilation; she swallowed a thick diesel odor with each breath.

Then the bus pulled off the interstate and slowed to maneuver the curve of the exit ramp, tires whining on macadam. Stone Face's eyes were still shut, her mouth open. Roxanne hesitated with her hand an inch from the woman's shoulder and decided that no matter what, from now on she was going to be nice to everybody; she would do things for people So she touched with two fingers. "We're stopping for breakfast."

The woman let out a sour yawn, shifted in her seat, and shielded her eyes with a forearm. Roxanne looked out past the matted grey hair and blinked straight into the sunrise. She had to squint to take in the layers of pink at the horizon. All around, on both sides of the highway, lay acres and acres of furrowed black soil, between seasons and empty. The highest structure for miles was the DX sign at the truck stop; it must have risen a hundred feet into the air, with the word "DIESEL" in letters as big as she was.

"Why is everything so flat?" she asked the woman.

The woman settled her glasses on her nose. "Because that's the way God made it." She said "God" like a curse.

The bus slipped between the tractor-trailers parked askew on the blacktop, some with cabs tipped forwards, some with engines idling, sunlight glinting off chrome, everywhere the smell of diesel. The driver stopped amidst the cars near the square, squat building of the diner. That's all there was: the building, four gas pumps, and blacktop with rows of painted lines everybody ignored.

A half mile or so down the road a few whitewashed houses clustered together around a silo. Three cows stood by a wire fence, chewing, switching tails, studying the bus with great brown eyes.

Roxanne let the woman off first and slipped into the aisle between Greybeard and Old Lady Aumuck, smiling and saying "Thank you" to no one in particular, then shuffled toward the front of the bus with the rest of them.

As soon as she entered the diner, she got a deep whiff of sizzling grease and felt her innards churn. She hurried back to the ladies' room and had only a short wait for a stall, then leaned over the toilet for five minutes but ended up just spitting a string of phlegm. When she sat to pee, she took the plastic pen from her bag and filled in a four-letter word until it looked like BOOK.

Back in the main room, she thought she could eat but found all the tables and counter stools filled. So she flipped through the listing on the jukebox, regretting all the cassettes she had left behind. But here she played no tunes, sure the others would give her funny looks. Except for a few little kids, she was the youngest person on the bus.

Roxanne moved to the rack of postcards, glossy scenes of cornfields, tractors bailing hay, lean white farmhouses, a map of the state with cartoons of corn, wheat, hogs, and cattle inside its borders. She slipped one from the rack and saw that nobody was looking. It would be so easy just to drop it into her bag.

But she stepped to the cash register and asked the woman, "How much?" Her fingers clicked a quarter against the glasstop. No more stealing.

She glued the last stamp from her change purse to the marked spot and wondered who to write to. She considered scrawling "I'm sorry" to her mother but then remembered she wasn't. Her leaving had been her message. And not yet to Tommy or Molly or Karen or Chuck or Fran. Not until she had a room and a job, a return address where she could invite her best friends: come see me, stay at my place, anytime.

When Roxanne looked again, two seats at the counter were empty. She took one and, moments later, the man she had named Buzzard slipped in beside her, straddling his stool as if mounting a horse. She pretended not to notice, even when he set his plaid hat on the counter near the sugar bowl and twirled it by the brim.

The waitress, a hefty woman with tight blonde curls, tossed coffeestained menus in front of them as she rushed past balancing a stack of dirty plates on a forearm. Hungry as she was, when Roxanne imagined biting into anything listed on the sheet, her stomach surged with an oily taste. By the time the waitress came back with a "What'll it be," she still hadn't made up her mind and began to stammer under the woman's glare. "Let me see . . . Let me see . . ." Then she noticed the pie plates on glassdoored shelves by the coffee urn. "A piece of apple pie," she said with triumph, the first food she had ordered in her new life.

"Why don't you get a big scoop of ice cream on top," Buzzard said, and when she turned to him, he cocked an eyebrow and winked again, a man with red-veined sunken cheeks and a mat of brown hair that looked like plastic.

She let out a quick cackle. "I'll get fatter."

He scanned her up and down with rheumy yellow eyes. "You look ok to me."

"Sure," she said in a disbelieving tone she hadn't used since she was ten.

"How about it, mister?" The waitress delivered Roxanne's pie and snapped up Buzzard's menu. He grinned back with missing molars. "Four eggs over light and easy, sausage, and ham. A pile of toast and a pot of coffee. I worked myself an appetite sitting on that bus." He patted his stomach as if he wasn't a scrawny man with wrists like doorknobs.

Roxanne took a forkful of sweet pulp and soggy crust.

"Name's Craig," he said to her.

For a second she wanted to make up something and then figured it didn't matter. "Roxanne."

"Pretty name."

"Sure." She looked up at their reflections in the steamy mirror, he with the hat on again and the red neck of a plucked rooster, she squarefaced and broadshouldered, breasts too small and too high, thinking again that she might have made a better looking boy.

He slurped coffee. "Going far?"

"Last stop."

"Long way to sit."

"Can't afford to fly."

"I like buses," he said. Nice way to see the country. Meet people."

"Not the one they got me next to.'

He threw his head back in silent laughter as the waitress set down his plate. He jabbed a point of toast in the yolks and watched them run. "Any friends where you're going?"

She nodded, pretending it was true.

"Boyfriend?"

"Maybe."

"Figured you would."

"Why's that?"

"Girl like you."

She glanced up at the mirror again. "What kind's that."

"Kind that gets boyfriends."

"Sure."

"Going to get married?"

"Me?" She almost spit out a mouthful of pie. She didn't like Buzzard, but it was fun to be talking to him, better than sitting next to Stone Face and smelling diesel.

"What's his name?" Buzzard asked.

"Tommy."

Tommy was as much of a boyfriend as she'd ever had. They'd hung out together since she was twelve and he eighteen, almost always with the gang, crowded six or seven into somebody's car or smoking on somebody's porch, listening to tunes, parading up and down the aisles of stores, stealing, sometimes breaking things just to do it.

"Is he where you're going?"

She shook her head. "Where I been."

"Then why're you here?"

"He's coming later." She blurted the lie and then felt her face break into a wide smile as she realized that it might come true. Not just Tommy. Karen, Molly, Chuck, Fran too--they really would join her wherever she settled. All of them away from the old shit in a new place. She imagined the scene of meeting them at a bus station, her friends dropping suitcases and dufflebags to slap palms, lock their arms around her neck in great hugs. "Hey, Roxanne," they would say, all piling into her car to head for her place. "Hey, Roxanne." She laughed out loud.

"You're one happy lady,' Buzzard said.

"Yeah."

"So what's this Tommy like?"

"Tall ... thin ... kind of blond." She groped for a description that a stranger could accept, knowing that other people thought Tommy was weird. More skinny than he was tall, with huge dangling hands, pale pimpled flesh, and brittle hair that seemed drained of color. A twenty-year-old guy who did nothing but hang out on street corners with sixteen-year-olds. Her mother hated him. She truly did.

"You got something going?" Buzzard squinted over at her.

"We're tight." Roxanne clasped her right hand over her left wrist. "Like that." And it struck her how much she took care of Tommy, how she gave him cigarettes and money, how she'd listen for hours to how his bastard drunk father used to beat him with a belt. What would he do without her? She brooded down at the bottom of the empty coffee cup.

Buzzard tugged at her sleeve. "Driver's signaling. Wake up."

'Yeah. Ok."

"Want to ride next to me? Seat's empty."

She looked up into his blood-streaked eyes. "Sure," she shrugged. "Why not?"

Roxanne wanted to stick out her tongue, wiggle thumbs in her ears. She could see the others sneaking looks at her sitting next to Buzzard. Stone Face seemed to take turns between glowering at her and scowling up at her canvas dufflebag jiggling in the overhead rack. Roxanne had spent hours decorating that bag with felt tips, marking both sides ROXANNE in letters that burst into multicolored flares.

Buzzard tapped his foot as if listening to a song. He wore scuffed black pointy toed shoes crusted with mud.

"You like music?" she asked him."

"Got a transistor radio in my suitcase."

"What kind you like?" "

"Loud. The louder the better."

"Rock?"

"Long as it's loud." He winked at her.

He seemed to be winking every thirty seconds since she sat down.

But Roxanne couldn't tell what those winks meant, the way she felt when everybody else was laughing at a joke she didn't get.

Buzzard's eyes were crinkled, his narrow mouth twisted in a grin as if he thought they were sharing a secret. Still it was better than sitting beside Stone Face and listening to her teeth rattle.

"Where you going?" she asked him.

"Ain't made up my mind yet."

"When will you?"

"When I see someplace I like."

"How could you know you like it with the bus moving so fast?"

"Then I guess I'll just have to keep riding."

She grinned back at him, liking him a little now for his game of banter. If they could keep it up, the day would fly and they'd be somewhere. Night riding was best. The day was nothing but looking at cornfields and counting telephone poles.

"Where's your home?" she said.

"Wherever I'm at. Right now this bus's my home."

"And when you find a place you like, will that be your home?"

"You got it." "

"How long you stay in one place?"

"Till I get tired of it."

"How much time that take?"

"Sometimes a couple of hours. Sometimes a month. Sometimes a year."

"Then I guess you don't have a girlfriend." Roxanne laughed, amused to be the one asking all the questions.

"You mean somebody like your Tommy?" She nodded.

"Nope. Girlfriends are like homes. Whoever I'm with, that's my girlfriend."

"What if she's got a boyfriend?"

He craned his head in all directions, looked up at the rack and under the seat. "I don't see no boyfriend."

She thought of reaching into her wallet to show him Tommy, but stopped with her hand on the clasp. She didn't want any of Buzzard's remarks. Tommy wouldn't pose for pictures, always covered his face when he saw a camera point at him. But one time Karen had caught him when he was sort of drunk, slouched openmouthed against the wall of Chuck's house pressing an icy beer can against the side of his head.

Buzzard snorted, made a gesture as if he was going to punch her, but just grazed her upper arm with his knuckles.

"You was about to show me a snapshot of Tommy, wasn't you?"

"I was. But I forgot. I left his picture behind."

"If I was Tommy, I wouldn't want no girlfriend of mine to forget my picture."

"He's going to send me a new one. He's having it taken."

"Maybe you'll forget what he looks like by the time it gets to you."

"Never happen."

He rolled his eyes and smirked. "You bet."

Instead of being angry, Roxanne was beginning to feel sorry for Buzzard, a man with no home, no girlfriend, nothing but a crap radio in a suitcase and ratty black shoes having to sit on buses half his life. And suddenly she wanted to weep.

"There's nobody in the world like my friends," she said.

All her mother did was bitch at her; the only sign she had a father were birthday and Christmas packages mailed by department stores. "I don't know where I'd be without my friends."

"You're here. They're there."

"Not for long," she insisted.

"You got this far without them."

"We look out for each other."

"Yeah." Buzzard wasn't smiling now. "I knew people like that once. They don't think about me no more, and I don't think about them."

"Me and my friends," Roxanne said. "We're different."

"How come you never call me Craig?" Buzzard asked.

Roxanne clamped a hand to her mouth and choked on her laugh, coughing and sputtering. He stared at her for an answer. "You don't look like a Craig to me," she finally said.

"What do I look like?"

"Like you should be ... ah, Willie."

"Willie?"

"Why not?"

"What's a Willie like?"

"I don't mean all Willies are the same. But—to me—a guy who

moves around as much as you do should be called Willie."

"What the hell's wrong with Craig?"

"I never knew a Craig before. It's kind of a fancy name."

"Maybe I'm a fancy guy."

Roxanne looked at his neck and his battered hat. "Maybe." She sputtered again. All she could hear in her head was the sound Buzzard, Buzzard, getting louder each time. She clenched her jaws shut for fear it would fly out if she opened her mouth.

"Christ!" His nostrils flared. "What the hell do you know?"

She shrugged.

Buzzard looked out the window. Roxanne noticed the long brown hairs that grew thick in his ears and turned to the opposite direction, looking out across the endless fields to a farmer alone on a tractor. What a scary way to live. All by yourself in the middle of nothing. Streets and stores and lights—that's what she needed. She could hardly wait to get to where she was going.

"I bet he's a fag." Buzzard suddenly turned and put his face up close to hers.

"Who?"

"That goddamn Tommy."

Her impulse was to laugh. But she stopped when she saw his eyes. "He's not."

"I bet he's got a tiny little pecker." Buzzard wiggled his right pinky and left it dangling. "Like a goddamned bob-tailed puppy." He snorted and flopped his head against the seatback, pulling the white head cloth loose. He wadded it in his fist. "The sonofabitch probably wears diapers."

Roxanne squeezed her eyes shut to fight the tears. She felt so sorry for Tommy. Instead of being angry at Buzzard, she hurt for Tommy, at how much he'd miss her. Oh shit! She didn't want to think about it.

"Why're you snivelling?" Buzzard's words were becoming slurred, like a drunk's, although she was sure he hadn't had a drop since they sat together.

"Don't talk about Tommy." She kept her voice soft and pleading.

"Can't he take care of himself?"

"No." The tears broke loose now. She didn't make a sound, but her eyes swam in tears. They ran down her cheeks into the corners of her mouth. She tasted salt; it burned into a sore on her lip.

The bus hit a pothole, springs bottoming with a great thump. She heard gasps from the other passengers but could not see past the blur of her eyes.

"That was some goddamn bump," Buzzard said, cheerful again.

"Yeah." She rubbed her sleeve across her face.

"What was you crying about?"

"You know." "

"That! Jesus! I was just teasing." He spread a hand on her thigh, hot through the thick denim of her jeans. When her leg twitched, he gave a quick squeeze. "Can't you take a joke?"

What would happen if she screamed? The shrill piercing plaint that had terrified all the kids when she was ten. She imagined herself screaming like a siren and the others snapping their heads to look out windows, pretending they'd heard nothing, the driver peering hard at the road.

Her duffle bounced in the rack above Stone Face. She watched it pitch from side to side.

"I'd better check my stuff."

She stood quickly and tried to step into the aisle, but Buzzard gripped her wrist and yanked her back down into the seat. "It'll be ok," he said.

He did almost all the talking now. Buzzard. The side of his face pressed against the seatback as he murmured toward her ear. His hand lay on the padded rest between them, an inch from her arm, ready to snap out. So Roxanne sat very still and nodded or shook her head when he asked for a response. Outside the window the sky was layered pink and purple at the horizon. If she looked ahead, all she could see was a dark strip of highway disappearing into the sunset.

" ... and she says to me," Buzzard was telling her, "Craig, if you do that again, I'll kill you. You know what I did?"

Roxanne shook her head. "

"The same damn thing all over again. Right in front of her. Did that bitch kill me?"

She rolled her head from side to side.

"Damn right, she didn't. She didn't do diddly squat. So I kicked her ass and told her to get the hell out. I didn't want no part of her."

His hand squeezed shut until the veins quivered around the white knuckles. "Weren't I right to do what I did?"

Roxanne waited until she felt the pressure of his fingers on her arm before she nodded.

"Knew you'd think so. We're two of a kind, ain't we, kid?"

Buzzard stopped talking to watch several men fishing in a creek by the side of the highway.

"What's asshole do?" he asked suddenly.

"Who?"

"Your fag boyfriend."

"Nothing."

"Nothing? What's he live on? His good looks?"

"He's not working now. It don't make no sense. He's going to be coming out to meet me." For the moment she believed that was the reason Tommy didn't work.

"I got a feeling," Buzzard said, "that he ain't going to be coming. That's it's all over with him and you."

She forced a laugh. "Why?"

"Cause he's there and I'm here."

This time her laugh was empty. "Sure. Big talk."

"I'll show you things an asshole like Tommy never even thought of." His hand covered the fist she balled in her lap.

"I've got someplace to go," Roxanne said. "People're waiting for me."

"Tell me another one. Only one's waiting for you are police hunting down another damn runaway."

She tried to pull her hand free, but he squeezed until her nails dug into her own flesh. She had to catch her breath.

"Do you know how old I am?"

"I've had 'em younger."

"You can't make me do what I don't want to."

"Kid, you'd never believe the things old Craig is going to make you do. For starters, you call me by my damn name." Now he bent her wrist back. "Craig," he hissed at her. "Say, 'Anything you want, Craig.'"

She clenches her jaw until she thought her teeth would crack.

"Buzzard!" she called, so loud all the others turned toward the sound. "Your name is Buzzard!"

He dropped her hand in his surprise, but just as quickly pinched the inside of her thigh. "I'll kill you, bitch."

Roxanne reached her other hand, the one that did not ache, into the pocket of her jeans, slid the match book up to the opening, and folded back the cover. She bent one match down against the striking surface, and, as she pulled the book out, snapped it with her thumb.

She tossed the flaring matches into a newspaper crumpled under a seat across the aisle. "Fire!" she screamed. And Fruitloop and Old Lady Aumuck screamed with her. "Fire! Fire!"

People were shouting, kicking at the floor, Buzzard too. The driver slammed brakes, skidding the ball of flame under Stone Face's feet.

Roxanne jumped up and ran toward the front of the bus, all the time shrilling "Fire!"

With one hand she caught the strap of her bag on the overhead rack, then heaved against the door, tumbling onto the shoulder of the road, rolling off into the weeds.

For nearly a minute she held her breath, expecting the others in pursuit, then only Buzzard stomping toward her in a fury. But the door closed with a hiss and the bus just stood there vibrating with a throbbing idle, its stainless steel glinting in nightfall, the tinted windows blacking out everything inside.

If the door opened again, she would drop her duffle and run into the fields. But the bus wrenched into gear and eased back onto the macadam.

Roxanne waited until the tail lights vanished, then stood up and picked the burrs from her clothing. She started walking in the direction the bus had gone, further from home with every step, shivering, feeling herself being swallowed by the night.

Stef

Although three taxis waited outside the hotel, Victor took the tube from Green Park to Earl's Court because that was the way Stephanie would have traveled. She lived on Hentee Crescent, off Warwick Road, her street just a squiggle on his London pocket map.

He checked the address again on the envelope his daughter had used to mail a birthday card two months ago, her first communication in almost a year. "Stef" she had signed in a new printing he didn't recognize. During the time they lived together—he and she and her mother—she was always called Stephanie and wrote her signature in a flourished script.

The card had annoyed him with its magenta flowers smeared on cheap paper under the words "Birthday Wishes." He didn't bother to read the rhymed message, throwing the card out in that night's garbage, unwilling to show it to Julia, to have her hold it at an edge with two fingers and arch a brow. But he had saved the envelope, stuffed it in a desk drawer with scribbled notes and business cards he'd been meaning to enter into a permanent directory.

Victor left the Earl's Court station via the Warwick Road exit, up a ringing metal stairway and past three lavender-haired punks hovering over the ticket machines. On the street he faced the grey front of the exhibition hall, again wondering why everything modern in London was so ugly. Julia wanted to believe London was a city of elegance, nothing but quality shops and glittering restaurants. She refused to notice the soot eaten into the marble facades or the trash trampled in the gutters. He hadn't told her where he was going, even that he knew where Stephanie lived.

He rarely mentioned his daughter to Julia and she never asked. Planning this trip, their first abroad together, he told himself there was no danger of running into Stephanie in the St. James chambers where his meetings would be held. He and Julia would travel in different circles. But that morning as he lay watching Julia's soft breathing beside him, though they had made love during the night, Victor felt he had no more right to touch her sleeping form than he did a stranger's. Before she awoke he left the hotel to look for Stephanie.

She and Arnie had split up. He'd heard that much. Her mother called him at his office whenever she learned another traumatic detail of their daughter's life. He didn't have the heart to tell her he'd rather not know.

At the corner of West Cromwell Road he stood at a traffic light for several minutes while a stream of lorries rumbled by, spewing diesel smoke and clanking chains against their undercarriages. He thought it must be the most unpleasant corner in the city, an intersection of two wide roadways glutted with hulking vehicles. When the light changed, he had to run across to avoid a van that swerved into a right turn.

Victor made several passes up and down the block, finally looking closely at his pocket map. Hentee Crescent didn't join Warwick Road; he could reach it only by cutting through an unnamed alley cluttered with rubbish bins. Though the word crescent had a graceful sound, evoking great sweeps of Georgian town houses, this one was a grimy cluster of squat dark-bricked buildings facing a narrow arc of pavement.

From where he stood he could see through an open window into a barren ground floor room, just a few wooden chairs on a scrap of carpet, the walls papered with a splashy design of oversized flowers that reminded him of the birthday card. Two women in purdah came out onto the front steps, jabbering harsh, throaty sounds. Stephanie's building was three down, identical to the others except for the shrunken white curtains hanging in all the windows. He checked the envelope again, hoping he'd made a mistake.

Only when he pushed back the frosted glass door and stood in the foyer did he consider that she might not be home, that she might be working or shopping or visiting. His daughter's life was a mystery to him now.

A brass wall plate contained narrow slots to identify the tenants, a small black button beside each slot. He expected to find Arnie's surname, but she had used her own—his.

He rang, waited a minute or two, and rang again. This time the inner door buzzed and he turned the knob to step into the hallway.

"Who is it?" Stephanie shouted down the stairwell, suspicious. "It's your father," he called.

"Oh."

Victor couldn't tell what that sound meant—relief, hostility, indifference?

"Where are you?" he asked her. "Second floor. Up three flights."

Victor climbed slowly. How easy it would be to turn and step back into the street. He averted his eyes from the dark hand marks smeared along the wall.

Stephanie stood in a doorway, an underweight girl wearing baggy ankle-tight jeans and an insideout sweatshirt from her old college, nap showing, the school name meaningless in reverse letters. Her light hair was tangled; the lack of makeup gave her face a blank look. He imagined Julia's judgment: with just a touch of blush and eye shadow she'd be a pretty girl. Stephanie watched him silently, reactionless at this first sight of her father in two years.

"Your card came," he said.

"You didn't have to fly three thousand miles to tell me that."

"It surprised me."

"I was staring at a rack and had an impulse."

"And picked me."

"A coincidence of the calendar. What brings you here?"

"I'm passing through. The first time since I visited during your junior term."

"Before Arnie." Her mouth twisted as if she had more to say. He didn't respond, wouldn't let her provoke him.

"Business this time?"

"Some business. Some pleasure."

"That must mean you're with what's her name."

"Julia."

"If you say so."

"Did your mother tell you about her?" Stephanie shrugged. "Where is she?"

"Probably shopping for silk scarves."

"But you're not."

"No, I'm visiting my daughter."

She braced a hand on her hip, narrowed her eyes. "Uninvited."

She was trying hard to look furious, but Victor knew it would be all right, no scene. Her threats had always been a bluff—except for Arnie.

"I've heard that Londoners are very hospitable people. Just ring a bell and somebody will offer you a cup of tea."

She turned and moved back into a room, no longer blocking the entrance. He stepped in after her and closed the door.

This wallpaper was terrible too, a repeated pattern of eighteenth century drawing room scenes, bare-shouldered women in gowns puffed with crinoline, periwigged men, the step of a quadrille, a curtsy, a bow. Whoever had hung the paper hadn't bothered to align the rolls; the room was filled with mismatched people.

Victor sat in an overstuffed chair, sinking with a twang of springs. He rubbed his hands over the threadbare fabric of the armrests. The front windows were closed, large panes vibrating from the lorry rumble on Warwick Road. Stephanie clattered through drawers of a tiny kitchen unit set in an alcove.

Besides the entrance, the room had one other door, closed shut, white enamel chipped down to bare wood. The only furnishings were a sofa even shabbier than the chair, some odd tables, a few throw rugs spread over linoleum, and a thin bookcase stuffed with college texts and warped paperbacks. The prints tacked on the walls were unusual, posters for exhibitions at galleries he had never heard of. Stephanie had always liked art, but these stark prints clashed with the ornate paper.

She filled a pot with water. "It's instant."

"Fine," he said, though he hated instant. "How long have you been living here?"

"Since Arnie. He had it first. Shared with a mate called Sid. Then I came along and poor Sid was out on the street. Arnie too now."

"What happened to him?"

She shrugged. "He turns up now and then. I thought it was him when you rang."

"Are you still friendly?"

She snorted, a mannerism that annoyed him, especially because he suspected she used it often. "With him? He downs four or five pints to build up nerve, then pounds on the door demanding to see his kid."

"Where is the baby?" Victor finally asked, though he'd been searching the room for signs of a child's presence, listening for a gurgle or a cry. Then he recognized the acrid diaper pail odor.

"The baby's name is Margaret."

"I know. Your mother told me."

Stephanie set two cups in their saucers, poured milk in a pitcher. "Since when did you two become so chummy?"

"We're in touch."

"That's news to me. The last I heard you were both ranting."

"We stopped being angry with one another a long time ago."

"Now you have news of my downfall to bring you together."

"We're concerned."

"Isn't it rather late for that?"

Victor stirred his tea, the clink of his spoon the only sound in the room. "Is the baby with a sitter?"

"Sitter? Why no." Stephanie assumed a genteel accent. "Margaret's nanny has taken her for a stroll through the park." Then in her normal voice, "She's having her nap."

"I'd like to see her."

"Granddad." She didn't smile.

"I suppose I am," he said.

Without a word, Stephanie opened the chipped white door and revealed a cluttered room with dark blue walls, a thick mahogany headboard, clothing heaped atop the bed quilt, and upended toys scattered across the floor—stuffed animals, bright plastic balls, dolls. She moved inside where Victor could no longer see her. He leaned forward and gave a start at the sudden wail.

Stephanie cooed. "Did I wake you up, lovey? It's all right. Mummy's here."

The sobbing slowed and quickly stopped, replaced by deep sucking sounds.

"She's wet," Stephanie said. "I have to change her."

Her murmurs were too soft for him to hear now. He saw a small foot kick into his line of vision, then disappear, heard a giggle.

Stephanie stepped back into the front room carrying a frail looking child with fine honey-colored hair and a large forehead. The baby stared at him through round blue eyes and drew on the pacifier that obscured her mouth. The skin struck him as too pale, the arms brittle.

"When was she six months?" Victor asked, wondering if he should offer to hold the baby.

"She isn't. Three weeks from now."

"She looks well-behaved."

"You've only seen her for ten seconds."

"Does she give you problems?"

"She's a baby, isn't she."

"I only meant that some are easier than others."

"So are some parents."

Victor clutched the armrests and dug fingers into the chair's padding, then pushed himself up until he was standing. When he approached them, the baby shrank against Stephanie's shoulder with a look of distress. The pacifier dropped to the floor. He expected bawling. But the baby just gazed at him with puzzlement when he stooped to retrieve the plastic ring.

"Should I wash it?" he asked.

"You have to be immune to germs to survive around here."

He reached the nipple out toward the baby's face and watched her mouth close around it. Her palm, small and warm, rested on his knuckles. He held his hand under her touch until Stephanie hoisted the padded backside and broke the contact.

"Is she healthy?" he asked. "She looks so thin."

"I feed her." Stephanie glared.

"I didn't mean that."

"She gets colds. We see the National Health doctor. But I think she picks up more bugs sitting in the waiting room with so many other kids."

"You can use the health services?"

"Of course."

"What's your status here?"

"I'm on the dole. The Council pays for this flat. A bedraggled social worker stops by now and then to fill out a form and then I get my charity. After all, I'm a Brit's mum." She bounced the baby with an exaggerated rhythm, chanting, "Margaret, Margaret, subject of the Queen."

Does Arnie help?" He expected the snort this time, didn't know why he had bothered to ask the question.

"Arnie's only good for one thing. The first time I saw him in that pub I knew. I didn't care if he had two bob in his pocket or could speak a complete sentence. And my instinct was right. For six months he was spectacular. Then we had an accident"—she held the child out at arm's length. "Somehow he was under the impression that if you stopped afterwards it would make the mistake unhappen."

"He doesn't sound like a mental giant."

"Arnie was the highpoint of my junior year abroad. Everybody else went home to be seniors. I stayed on for independent study . . . Being Margaret's mother." She sang the words, then tossed the baby and nuzzled her cheek.

"Is it worth it?" His eyes scanned the room.

"Margaret, are you worth it?" The baby's mouth pulled at the pacifier. "And how's your life?" she asked Victor. "You didn't pick up Julia in a pub." Although Victor said nothing, she held up a hand to silence him. "Don't tell me. She's witty, elegant, sensual, and very well dressed. All her undies are in Burberry plaid."

"Exactly right." He couldn't help smiling. "Except for the plaid. Though she may be buying those right now."

"Does she know you're seeing your ne'er-do-well daughter?"

"Yes," he lied.

"I suppose hers are models of elegance and grace."

"Sons. Two of them, both in college."

"They'll never be permitted a junior year abroad."

"In fact the older one will be here next term."

"Be sure to have him look me up. Sample some local color."

"It won't be his first visit."

"I should have guessed a classy woman like Julia would be well-traveled. How does she stack up against my mother?"

"They're very different." "In whose favor?"

"Julia is much more at ease with the world. Your mother is a shy woman."

"And you've always wanted someone with style."

"Only if there's substance."

"Poor Granddad." She spoke to the baby, looking down where the

drooling had left a dark circle on the reversed sweatshirt. "Disappointed by wife and daughter. We could live in Mayfair with what he spent
on country day schools. No tuition too high in his quest for the ideal
offspring. All he got for his money were bad reports—'Stephanie has
a rebellious streak.'"

"The euphemism was 'high spirits.'"

"Exactly what Arnie found so fascinating." She cradled the baby
and rocked her from side to side. "Will you and Julia marry?"

"Unlikely."

"Maybe you should adopt her."

"She's fine the way she is. We're perfect together in small doses."

"Before reality can intrude its ugly head . . . the reason you and
Mother divorced."

"What reality?"

"Arnie." She touched the tip of her nose to the baby's. "Grandma
and Grandpa couldn't bear having a daughter who bedded down with
a common navvy. So they punished each other by getting divorced."

"It didn't happen that way. The only thing you changed was our
timing. We'd planned to wait until you graduated."

"Well, thank you for wanting to shelter your little girl from life's
cruelties."

Victor's blood surged. "You enjoyed rubbing our faces in Arnie!"

"At least he pretended to love me!"

Her face flushed, nostrils quivering, eyes glazed with tears. The
baby, frightened, burst out crying.

He reached out toward the child, but Stephanie swung away from
him, clutching her daughter tightly. She pretended to study one of the
prints, a dark semi-human shape with swirl of black ink for a face.

Victor sat again, on the sofa this time. "Why do you sign yourself
Stef now?"

For a moment he thought she wouldn't answer. Then she said,
"That was Arnie's name for me."

"But you're not with Arnie any more."

She turned toward him, approached the sofa. "It's more appropriate for somebody on the dole." He thought she would weep and
quickly stood up beside her.

Her head hung and her hair fell limply over her eyes. He wanted to push the hair back, to close both hands over the bones of her face. But she just swallowed hard and pressed her mouth to the baby's head.

Victor remembered his rage when she called about Arnie and dropping out of school, how he had cursed her name and smashed down the receiver. Now her vulnerability made him feel ashamed.

"May I hold her?" he asked after a silence.

"It's Arnie's daughter you know."

"That's not her fault. We don't choose our parents."

"And we're stuck with our children."

He held out his arms.

"She's wet again," Stephanie said.

She passed the child to him and at once he felt the warm dampness seeping through the cloth of her playsuit. The baby squirmed in his unfamiliar arms, face trembling at the verge of collapse. Then he recalled a lesson Stephanie's mother had given him when their daughter was an infant: hold a baby tightly, tuck it firm against your chest, let it feel your heartbeat. When he did, the child calmed, rested her head against his throat. Her hair smelled of sour milk; she needed a bath. Wet and stinking, his granddaughter. "Margaret," he said, testing the name, and again, "Margaret," making it a soothing sound.

He pictured Margaret where they once had lived, the tiny fingers touching flower petals, the blue eyes entranced by the ducks on the pond.

"She usually doesn't take to strangers," Stephanie said.

"You could go home," he told her, his middle knotting with anxiety even as he spoke. "Finish college. Other girls with babies do it."

"You used to say London is the most interesting city in the world."

"Not this way. Not when you live on Hentee Crescent."

"Thanks for the offer. But I'll stay where I am."

"For God's sake, why? There's plenty of money. You know that."

He had spoken too loudly, made agitated sounds. The baby stiffened, drew away, and began to whimper. Stephanie lifted her from him, smacking kisses until the child was cooing again.

"I made my choices," she said, "and here I am."

"That's nonsense. We're free to change our lives."

"I haven't worked out this one yet."

He lifted a hand and watched himself hold it poised out in front of him. He saw that she was watching too. All he had to do was touch her and make himself say, I want you back.

"Do one thing for me," she asked suddenly.

"What?"

"Bring your friend Julia to dinner some night. Let her sample the native cuisine."

Victor looked to the doorway as if Julia were poised on the threshold for his answer, adjusting white gloves, one finger at a time. "She may have plans."

"She doesn't know you're here, does she?"

"No."

Margaret stroked her mother's cheek as if fascinated by the feel of her. Stephanie cupped her hand over the baby's fingertips and looked hard at her father.

"All right." Victor nodded, already dreading the evening. "I'll bring her."

For the first time Stephanie smiled at him.

Pleasure

They flew down the snow-packed hill on aluminum disks, plastic sheets, tiny children's sleds, crashing into drifts, each other, rolling over and over until they lay spreadeagled at the base of the trees, the cluster of Sally's friends Michael had just met that afternoon, one more stoned than the next, screaming into the wind. Michael couldn't remember any of their names or who was supposed to be with whom. The bloated babyfaced man in orange earmuffs was Leroy or Leslie, his wife one of two scrawny little women, either the one jabbering some incessant anecdote about her cat or the one whining about having to go to the toilet. Harry or Henry, who stood heaving snowballs at the others, was supposed to be hopelessly in love with Emma or Edna, a selfish bitch, now off flirting with somebody named Don or Tom, whose wife had stayed home in protest. Sally had talked of these people for hours, the tangles of their relationships, the traumas of their lives. Finally meeting them, Michael could not associate their faces with the tales of alcoholism, adulteries, breakdowns, and attempted suicides. They all looked so ordinary. He watched Sally rush from one to the other—hugging, squeezing gloved hands, kissing cheeks. Then he shrugged and flopped into a snowpile, lying motionless in the powdered chill until Ed or Ted or Fred pulled him out.

He liked to call Sally, listen to her say, "Hello, Michael," as if really pleased that it was him. Her voice was soft and sensual, warm with a throaty pleasure. More than anything else he enjoyed hearing her on the phone, when his imagination could make her into anyone he wished. Some nights he would sit in darkness and dial her number again and again just for the sound of her greeting.

On a whim, Michael decided to introduce Sally to Gene, a courtly Southerner he had known for years but usually avoided. They sat around a table littered with lobster shells and wine bottles, Michael snapping at Sally's nose with a hollow claw while Gene sprawled back in his chair and stretched out his long legs. "I did it with a woman once," Sally was telling Gene, who had introduced the question of sex. "I wanted to find out whether I'd like it." "Did you?" Gene asked. "No. It was weird. Women aren't the answer for me." "Is Michael?" Sally just smiled, but Michael laughed so hard that even the waiters stared.

With his wife Michael had never done anything. "Sat home and watched the kids grow" was what he told people after they separated, remembering how one night he went out into the yard and howled his boredom at the moon. He would demonstrate the sound for strangers, again and again, until Sally clamped a hand over his mouth and pinched his nostrils shut.

Sally threw a party for herself because her birthday came a week before Christmas and never received enough attention. Michael set up the bar while she warmed the hors d'oeuvres. Within a half hour the apartment was jammed with people, most new to him. Lois and Carl were there, Harvey too. Someone named Leonard came wearing lipstick, and that upset Tim, who spent the whole evening in handclenched agitation. Ruth danced on the coffee table and stepped high heels into the avocado dip. Joe and Elizabeth had an argument, and she insisted on telling everyone about his premature ejaculations. Ralph and Vera made out behind the drapes, while Ralph's wife, Terry, tried to paw at Will, who was more interested in setting up Sally's bong. Lenore crashed into the tension pole shelves and scattered knickknacks. People kept turning up the stereo, and the neighbor below pounded on the ceiling. Someone reported that Lou had passed out in the parking lot, his cheek frozen to a hubcap. Charlie and Vic went to look. Sally tripped on her way from the kitchen to the living room and dumped a pan of steaming lasagna onto the shag carpet. When everyone was gone, she told Michael it was the best party she had been to all year.

Before driving out into the winter night they had spent half an hour sucking smoke from the syrupy residue in Sally's hash pipe. Now they couldn't find their way to a party at a place they had never been before. Headlights, traffic signals, neon signs all fragmented and multiplied in Michael's vision. Blazes of green, blue, yellow, red. At an intersection, dazzled, he swerved into a sudden left turn. For an instant another car faced them head on, then veered with a shriek of tires. Michael slammed brakes and spun a circle on the icy shoulder, spraying gravel against the undercarriage. Sally sat beside him in rigid silence, but he blared the horn because they had come within a hair of being killed.

Her back to him, just beyond the reach of his fingertips, Sally kicked out of her jeans, pulled off her tee shirt, and dropped a gown over her head. From the pillows Michael saw her through smokestung eyes, a grey shape in the first glow of dawn. The mattress sagged them together as she climbed under the covers. When their legs tangled, he touched her arm and she slid against him. Her warm flesh softened, but he would not tighten his grip, would not close his eyes. She rolled away and within moments sprawled in openmouthed sleep, while Michael lay awake listening to the soft whistle of her breathing and staring out at the litter of objects that emerged from the darkness—a sweater balled on the dresser, a brassiere dangling from a lamp, letters stuck into the mirror frame. He wondered who she wrote to, who wrote to her, what she had to say to anyone.

Telling Stories

OTHER THAN JULIA, RUSSELL DIDN'T KNOW THE PEOPLE seated around the dinner table. They were her friends from the time of her marriage, and he knew he should have remembered what she had said about them. He also knew it would be a big mistake to ask her now even if he had been able to lure her into a corner for a hurried whisper, an admission that he hadn't paid attention. "Are you aware you do most of the talking when we're together," she told him once in the quiet after lovemaking, "and it's really not about you, just stories that I never know are true." "I'm a writer," he had said. "I write stories." "Well, don't write about me." She had pressed a hand to his check, and Russell couldn't decide if it had been a touch or a blow. In the dark he hadn't been able to read her face.

Here at this table he kept deliberately quiet, not silent, just smiling and offering a reinforcing comment when one of the others said something interesting. The food was good and the wine even better. They were dining on a large glassed-in sun porch that Carol, the wife, kept calling an atrium. Glowing night lamps gave a soft illumination to the deep green lawn, thick leaves of tall trees shimmering in the moonlight. Russell kept looking past the others to the garden, drawn by the colors of the vegetation and the dark shadows that seemed to be creatures rushing across the lawn. They certainly lived elegantly, Carol and Jerry. Russell wished he could recall what Julia told him they did, how they made their money. He'd Google Jerry at home when he learned their last name.

The other couple, Evelyn and Alan, didn't seem to belong together, not the way Carol and Jerry did, both sandy-haired and ruddy, a bit overweight, but solid, as if they spent hours doing something physical like playing tennis. Alan sat erect on the padded chair, thin, taut, and sallow, occasionally smiling as if on a timer. When he spoke, it was extremely precise and informed. He seemed to know a lot about a lot of things, and he wasn't the kind of man you could kid about his knowledge, the way Julia, a friend from way back, did Carol and Jerry. What Julia said was just silly, and Russell wished she had more wit.

Evelyn puzzled Russell, reminding him of a woman from his mother's generation, her gray dress out of style, her faint blonde hair pulled back in a tight bun, her glasses in a thick pink frame. She certainly wasn't fat, but beside her husband she looked thick, perhaps because when they all had been standing in the living room, Russell noted that she had wide hips and heavy thighs. He let her walk ahead of him to the sun porch and saw that she seemed to wobble in her low-heeled old ladies' shoes. She had a long face, a large jaw, and spoke with what he took to be an accent, but not foreign, not British, though she reminded him of someone from a black and white postwar film, a plucky housewife making do.

Julia reached under the table to touch Russell's hand, looking straight ahead and saying something to Jerry about a car he had owned years ago. Russell squeezed her thigh, flattened his palm against it as Jerry laughed and said, "Oh, that one. I could have made lemonade out of it."

Carol pretended to punch his arm, and Alan and Evelyn smiled, but Julia laughed out loud, her animated face making her especially pretty. Russell told himself he didn't want to do anything to spoil things between them, not here, not with people—Carol and Jerry— she liked very much, people he still was trying to decipher.

Evelyn and Julia helped Carol clean up the desert plates despite Carol's pleas from them not to bother. Russell wondered if he should volunteer too, looked for a sign from Julia, but she was focused on collecting the china. When Jerry and Alan sat fixed in their chairs, he didn't offer. Evelyn rattled cups, looking nervous as she stepped toward the kitchen, as if fearful of dropping the stack in her two hands. Russell had a thought: she's terrified of dishes. He couldn't write it down then and there but would tap it into his iPhone when he no one was looking.

The idea might fit into a story. He wrote stories as much as he could, trying to get up very early for a few hours before he had to drive to his work, but managing to do that only a couple of times a week. He did write weekends, though in the months since he met Julia he had decided he'd rather be with her.

Several of his stories had been published in magazines he called respectable, clearly not any he'd feel shame about. People, friends at work and from college, said nice things about them, and he could tell they weren't lying. In fact, some seemed impressed at his modest success, as if he were the real thing. Whatever that meant. At least he knew he wasn't deceiving himself, wasting his time. He had been writing stories in his head all his life until he finally worked up the nerve to put the words on a screen before printing the pages he marked up with green ink. Now, more so after the publications, he sought story ideas, germs of material.

He hadn't shown any of his stories to Julia, though she knew about them and even asked to read some, offhanded, not with what he took to be genuine eagerness. Sure, he'd tell her. I'll bring one next time, though he always managed to forget. He often thought how odd it was that they could be so intimate in bed, so unashamed, holding back nothing, and yet so tentative about his writing. Was that the reason she said what she did about him telling stories? Had she been teasing or testing? He didn't want her judging the stories, judging him. Not yet.

When the women came back from the kitchen, Jerry brought out several cognac bottles. Russell was about to say, No cigars? But he swallowed the words, covered his mouth with a linen napkin when he coughed.

"I know what we'll do know," Carol said. "Let's tell each other about our childhoods. Some of us don't know each other well, and you can learn so much from what we did as kids."

"Great," Julia said, "I'd really like that."

Russell suspected she and Carol had planned that in the kitchen, if not before. He could see Alan contemplating, Evelyn's eyes darting. But never in Alan's direction. He thought of making up a tale, something about setting a school lab on fire and ending up in juvenile detention. Actually, he'd fantasized doing that every day in chemistry class. The fire, not detention. Of course, he wouldn't speak that fabrication, not with Julia there, not with the way he was looking forward to the end of the dinner party and their time in bed, the house to themselves, her kids off visiting their father. He'd do nothing to spoil the evening. But he'd make notes about that idea, a tale about an alter ego.

He found himself eager to hear what Julia would reveal, with the thought of teasing something deeper, more intimate, out of her later in the dark, touching spots that would make her moan. But Carol volunteered to go first. "After all, it was my idea."

Jerry gave her a peck on the cheek. "And I'll fill in the details."

"Maybe I'll surprise you."

He winked at the others. "I can hardly wait."

Carol began. "We moved halfway across the country when I was eleven. Dad's job. And I was devastated. I loved our house. I loved my room. My stuffed animals. Tons of them. My brothers were only toddlers and had no idea what was happening. But I cried for days. When the movers loaded the van, and my parents were ready to drive away, my father had to carry me to the car, me kicking and screaming. He didn't yell, though. He just said, 'I know you're upset. I'd be too, but it will be great where we're going. Even better than here.' I've never forgotten that."

Even though she was smiling, Russell suspected she was close to bursting into tears.

"Her father is a great guy," Jerry spoke quickly. "One of the kindest people I've ever met." He reached to take Carol's hand.

"And was your dad right about the new town?" Julia asked, though Russell was sure she already knew.

"Absolutely. I loved it even more. We had a much bigger house, a bigger yard, and my room was great. Dad told his company that was the last time. We wouldn't relocate again. And that's where I lived even after I came home from college, until I met Jerry."

"It wasn't easy to get her to make up her mind—me or that bed with all the stuffed animals."

"You had toys in bed after college?" Julia's voice rose.

"Still does." Jerry winked at the others. "Only now it's me."

"My boy toy." Carol stroked his arm.

They really love each other, Russell thought and had to look away.

Julia insisted that she go next. "It's hard to come up with something Carol and Russell haven't heard before." She looked at them. "Did I tell you about my dance recital?" They shook their heads, and Russell sensed they would even if she had.

She was supposed to have the lead role in a performance but tripped over a teammate during a gym volleyball game and wrenched her knee. Her mother wrapped the knee with icepacks for several days, keeping her home from school. Though she still had pain, she went on stage, and people—her teacher—told her she'd been wonderful. "

"So you had a career," Russell said, assuming she'd danced for years.

Julia shook her head. "No. I quit lessons right after that as much as my parents and my teacher wanted me to go on."

"Why?" Evelyn spoke softly, as if her question were an intrusion.

"Because I knew I'd never be good enough."

Carol picked Alan to go next. He told about winning a science project as if giving a formal report, and Russell remembered that Julia said he did important research, though about what for whom he had no idea. It seemed to have been a major competition, resulting in a prestigious scholarship. Alan made it all sound very dull.

Jerry's story was about coming off the bench in a big game to replace an injured quarterback and throwing a long, long winning pass, the ball wobbling as if tossed by a five-year-old. But it didn't come off as bragging, more like something he still couldn't believe had happened, Jerry still shaking his head as he dramatized the details, arms reaching toward the ceiling as his fingers snatched an invisible object. "My hero!" Carol said and wrapped arms around him. Julia clapped. "Full disclosure," Jerry said. "The quarterback recovered, and I never got in a game again." Carol booed.

Russell realized he should take his turn. He wondered if Julia had told Carol and Jerry about his writing, if they expected something special from him, clever and inventive. But he decided not to try, fearing he would come off as pretentious. So he talked about the hours he spent drawing comics as an eight-year-old, adventures of a superhero called Bullet Man with a bullet-shaped head and bullet-shaped car that could run down gangsters. "The main problem is that I have zip drawing talent. In fact, I'm as bad now—worse—than I was then."

Julia gave him a puzzled look as if unsure whether he was improvising on the spot. He put a hand across his heart. "Honest," he told her, relieved when she smiled.

"And you're last," Carol told Evelyn, who seemed to be shrinking into herself under the others' attention. "Batting cleanup," Jerry added.

Russell looked to Alan for his reaction, but Alan seemed to be studying his distorted reflection in a coffee spoon.

"I'm not good at this," Evelyn said, speaking so softly the others had to lean toward her. He was glad that Carol did not ask her to be louder and almost suggested that they let her skip. What did it matter anyway? Then he realized he was curious, especially when he saw how pale she had become, how she stared straight ahead at a blank wall.

"I wasn't a very appealing child," she began. "Overweight and ungainly. My parents had me late in life. It may have been the only time they had sex."

Russell expected her to laugh, as if she had made a joke. But she didn't, and none of the others changed expression. They seemed embarrassed, even Alan, his fingers twisted around the spoon.

Evelyn paused, and Russell thought that was it, that she had said all she would, but she swallowed and went on. "Have you ever been to a funeral home?" The others all nodded. Carol breathed out a yes. "All those undertakers in dark suits and solemn faces standing silently in doorways, never speaking above a whisper, trying to pretend they didn't exist. Well, that's how it was in my house. My father should have been an undertaker. But he was a small town banker, always calculating, letting others deal with people. Except on Sundays." She repeated, "Except on Sundays," and then stopped.

Russell realized he wanted her to go on. "What happened on Sundays?"

"Sunday is when I poured tea. They started me at the age of five. In the afternoon after church people would assemble, people like them, men in dark suits, women in gray dresses. I cringed every time the door chimes sounded. But I was already waiting in the kitchen, sitting on a stool in my starched dress, the pleats puffed over a crinoline petticoat, my Mary Janes gleaming. My mother had braided my hair, pulling so hard I wanted to scream. But I wouldn't. Couldn't. When everyone had arrived, my mother would speak my name. Evelyn. Just once.

Never twice. And I would push out a mahogany cart with our best serving China, stopping in front of each person and asking, 'Would you like tea?' 'Please,' they all would answer, the same word in the same grim tone, and I would pour, trying not to show how terrified I was, how my hands shook.'"

Russell found himself clutching the bottom of his chair. When she paused the sudden silence was like a roar in his ears.

"But I never spilled," Evelyn said, almost a whisper. "In all those years I never spilled."

Russell knew he would write the story, saw in his mind print on pages in a very good magazine, but the way he would tell it the girl, the character, would smash cups in an outburst. He didn't think he would have her run out the door. That would be too much. She'd just glare at her parents and smash cups.

Evelyn spoke again, her jaw set, loud this time. "I never spilled a fucking cup."

Russell heard a gasp, unsure whether it came from Carol or Julia. He couldn't look away from Evelyn's face, grasping at every detail of her expression. "My God!" he said. "What a story."

Evelyn pushed back from the table and stood, her face red, her body trembling. She shouted at him. "It's not a story. It's my life!"

She bolted toward a glass door, threw it back, and ran out into the yard. Russell could see her far back in the glow of a night lamp, a dark shadow hunched and shaking. He felt sure she was weeping.

Carol and Julia stood to go to her, but Alan waved them off. "It's better for her to be alone when she's like this." He stood too, smoothed his jacket. "I think we'd better leave now. I'll say goodbye for Evelyn too. We'll just walk around the side of the house. Thank you for inviting us." Her slid the glass door closed, carefully, waiting for a click.

Carol and Jerry just sat, hands folded on the table.

Julia looked at Russell. "That was awful," she told him. "Cruel."

"I'm really sorry." At that moment he meant it. "Should I go after her and apologize?"

She shook her head. "That would be worse."

"You know," Jerry said, "I was thinking the same thing. A story."

Carol nodded. "I wonder if she's ever told other people."

"Alan," Julia said. "She must have told Alan."

Russell sensed she was softening but knew not to reach for her hand. He was thinking how, in the morning, he would start the story, perhaps with an image of cups and saucers stacked on a polished cart. Or perhaps the small girl terrified to squirm in that starched dress.

Jerry reached for a cognac bottle. "Another?" The others nodded. "It's funny," he said as he poured. "I gave up football, Julia gave up dancing, and Russell gave up drawing comics."

"And Evelyn gave up pouring tea," Carol added.

Julia smiled, and Russell knew it was all right. Soon they would go back to her house, the children gone, and they would have sex. Even now at this table he anticipated her sounds of pleasure. But he sensed this would be the last time, that she would be hesitant the next time he called. And he knew he would write about her, not sure whether he would include the graphic details of their lovemaking. Those he might save for another character, some woman he created in the future.

About the Author

Walter Cummins has published seven short story collections—*Witness, Where We Live, Local Music, The End of the Circle, The Lost Ones, Habitat: stories of bent realism, Telling Stories: Old and New*. He also has four collections of essays and reviews—*Knowing Writers, Death Cancer Madness and Meaning, Irresponsible and Maladjusted*, and *Seeking Authenticity*. More than one hundred of his stories, as well as memoirs, essays, and reviews, have appeared in magazines such as *New Letters, Arts & Letters, Kansas Quarterly, Virginia Quarterly Review, Under the Sun, Confrontation, Bellevue Literary Review, Connecticut Review*, in book collections, and on the Web. With Thomas E. Kennedy, he is founding co-publisher of Serving House Books, an outlet for novels, memoirs, and story, poetry, and essay collections. For more than twenty years, he was editor of *The Literary Review*.

His other publications include *Our Literary Travels* and *The Literary Traveler*, co-written with Thomas E. Kennedy; *Programming Our Lives: Television and American Identity*, co-written with George Gordon; and collaboration in five books on the Vanderbilt-Twombly Florham Estate.

He is a professor of English Emeritus at the Florham Campus of Fairleigh Dickinson University, where he taught in the MFA Program in Creative Writing and the MA Program in Creative Writing and Literature for Educators. His degrees are a BA in English from Rutgers and an MA in Humanities, MFA in Creative Writing, and PhD in English from the University of Iowa.

www.ingramcontent.com/pod-product-compliance
Lightning Source LLC
Chambersburg PA
CBHW021136190726
48288CB00008B/2687